Praise for *Hola and Goodbye: Una F*

Hola and Goodbye is a marvelous and ass
Each story is surprising, moving, humorous, ...
deftness and nuance, Miscolta captures three generations of one American family and their sometimes-flawed humanity as each generation works to find their place in the world. There is a poignancy as every generation, with their singular desires, strives to create their own lives, all while experiencing different kinds of dislocation. Miscolta isn't afraid to tackle race or gender—she is unflinching. This book tells a new kind of immigrant story, a new kind of story about what it means to be a family. This is a superb collection whose range is not only impressive, it's remarkable.

—Nina McConigley, author of *Cowboys and East Indians*

Donna Miscolta brings the old streets to burning life. I can hear these voices, I can smell the cooking. The ghosts step out of these alleys as if they'd never left. Wonderful stuff.

—Luis Urrea, author of *Into the Beautiful North* and *Queen of America*

"Life," Donna Miscolta writes in *Hola and Goodbye*, "was not about running away, but running toward something." The characters in this intricately linked and exquisitely structured collection of stories do just that. For better or worse, they rush toward life, future-minded despite the past whispering from behind, and fueled by the clashing forces that make us human— courage and recklessness, wisdom and hope, the need to belong and the undeniable instinct to strike out on your own. Miscolta writes with the precision demanded by the short story, but with the range, scope, and generosity we crave in the novel, and what results is an unforgettable reading experience. *Hola and Goodbye* is a thoroughly satisfying book from a very talented writer.

—Lysley Tenorio, author of *Monstress*

Hola and Goodbye

HOLA AND GOODBYE

Una Familia in Stories

Donna Miscolta

CAROLINA WREN PRESS

© 2017 Donna Miscolta
Cover Design by Laura Williams
Interior Design by April Leidig
Typeset in Garamond Premier Pro by Copperline.

*The mission of Carolina Wren Press is to seek out, nurture,
and promote literary work by new and underrepresented writers,
including women and writers of color.*

This publication was made possible by Michael Bakwin's generous establishment
of the Bakwin Award for Writing by a Woman and the continued support of Carolina
Wren Press by the extended Bakwin family. We gratefully acknowledge the ongoing
support of general operations by the Durham Arts Council's United Arts Fund
and a special grant from the North Carolina Arts Council.

The following stories originally appeared, in slightly different form, in the
following publications: "Lupita and the Lone Ranger" in *Kweli Journal*, June 2016;
"When Danny Got Married" in *Bluestem*, June 2014; "Ana's Dance" in *The Lascaux
Review*, 2014; "Irma the Practical" in *Hawaii Pacific Review*, January 2014; "Fleeing Fat
Allen" in *Conversations Across Borders*, March 2012; "The Last Canasta" in *Connecticut
Review*, Spring 2011; "Strong Girls" in *Calyx*, Winter 2008; "Rosa in America"
in *New Millennium Writings 2006–2007*.

Library of Congress Cataloging-in-Publication Data
Names: Miscolta, Donna, 1953– author.
Title: Hola and goodbye : una familia in stories / Donna Miscolta.
Description: Durham, NC : Carolina Wren Press, 2016.
Identifiers: LCCN 2016036274 | ISBN 9780932112644
Subjects: LCSH: Mexican American families—Fiction. | Mexican American women—
Fiction. | Mexican-American Border Region—Fiction. | Domestic fiction.
Classification: LCC PS3613.I843 A6 2016 | DDC 813/.6—dc23
LC record available at https://lccn.loc.gov/2016036274

For my mother,
Dolores Camacho Miscolta,
and my grandmother,
Francisca Camacho Alzona

Contents

Hola and Goodbye

1

Four Women

Lupita and the Lone Ranger

————————— ❖ —————————

LUPITA WAITED AT the bus stop. Her fingers worried the mesh bag that held her lunch, her wallet, her keys. She resisted the impulse to glance first one way for the bus and then the other way for Rosa. Some mornings she`scolded Rosa for nearly missing the bus. Other days she was harshly silent. And on the days that Rosa did miss the bus, Lupita cursed her as she went to work alone.

California. USA. The words that once played in her head like a song or a prayer now bullied with instructions: Speak English.

Refusing to look for either the bus or Rosa, Lupita looked straight ahead at the shuttered market across the nearly deserted street. Mrs. Dawson would open at nine just as she did on Saturdays when she greeted Lupita for her weekly shopping. Just after Mrs. Dawson jangled open the double padlock, just after she turned the sign in the window from *CLOSED. PLEASE COME AGAIN* to *WELCOME*, Lupita entered the tiny, cramped store where the eggs were fresh but the lettuce just shy of wilting, where the light was dim and the smell of the ammonia-washed floors rose to meet the tang of herbs. If Lupita wasn't so picky about the size of the onions or the firmness of the tomatoes she wanted, she could send one of her girls to do the shopping. Instead, she always had to rehearse her English ahead of time, scripting what she'd say to the talkative shop lady. But Mrs.

Dawson asked different questions each time. Not easy ones about the weather. No, she wanted to know what Lupita thought about this or that complicated, inexplicable thing. Sometimes Lupita could do no more than smile politely.

Her tongue seemed incapable of forming the sounds of English, her mind confused by its structure, her heart despairing of the effort. Besides, what use did she have for English, sorting fish in a cannery that employed so many Chinese workers? Better for her to learn Chinese.

Ever since the foreman put her and Rosa on separate lines and staggered their breaks, she heard Chinese all day long. Even while the foreman barked at the Chinese workers about the English-only rule, there was little he could do to enforce it. He was outnumbered, which made him angry, so he took delight in exacting compliance from Rosa and Lupita, cupping his hand to indicate their Spanish reply did not register in his American ear, feigning incomprehension when they answered *sí*, or walking away and ignoring them altogether. As if they didn't exist.

She told Sergio of the foreman's behavior through bitter tears, wanting him to be indignant on her behalf. At first consoling, drying her cheeks with the back of his hand, cooing *está bien, está bien*, now he only sighed and shook his head. She knew it was because he expected her to learn English. After all, he had acquired a stammering but intelligible fluency, even picking up the slang he heard at the bowling alley where he worked nights wiping up spilled beers and sweeping up Cracker Jack pieces. Her children knew English, too, following the shows on the radio and retelling the latest episode of the *Lone Ranger* at the dinner table until Milagros remembered to turn to her and explain in Spanish. Lupita nodded, said, *Good, good*, meaning both that the program was good and that she was on the side of good, the side of the Lone Ranger, the one who came to the rescue. But her intent was lost on her children, who had already resumed their imitation in English of the radio characters.

Rosa was the only one she could count on. Though recently Rosa had begun to be more mindful of the foreman and his rule. Where before she had been silent whenever he passed her as he patrolled the lines, she now tossed out some phrase in English to her co-workers. *Careful, now* or *Let's keep up the pace.* Things she had heard the foreman himself use. Lupita had only heard her do this once, on her way back from her break. But she felt certain that Rosa had made a practice of it, and it worried her, though she wasn't sure if her concern was more for Rosa or for herself. If the foreman decided that Rosa was mocking him, he could punish her. And wouldn't it serve her right? If Rosa's English met with approval, well, there was only so much Lupita could do if Rosa decided to abandon Spanish. Only so much.

When she heard the bus approach, she looked up quickly to search for Rosa and saw her running awkwardly in high heels, her work shoes in hand. Her mesh bag was slung around her neck and shoulder so that the strap separated her breasts, which rebounded with her trot.

The bus reached the curb before Rosa did, and when the door swung open, Lupita let her bag slip to the ground, knowing that the orange inside would be ruined and taste bitter when she ate it later. By the time she retrieved her bag and faced the exasperated driver, Rosa arrived panting through painted red lips, the smell of the sweat beading at her temples and spreading at her armpits overtaking the scent of her cheap perfume. They boarded the bus and paid their fares, Lupita ignoring the driver and Rosa offering a deferential smile. They sat where they liked in the morning because there were few people on the bus, and if they wanted, they could speak Spanish in normal rather than hushed tones.

This morning, though, the conversation moved slowly, with Lupita meeting Rosa's chatter with the same indifferent nods and shrugs they were often treated to by the gringos at the bank, the post office, and here on the bus. But Rosa was not deterred and talked and talked and talked about nothing, or at least nothing about which Lupita cared to hear. Lupita folded her hands tightly in her lap, wondering if Rosa was truly unaware of the effect of her tardiness.

There were many things Lupita forgave Rosa for, a good number about which Rosa was clueless. She overlooked Rosa's wasteful spending on lipstick and rouge, and her useless application of them. Then there was her tendency to chatter on about her dreams for the future. Lupita was tolerant there, too—for everything but Rosa's wish for a gringo husband. There was no need for such ambition—even in Kimball Park. She let an unconcerned grunt fall from her lips in response to something Rosa said and turned to watch the growing traffic. She felt the bump of an elbow as Rosa rummaged in her bag and withdrew her knitting. For the first half of the forty-minute ride, Lupita was silent while Rosa hummed a *corrido* and her knitting needles clacked a tinny beat. But then Lupita relented and looked away from the window, remembering that Rosa was, after all, her long-time friend, remembering also that once she got to the cannery, she would not speak Spanish until she was on the bus back home with Rosa.

She fingered the ball of ocean-blue wool in Rosa's lap. "¡Qué bonito color!"

Rosa draped the half-finished shawl across Lupita's shoulder. "Sí," she said, smiling.

Lupita, feeling guilty now that she knew the shawl was for her, complimented Rosa on her earrings, bracelet, and necklace, all of which she would have to remove once she got to work. Lupita found it ridiculous that Rosa bothered with jewelry, high heels, and makeup for the morning ride. She was too tired at the end of the day to wear anything but her work shoes, too saturated with the smell of fish to care whether bracelets adorned her wrist, and her makeup had long since dissolved in the heat of the cannery. Still Rosa persisted in her morning routine, which made her late for the bus. But Lupita admitted there was something in this futile effort that aroused a tenderness for her, a feeling of protectiveness for their relationship. It was this feeling that often led Lupita to turn the conversation to their years in Mexico where they, their friendship, and their dreams originated. "Do you remember," she asked, enumerating the Sunday strolls through the plaza, the outdoor market where they bartered eggs and vegetables for meat, the time they sneaked into the movie theater?

But this last was the wrong memory to rekindle. Rosa told again how once at the fiesta de San Blas she was mistaken for a famous Mexican movie star. Again there was the wistful musing whether she would have graced the screen herself had she stayed in Mexico. "Here todo es English," she said, mixing her languages, a new habit.

As if Rosa could be a movie star in America even if she learned flawless English. Lupita shook her head. There were no limits to Rosa's foolishness. But Lupita didn't say so. She let Rosa continue talking of movies and movie stars, roles she might've been suited for, costumes she might've worn, because in her excitement only Spanish tumbled from her mouth.

When they got off the bus, there were five blocks to walk, but already there was a change in their mood and conversation. They spoke more quietly, their exchanges less frequent. By the time they reached the gate of the cannery where they joined other arrivals, most of them Chinese chattering in their piercing dialect, they stopped speaking altogether. They clasped hands as they made their way with the rest of the shift to the dented, rusty lockers where they stored their lunches, and Rosa changed her shoes and stripped herself of her jewelry. Before they separated to take their places at their lines, Rosa leaned in Lupita's ear and whispered, "Que tengas un buen día."

"Igualmente, hermana," returned Lupita, who was always heartened by this reference to their sisterhood that was not a blood tie, but one of spirit and circumstance. And obligation, she thought.

Lupita followed a group of Chinese women heading to Belt A. As she walked down the corridor behind them, she turned her head slightly to avoid the smell of Chinese cooking that they seemed to wear like clothes. Lupita wondered what odors she carried on herself. Whatever they were, they were obliterated soon enough by the reek of tuna, which seeped into her pores, the weave of her dress, her nostrils, and her scalp almost as soon as she stepped onto the factory floor. She quickened her pace, as did the women ahead of her. One of them was Maxine, at least that's what the foreman called her. She was Mei Xing to her Chinese friends. Lupita liked Maxine, a good worker who had used her favor with the foreman to intercede on behalf of others—for a slower worker just learning the belt, or someone for whom the language barrier had her discarding heads left and tails right instead of the other way around. Maxine had never had to mediate on Lupita's behalf because

Lupita's work was equal to Maxine's. There was a mutual respect that could also be a friendship, if only Maxine would not assume that Lupita's inability to speak English also was a failure to comprehend it, prompting her to communicate with Lupita through exaggerated signs of hand and face.

They were barely at their places when the machines started rolling and the foreman marched by shouting, "All right, ladies, let's get to work," a needless exercise of his vocal chords, the women having already responded automatically to the cue from the engines. Lupita's hands moved swiftly in the pattern she had devised, an efficient sequence of motions. Her hands were themselves like fish in their sinuous movement, their sea-salt smell, even the scaliness of her chapped skin. She filled her head and tail buckets ten times before the morning break.

As she followed her line to the break room, the foreman stepped in front of her, his name badge insinuating itself in her eyes as she lost sight of Maxine and the others headed for the tea and sesame crackers they shared among themselves. She thought of the orange in her bag, longed for its bitterness, and felt the anger rise in her as this man stole the precious minutes of her break. She faced Mr. Lewis. He was unimposing in size, and despite the yellow-brown tinge of his scant hair and small eyes, his looks were colorless. Lupita realized that it was the language he spoke from his thin-lipped mouth that gave him power over her, and she concentrated hard on her own words, their sound and shape.

"Can I help you, Mr. Lewis?" She managed a polite smile, hoped he didn't notice that she said *Loo-ees*.

"Glad you asked, Lupita." He pronounced it *Lapida*, and she was sure that his pronunciation caused him little concern. "I've been wondering, how do you say 'gimme a kiss' in Spanish?"

Lupita watched the leer warp to displeasure as she answered. "At work I speak only English." She emphasized *work* to remind him of her importance on the belt.

Mr. Lewis moved aside to let her pass. "Never mind," he said, "I'll just ask your friend Rosa. She likes to talk to me."

Throughout the day, Lupita tried to catch Rosa's eye, but the foreman stalked the lines like a dog. Rosa, ever mindful of Mr. Lewis's presence, took every opportunity to demonstrate her English. While Lupita couldn't hear the words, she was convinced by the slow, exaggerated movements of Rosa's lips that it was English she spoke, eager and ingratiating. There was a moment when Rosa's back was turned and Lupita had only the grin on Mr. Lewis's face to suggest the sum and substance of the conversation.

At the end of the day when the machines ceased their clamor with a reluctant groan, the quiet was almost overbearing. Some of the women tested it with whoops and laughter, but most talked in near whispers or not at all until they were clear of the factory floor. Lupita found Rosa at the lockers changing into her high heels, her jewelry already dangling from her ears, neck, and wrists.

"¿Qué estás haciendo?" Lupita demanded.

"Just because I work in a cannery doesn't mean I shouldn't care about my appearance."

"We'll miss the bus," Lupita warned.

"I'm ready." Rosa led the way, but when Lupita edged ahead of her and easily overtook her by several steps, Rosa said brightly, "If we did miss the bus, I bet Mr. Lewis would drive us home."

The words almost caused Lupita to stop in her thick-soled tracks, but she made herself continue walking, though not so fast as to leave Rosa behind. When they were on the bus, conscious of the smell of fish they brought and seated in the back, away from the contemptuous stares of the other passengers, Lupita let loose her anger in a loud rush, drawing attention to them after all.

"¡Qué tontería! ¿Estás loca, mujer?"

It was the wrong approach, Lupita knew. But it was too late. She had already sent Rosa to the precipice of her pride. But instead of trying to coax her back, Lupita retreated without her, sat stiffly on her half of the bench, girdling herself with crossed arms. Rosa pulled her knitting from her bag, made a show of spreading the half-finished shawl across her lap, the shawl she was making for Lupita.

After a moment Lupita tried again. She couldn't help it. It was as if the steady click of Rosa's needles goaded her to persist. "Mr. Lewis is not a kind man," she said evenly, matter-of-factly, her teeth nearly clenched. She resisted an urge to shake her finger at Rosa.

Rosa continued to knit, her eyes intent on her work. Then, with a clash of her needles said, "You think you're always right. But you're not."

"Vamos a ver," Lupita said mostly to herself since Rosa had begun to hum her *corrido* loud enough that some passengers turned to glare at her. Rosa disregarded them all. She might as well ignore the whole world if she ignores me, thought Lupita. She was struck by her own arrogance and how risky it felt. But then, she was right. She knew she was.

When they got off the bus, Lupita made a weak show of reconciliation, patting Rosa's arm as she said, "Hasta mañana."

"Tomorrow," replied Rosa, and Lupita watched her clip-clop away in her high heels, a portion of the half-knitted shawl flapping from the bag at her shoulder.

Lupita walked briskly, head down, past the little market so as not to be waylaid by so much as a wave from Mrs. Dawson.

At home Lupita was met by the sound of the radio program in English that had her children hypnotized. They were sprawled on the rug, their eyes distant even as they gave a quick glance and half-smile, or some other sign of welcome that Lupita insisted as her due. Lupita didn't playfully kick the shoe of the child lounging closest to her foot as she did some days.

Today she only shrugged, willing, almost eager to feel that sense of loss, that her children were as absent to her in the evening when she came home from work as they were when she left them sleeping in their beds in the morning. It gave her more fuel for her resentment at Rosa, and as she headed into the kitchen she was almost disappointed that Sergio had remembered to turn the flame off under the beans. It was what she reminded him of each morning before she left for work, because once he did forget and let them cook until they stuck, a thick crust of brown, to the bottom of the pot. She had been angry about coming home from work and having no beans for dinner. But more than that, she had been upset at Sergio's neglect of something so basic and necessary.

Sergio came in buttoning a clean shirt and paused to kiss Lupita's cheek and ask about her day. Lupita sank into a chair, wanting to tell her story, wanting Sergio to be on her side, but all she managed was "Como siempre," as she watched him match the last button to its hole and straighten the fit of the shirt over the slight buldge of his belly. He would've liked one of the shirts that had *Victory Lanes* emblazoned on the back and his name on the front above the pocket. Only Jake and Hoyt who worked at the counter, assigning lanes to the bowlers and ringing up totals on the cash register, were dressed in the official shirt. Sergio was the janitor.

"You deserve a shirt," she noted.

"So what's new?" he asked, though she could tell he was grateful for her words.

Lupita went to the refrigerator and took out the chicken soup she had cooked the night before. "There is a problem with Rosa," she said as she set the pot on the stove, startling even herself with its clang.

Sergio raised an eyebrow, waited for Lupita to continue.

"She is becoming too friendly with the foreman. It is only trouble for her." Lupita stirred the soup, ready to explain the whole situation to Sergio, to show him how she was being wronged by Rosa.

But Sergio only patted her on the shoulder. "Be her friend."

Yes, thought Lupita, *and shouldn't Rosa do the same?*

Dinner was hurried, with Sergio leaving early for the bowling alley and Lupita already chopping vegetables for tomorrow's stew before clearing the table. The children were back in the living room, their heads cocked to the strains of the *Lone Ranger* theme, which Lupita knew was the sound of rescue and triumph. While she waited for the cooking oil to heat, she cleared the table and piled the dishes in the sink to be washed, and these tasks of setting her kitchen in order, of putting things in their place, helped her decide how she must deal with Rosa. She must let Rosa go her own way, and Rosa must know that she will not follow. It was not an ultimatum. It was just the way it was.

Lupita tested the oil, and when it sputtered at her, she dropped the onions in and then the carrots and celery to sizzle—a long hiss that she finally doused with water. She covered the pot and left the vegetables to simmer.

When she was done in the kitchen, she sat with the children while Milagros read them a story. She read in English, of course, and Lupita was proud of her prowess with the language of hard consonants and confusing array of vowel sounds. Lupita praised her in Spanish, as if offering its soothing rhythms for contrast.

The next morning Lupita and Rosa arrived at the bus stop at the same time. As they approached from opposite directions, there was no direct eye contact. Each held the other in broad focus, Lupita peripherally registering the red blot of Rosa's mouth at a distance but up close failing to contain the urge to scan her face. They exchanged greetings, smiling and cordial, and when the bus pulled up, it was as if everything was the same. Except that Rosa didn't have her knitting. Her plump hands rested in her lap as she hummed her *corrido*, and Lupita turned to the window. The bus headed west toward the bay, through the residential neighborhoods lined with shaggy palm trees or drooping acacias, past the business district with its barred windows and chained doors, and into the industrial area with its gray and brown factories, the color of slugs and moths.

At the cannery they parted even before they got to the lockers, Lupita falling in step with Maxine, who employed emphatic gestures even to ask, "How are you today?" Lupita responded quickly to prove her understanding, "I'm very fine, thank you, and how are you? It's a very nice day, isn't it?" And she conceded to herself that English was necessary at times, that she couldn't always cling to her Spanish.

At the end of the day when Lupita picked up her bag at her locker, Rosa was already there waiting for her. Her hair was combed neatly, her makeup was freshened, and she was wearing her high heels. Though she sat decorously on the wooden bench, when she spoke, it was with childish excitement. "Mr. Lewis has offered me a ride home. And you can come, too."

When Lupita responded with a severe stare, Rosa explained what she thought Lupita must've been missing. "We can go together." Though her voice was bright, there was a note of pleading.

"Did Mr. Lewis invite me?"

"No, but it's all right," Rosa said. "He said if I need anything, just ask." She blushed with pleasure underneath her rouged cheeks.

Lupita thought Rosa a pitiful sight. Wanting to both save and punish her, she was confused for a moment by these two impulses. But then she blurted harshly, "Go, if you want."

"Bueno." Rosa rose on her high heels to leave. "Hasta mañana." She waited for an answer, but Lupita stubbornly persisted down the path she had veered and merely waved her off. She didn't watch Rosa walk away, but waited until the sound of her high heels no longer echoed above the bustle of the other departing workers, and so missed her bus—a misfortune she could blame on Rosa, and which was easier to think about than any misfortune Rosa might encounter on her ride with Mr. Lewis.

When she got home, Sergio met her at the door, looking at her with worry.

She told him she missed the bus. "No es nada," she said, relieved that he was ready to leave for the bowling alley.

But he didn't go just yet. He hadn't stopped looking at her, though the worry on his face was now mixed with doubt. "And Rosa?"

"No," replied Lupita, "she didn't miss the bus."

Apparently unwilling to ask any more questions and not wanting to be late, Sergio gave Lupita a gentle kiss on the cheek and left. She went inside and kissed each of her children in turn. The looks of puzzlement she elicited she accepted as readily as if they had kissed her back. She went about her evening tasks with great concentration, but every so often she heard Sergio ask, *And Rosa?* until she was so anxious for the next day that she sent the children to bed early, producing not only more puzzlement but protest, a distraction she welcomed and even prolonged, engaging in squabbles over tooth-brushing and face-washing. When she went to bed herself, she did so with the satisfaction of knowing that she had acted in their best interest. Still, she slept poorly and was awake when Sergio came home at 2:30, even though she pretended to be asleep.

In the gray morning lit only by the blue flame beneath the simmering beans, Lupita prepared a sandwich of hardened cheese and a thin slice of ham. Her hands trembled for lack of sleep and her head was thick and dull. But she was prepared to struggle through the day. It was a matter of survival. She wrapped the sandwich in a sheet of brown paper, then dropped it along with a musty orange into the mesh bag. On the other burner she warmed a tortilla, doubling the glow of light in the kitchen. She absorbed its warmth and comfort to fuel herself for the day ahead. She ate standing, but not hurriedly, allowing herself a few minutes of longing for Mexico. Not for the hard-scrabble life that was hers in Acaponeta in the years since the revolution, but for the music that dwelled even in bare rooms, forced from scratchy phonographs, blared from cantinas, warbled by her neighbors. It was music she had yet to find in her new home, a town almost as dusty as her old one, but with no poetry to save it. There was only English.

Lupita finished her breakfast and set out a stack of tortillas and a box of cornflakes for her family. Reluctantly, she left the kitchen, where the smell of beans had begun to fill the room and the slow flame underneath the pot burned steady as a friend. In the bedroom she shook Sergio until he opened one eye. "Me voy. No te olvides de los frijoles," she told him. "Los frijoles," she said again and waited until he opened both eyes to reassure her.

She stopped to look in on the children. Petra clung in her sleep to the side of the bed while Milagros sprawled over its width, one arm flung across her sister's neck. Consuelo was on a mattress on the floor, curled around a pillow. They were growing so fast, but there would be more children to come. She was not finished birthing babies to keep her company in this new land. She blew kisses at their sleeping faces.

She waited at the bus stop, kept herself from pacing by concentrating on Mrs. Dawson's store across the street, planning the conversation they would have on Saturday, anticipating Mrs. Dawson's questions and devising possible English answers.

When the bus pulled up, she was still mouthing English phrases. Though she boarded the bus without looking around for Rosa, she could no longer ignore her absence. It was Rosa's absence that accompanied her on the bus and into the cannery. When Mr. Lewis passed her as he inspected her line, he stopped to ask, "Where's your friend, today?" His tone was neutral and businesslike, but his look was triumphant, sending a chill of remorse through Lupita who answered what they both knew must be true, "She isn't well today."

He clucked with mock sympathy, then winked at her as he would to someone with whom he shared a secret. "You just see that she feels better soon."

All day Lupita worked like the madwoman she was, venting

her anger at Mr. Lewis, her worry about Rosa, her defiance that grew from a small nub of shame beneath her breastbone as she heaved fish heads and tails with such frenzy that scales flew in the air around her, catching in the net that covered her head and landing on her cheeks, which she didn't scrape away.

That evening Lupita rode the bus home alone for the second day in a row, grieving the losses, lamenting the sacrifices that came from living in a new country. She was too lost in her misery to remember to hurry past Mrs. Dawson's. A rap from inside the store window jerked Lupita's attention to Mrs. Dawson's beckoning hand. Lupita was not in the mood for small talk, which Lupita called "tiny talk" not just for its lack of substance but for her own lack of English that limited her conversation to a few reliable phrases. Lupita smoothed her dress as if the gesture might also erase the crease in her forehead and ease the tautness at her jaw. She entered the store, the bell above the door clanging.

There were a few customers assessing the freshness of the meats or the remaining shelf life of the bananas showing the faintest of spots. Mrs. Dawson was behind the counter, wiping its chipped surface with a rag. She talked fast. It was her nature, and Lupita appreciated that she didn't slow down her speech to distorted syllables, didn't shout to aid Lupita's comprehension. Lupita waited out Mrs. Dawson's monologue, which began with news of an unexpected delivery of tripe should Lupita need any for that soup she made, then rambled on about bread prices and stray cats and broken street lamps. Lupita understood most of the words but today had no energy to search for English replies from the crevices of her brain, which were filled with just one word: *Rosa, Rosa, Rosa.* Suddenly, Mrs. Dawson stopped talking and peered into her face, pressed her finger to

Lupita's cheek, and removed a fish scale. She studied it, a translucent flake, then wiped it on the rag she had used to clean the counter. "For a moment, I thought it was a tear," she said with a laugh.

"No, is not," Lupita assured her, dry-eyed and determined to stay so.

When she got home, the radio was on as always, but it was not yet time for the galloping music of the *Lone Ranger* show. It was another program—one with singing and laughter. The children sprawled on the floor and furniture, eyes glued to the wooden box as if they could see the words pouring from it, and for a minute Lupita stared at the box, too, until she noticed Rosa's slouched figure in the corner. Like the children, Rosa faced the radio, but her face was not alert to its chatter. She sat vacant-eyed, her knees bumped against each other and her ankles wrapped around the legs of the chair.

Lupita approached, loosened her from the chair and led the way to the kitchen. They walked past Sergio, and Lupita avoided his gaze. Her concern at the moment was Rosa, who needed her.

Rosa in America

———— ❧ ————

ROSA WAITED UNTIL Lupita's back was turned before she lit the cigarette. By the time Lupita shot her a look of disapproval, Rosa was dragging deeply, her head filling with the comforting cloud of tobacco, and her friend's opinions mattered a little less to her. It was Lupita's kitchen, and Rosa as usual had just eaten Sunday dinner with the Camacho family in their two-bedroom stucco on Palm Street, with St. Rita's at one end of the block and the corner grocery store at the other. It was a home of permanence with the smell of onions and frijoles deep in the wallpaper and the old family photographs nailed in a gray line along the threshold of the dining room.

Rosa aimed at the ceiling and exhaled, watched the smoke dissipate just before it reached the crack in the plaster that looked annoyingly like a heart. She let herself be distracted by the shrieks and scrambling of the Camacho children trapping moths on the porch with Lupita's old hairnets. She heard Sergio yell *Cállense* and then turn the volume up on the radio in the living room. He and Camilo, also a regular at Sunday dinners, were listening to the fights.

Lupita sat down across the kitchen table from her, and Rosa brought the cigarette to her lips again, rested it there and narrowed her eyes to see through the smoke. She was a modern woman in a modern country and she had modern dreams, fiercer and more urgent now than ten years before, when she crossed the Mexican border, her arm linked in Lupita's, each of them with the American dollars that would pay the head tax, visa, and medical fees sewn into the hem of her dress for safekeeping. Even now her English was scant, though far better than Lupita's, and though she couldn't explain the New Deal of *el presidente* Roosevelt that she saw in the headlines or heard mentioned on the radio, she had put her own meaning to the words.

"¿Por qué, Rosa? Why do you treat Camilo that way?" Lupita was shaking her head at her, while in the living room Sergio and Camilo shouted complaints at the announcer calling the fight.

"He tries too hard to please." Rosa mimicked Camilo's wide grin, smoke issuing from the corners of her mouth.

"Don't be cruel," Lupita scolded.

Rosa obeyed at least for the moment. "Dinner was good," she said. "You should teach me."

"You should want to learn," Lupita snorted, pushing an ashtray toward Rosa, who rested her cigarette so that the smoke rose up between them. "What will happen when you marry?"

Rosa wanted to give Lupita's words back to her, *Don't be cruel.* Lupita didn't know how the words pierced Rosa inside in a place where she reserved both envy and blame for her best friend. Rosa only sighed, "God knows."

Lupita was relentless. "God knows you won't marry when you ignore the attentions of a good man."

"Good but dull," returned Rosa, taking a puff of her cigarette.

"He's loyal."

"Like a puppy."

"He's gentle."

"Soft como flan." Rosa giggled at the comparison. Then she was moved to comment on his eating habits, the way he tipped the food in his mouth from the end of a fork, his wrist flicking to send frijoles past his large teeth. And must he talk with his mouth full?

"Ahora, te entiendo," Lupita nodded accusingly. "He's not good enough for you. He's not a gringo."

Rosa was silent, as if struck by Lupita's palm, the same harsh palm that slapped tortillas flat with such vigor. Rosa flinched as something swirled in her stomach, lurched, then bubbled down slowly. She knew she was being watched by Lupita, whose voice suddenly softened as she pleaded Camilo's case.

"Do you feel nothing for this man who adores you?"

Rosa softened also as she admitted to feeling something. "But not passion," she said firmly as she thought to herself that Camilo had no dreams.

Then Lupita's words came without warning. "Did you feel passion for Arthur Lewis?"

Rosa felt the color drain from her face, wondered if the look of her lipstick was as vivid as its thick taste on her mouth. An emptiness expanded inside of her to replace the bloated sensation of a few minutes ago. With hazy eyes, she saw Lupita turn quickly away. Ashamed for herself? Or for Rosa?

They had never discussed the subject. Rosa, who ached from an invisible burden, had told Lupita nothing, feared what she guessed.

Suddenly the radio noise reached the kitchen in a loud outburst. Sergio and Camilo added their cheers to the roar from the radio as the fight came down to the final round. Lupita leaned across the table and told Rosa in a loud whisper that Camilo planned to speak to her tonight when the fights were over.

"¿Sobre qué?" Rosa asked.

"Sobre el futuro," Lupita replied slyly, a finger pointing knowingly at Rosa, who waved it away with an agitated hand.

The future seemed at once to loom insidiously near and painfully out of reach. Rosa clutched herself around the waist with one arm and with the other gripped the end of the table and waited for a spasm to pass.

"You must think of what you'll say to him," Lupita advised.

The spasm over, Rosa placed both hands on the table. "I'll say nothing to him, because he'll say nothing to me."

"You're not getting any younger," Lupita said.

Her last words were suddenly loud because the fights had ended and the radio turned low. Rosa recognized the lush sounds of a Guy Lombardo tune and imagined herself swaying in someone's arms. They heard Sergio shepherding the children to bed as Camilo wandered into the kitchen and stood shyly against the sink.

"¿Quién ganó?" Lupita asked.

"Muñoz."

"I knew it."

"Very quick. Good fakes." Camilo tried to demonstrate, danced a few steps, a poor foxtrot, as he ducked and jabbed, and Rosa thought how small he was, how silly they would look as a couple. Then Camilo ceased his dance and looked at Rosa, who rose quickly from her chair, exclaiming, "¡Mira qué hora es!"

Both Camilo and Lupita looked at the clock with a collective motion that Rosa thought was surely rehearsed.

Camilo held out his hand. "Bueno, te llevo a casa." His voice was polite and encouraging, his eyes hopeful. Rosa took a deep breath, which renewed her earlier spasms, though more forcefully this time. She saw Camilo's hands rush toward her, spread like two open fans and looking as delicate. They appeared to flutter, and then she lost sight of them altogether as the kitchen somersaulted around her.

Later, as she rested, feet elevated, on Lupita's living room couch, Lupita told her, "He was mortified when he caught you as you fainted and his hand stuck in your armpit and clamped at your breast." She tucked a blanket around Rosa. "Duérmete. We'll talk tomorrow."

Rosa closed her eyes, and when she opened them a moment later the house was all shadows. She listened to the muffled voices of Sergio and Lupita from behind the bedroom door but made no effort to distinguish their words. When their conversation ended with a final emphatic mumble from Lupita, Rosa became aware of the sound of her own breathing, a soft pant, and the sound of her heart, a jittery thump. She was aware also of a sensation in her abdomen, something small and barely palpable, deep below her navel, and she pressed her hands there, tried to massage it away.

She thought of Camilo's hand on her breast, and she folded her arms across her chest as if against a chill. Her body shuddered with the memory of that evening with Arthur Lewis those few months ago when he had offered her a ride home from the cannery and she accepted against Lupita's stern advice. Her jealous advice, Rosa thought then.

He bought her dinner first, roast beef sandwiches and beer that they ate in the car, parked beneath a filigreed shroud of acacias at the far end of the lot. "Call me Arty," he said. He talked while he chewed, sprays of lettuce or strings of meat dangling at the corner of his mouth, and she attributed this apparent lack of manners to a hearty American appetite. She nodded and smiled at what he said, though she understood little, so when he started using Spanish words, mangling them mercilessly with a tongue made thick from beer, she appreciated even this attempt at conversation. "Sirvayza," he grinned, holding up his third bottle of beer. "Grashas," he responded, encouraged when she said, "Sí, muy bien."

But when he rasped, "beso," the only word he pronounced with any accuracy, she shrank back with an embarrassed giggle. His voice turned low and coaxing, his words were full of ·compliments, or so she believed, and she was flattered. When his hand touched her cheek, a shy smile escaped her, which made the grin he wore enlarge with anticipation. And as his hand migrated from her face, down her neck, across her breasts, becoming more aggressive in its advance on her body, Rosa tightened her muscles and kept her eyes wide open to concentrate on the ceiling of the car, at the blankness there.

When he pulled away from her, she couldn't look at him. Even as he smoothed the hem of her dress back down over her knees, she stared straight ahead where a branch splayed its thin acacia leaves against the windshield, and she busied herself with counting the delicate veins. She heard him zip his pants, a sound that ripped the silence in the car. Then he started the engine, switched on the radio, and, cursing himself at having forgotten it was broken, accelerated out of the parking lot. He began to whistle, at first it seemed from uneasiness, but gradually his tune became relaxed, and by the time he pulled up to the gray rooming house with the row of anemic geraniums in the second floor window box, it was smug and loud. He leaned across her to open the car door. And while the open door was a welcome sight to her, Rosa knew it did not really offer escape. She wanted to bolt from the car, but something held her rigid to the red vinyl upholstery of Arty Lewis's impatiently humming

Ford—a dim hope that what had happened could be explained with the right words. She sat and waited, counted three passing cars on this street that saw only occasional traffic and waited for a fourth. Still Arty said nothing, only examined the part in his hair in the rearview mirror. So Rosa set one wobbly foot on the pavement and then the other, and when she had walked a few steps slowly and deliberately to keep her knees from buckling, Arty slammed the door behind her and drove away.

Rosa lay on Lupita's couch, her knees drawn up, arms crossed over her chest. She tried to imagine her future. She would like to work as a hairdresser or in a department store selling perfumes. She would like to be married and have a family, like Lupita. A car passed outside and the headlights swept the ceiling, then left the room abruptly in darkness. Rosa let it cover her like a blanket, let it wrap itself around her—this knowledge that she was pregnant.

For the next five days, Camilo visited her after work, each time bearing a gift and an apology for the indecorous way he had broken her fall when she fainted. She accepted each gift as if it were a duty—the bouquet of carnations that surely came from Lupita's garden, the combs for her hair that she recognized from the Woolworth's window and not the boutique uptown, the scarf that clashed with her lipstick color, the bracelet that clasped her sturdy wrist a little too tightly, the ceramic mermaid that she could find no use for. She took them all with simply a nod or a shrug, the most acknowledgment she could offer.

She was uncertain if she meant it as acceptance or rejection of his apology—until Saturday, when he didn't come. She felt first abandoned, then angry at his absence, distraught at her predicament and somehow blaming him for it. She gathered the combs, scarf, bracelet, and mermaid, and a petal rescued from the recently expired carnations in the trash can. She set them in a heap on her bed. In a sweep of her arm, she sent them tumbling onto a square of brown paper laid out on the floor. She folded a neat package, scrawled Camilo's name across it, and tied it with a ribbon. She carried it to the little table by the front door, ready for her to take and place in his hands if he should happen to show up for dinner at Lupita's tomorrow.

She didn't count on his coming to her house first on Sunday. Camilo, his hair glistening and perfumed, stood at her door, his lips straddling his oversized teeth in a careful smile. Unprepared for this event, she blushed and spoke in an almost hysterical key.

"What are you doing here?"

"I've come to walk you to dinner." The words apparently gave him confidence, and he stepped forward past the threshold. Rosa, noticing he didn't carry a gift today, motioned him toward her one upholstered chair.

"Siéntate, Camilo." She heard the tenderness in her voice and wondered at its source. "I'll be ready soon." She motioned to the chair again, wanted to settle him deeply inside its worn cushion.

But he waited to sit down until she began to exit the room, which she did by walking backward a few steps and then emitting a silly shriek when she bumped into the wall. She turned and hurried into the bedroom, leaned into the mirror above the dresser, saw the anxious excitement reflected there. She brushed her face with powder to mute the flushed cheeks and applied her lipstick, making boundaries for her mouth as if to put limits on what her smile or speech might reveal. She twisted some curls to frame her freshly dusted face and then circled her shoulders with the black fringe shawl she saved for special occasions.

Breathing slowly to pace her steps back into the living room, she was so focused on making a demure and dignified appearance that Camilo's image did not register an impression until she was almost near enough to reach out and touch the knee on which the brown paper package was spread open. Camilo's gifts from the past week lay there in a sorry sprawl. Rosa noticed a piece of the mermaid's tail was chipped off.

He looked up at Rosa. "It had my name on it," he explained, an apology.

"Oh, Camilo," Rosa emitted in a strained whisper. "Lo siento. It was very bad. I didn't mean—"

She didn't mean to wail, but the sound poured out of her like water from a broken pipe. Her hands at her temples, fingers splayed over her eyes, didn't quite obstruct her view of Camilo, whose expression was that of the stray cat in the alley when she hurled a rock in its path.

"You didn't come yesterday," she said in gaspy, pitiable breaths that coaxed Camilo back from his recoil. Rosa was relieved at the look of understanding she saw in the flat black of his eyes that until now had seemed so lacking.

"You thought I had given up?" he asked.

Rosa nodded dumbly, hiccups preventing any speech.

"Rosa, you cannot doubt my feelings." It was half question, half command.

Rosa shook her head to show that no, she did not doubt, but then became confused and changed back to a nod to show her agreement, and the motion tilted her forward, made her slightly dizzy. "Tienes razón, Camilo. I was wrong. Discúlpame," she pleaded, her voice attaining its previous high-pitched note, her hands now clutching her shawl at her heart.

Camilo made small shushing sounds. He dropped the gifts and the wrapper on the floor and stood up next to Rosa's wheezing body. "Cálmate, Rosa," he soothed over and over, patting her back gently until she finally quieted.

Too ashamed to face Camilo just yet, Rosa looked down only to see the gifts scattered on the rug.

"Those are just trinkets," he said, waving his hand as if to shoo them away, then kneeling down to gather them in the paper wrapper and crumple them together in a clumsy bundle. Before Rosa could protest this, Camilo, still on his knees, grasped her hand and locked it inside both of his own with such assertiveness that Rosa became curious enough not to object.

"I have something more to give," he said, letting go of her with one hand to reach into his pocket.

Rosa watched Camilo withdraw a handkerchief folded over and over into a thick square, the outline of something small and circular making a slight bulge in the cheap white linen. He held it out to her, but she could only stare, both fearful and hopeful of what it might contain.

"Por favor, Rosa. Toma." Camilo moved his hand closer to Rosa's.

She let him slide the handkerchief into her hand, let him guide her into the chair while he remained on his knees, a posture that for a fleeting moment made her feel regal and empowered until a sense of entrapment took over. As if Arty Lewis's abuse and Camilo's devotion, both so undeserved, had become partners in a conspiracy.

"Ábrelo, Rosa."

She unfolded the handkerchief on her lap and found the ring.

"Will you, Rosa?" asked Camilo.

Without looking up from the ring that appeared too small for her finger, she answered, "Sí."

When they arrived arm in arm at Lupita's door for Sunday dinner, Rosa was already accustomed to the idea of marriage to Camilo and had found that the shame and guilt she felt about accepting his proposal were readily dissipating to relief that she would, after all, have a future. When Lupita beamed at the couple, Rosa basked in the fondness and approval. Later in the evening, when Sergio asked when the happy event would occur, Rosa was quick to agree as Camilo exclaimed, "As soon as possible."

In the days that followed, Rosa was occupied with two plans: her wedding and her confession to Camilo, the first quickly overtaking the second for her attention. Though the wedding would be small and simple, there was the urgent matter of a new dress, not to mention a new hairdo. There was the matter of the guest list, of who would be asked to witness the exchange of vows and share in the food and drink to be served afterward in Lupita's living room. Camilo was content to leave the arrangements to Rosa, saying with a wink to Sergio and Lupita at the next Sunday dinner, "Just as long as when it's over Rosa is my wife."

"It's about time," Sergio joked.

"It won't take us quite so long to have a child if I have anything to say about it," promised Camilo, displaying more boldness since Rosa had accepted his proposal.

"A child? Already you think of babies," Lupita chided, though with a smile. "And what does Rosa think of this?"

They turned to look at Rosa who refused to meet any of

the eyes aimed at her, lifting her own instead to the ceiling, to the heart-shaped crack in the plaster. "It's in God's hands," she said. It came out as a whisper, and they laughed because they thought she was being playful. And while Rosa covered her face with her hands to stop the tears, her shoulders trembled and heaved just as they did when she was overcome with giggles.

"Basta, Rosa," said Lupita. "We have work to do, a wedding to plan." She rose from her chair and Rosa, still shielding her face with her hands, allowed herself to be prodded to the bedroom.

Rosa sat on the edge of the bed, dabbed at her eyes with her pinkie, while Lupita bustled around the room collecting cloth and ribbon samples and the lists they had compiled—guests, menu, honeymoon possibilities. The last was the shortest since there were few options suited to Camilo's earnings. A cheap motel near the beach, a cheap motel near the mountains—Rosa was indifferent to them both.

Lupita arranged everything in piles on the bed and Rosa observed them with unfocused eyes so that they appeared to waver, as if they could separate at will from the yellow bedspread and float into tiny specks of dust.

"¿Qué pasa, Rosa?"

"I don't know," Rosa cried, clutching her abdomen to contain the fear there that was growing, that seemed to be pushing its way out. She stood as if to try to escape it and a gush of blood dropped between her legs. She looked at Lupita, her own horror reflected in Lupita's face as they both realized what was happening.

"Dios mío," breathed Lupita, and Rosa wondered if the slow shake of Lupita's head was in shock or sympathy. The dull throb in her belly was pierced by something sharp and rupturing, and she dropped to her knees with a moan. Lupita dragged Rosa to the bathroom and positioned her doubled-over body on the toilet. Rosa continued to moan softly while Lupita, midwife to her miscarriage, massaged her neck and shoulders, moved her hands along the length of her spine to press on her lower back.

It took only twenty minutes for the fetus to be expelled in a splash of blood and tissue. Rosa didn't look at it, but Lupita inspected it, judged it to be intact, and wrapped it in newspaper. Then she ran a bath for Rosa.

As Rosa sat in the warm tub, she watched Lupita scrub the toilet and the bathroom floor, waited for her to speak. *Were you going to tell Camilo? He would have married you anyway. No use telling him now.* Rosa waited to hear all of this from Lupita. But after Lupita wiped the last spot of blood from a crack in the floor tile, then washed her hands at the sink, she turned to Rosa. "Don't take long. There's a wedding to plan."

Alone in the bathroom, Rosa could only stare at her body—large breasts, thick middle, heavy thighs, bunions forming on her feet. You're not getting any younger, she told herself as she contracted her body, drew her legs up to meet her chin. The door opened and Lupita came back in, knelt down next to the tub, and took a sponge to Rosa's shoulder. Rosa began to lather her arms.

Ana's Dance

———————— ❦ ————————

THE WINDOWS WERE open to the blue-black sky, but there was no breeze to move the heavy air inside the apartment. Across the street, the diner blinked its electric-blue sign. *EAT*, it urged. *Eat*, Ana repeated to herself, only to practice her English vocabulary, knowing that the craving she felt was not for food.

She sat rocking, the squeak of the chair chorusing with the sucking of the baby at her breast. She stroked Carmela's head as she turned to watch Rudy. He was in front of the bathroom mirror performing—yes, she thought, performing—this Saturday night ritual, begun in the months after Carmela's birth.

He was wearing just his underwear. His suit hung smartly on the hook of the bathroom door, the stiff creases in the trousers giving them a look of alertness, as if wary of Rudy's muscular body. Rudy leaned over the bathroom sink, inches from the mirror. He stretched his upper lip down over his teeth, snipped at the hairs of his elegantly thin mustache, retracted his mouth in a smile. He rubbed hair cream in his palms, sniffed at its glistening whiteness, then massaged it into his black hair one, two, three times—a calisthenic that worked the muscles in the taut curve of his arms and shoulders. He swigged mouthwash from the bottle and, posed like a garden statue, spit like a fountain into the sink. With rapid hands, he spanked his face and throat with cologne. Invigorated by the self-administered slaps, he drew himself into his fighter's stance, bounced on the balls of his feet toward his reflection, and protected with his left while he delivered several mock blows with his right. He whirled to spar with his suit hanging on the door. Prevailing against both opponents, he leapt into the middle of the room, arms raised above his head in victory, and Ana, still watching, made her mouth smile while something clenched in her throat.

Perhaps it was indigestion after all, this feeling that squeezed against her belly and throat and made it difficult to breathe.

Heartburn, indeed, had been Irma's mocking reply when Ana had foolishly related her symptoms to her cousin. Irma, ten years older than Ana and married to a silent and feature-less gringo, had taken Ana in when she first arrived in Kim-ball Park. Though Irma had appointed herself chaperone to Ana, following her conduct with a severe eye, Ana had not left the dusty streets of San Blas to be smothered by her cousin's conventions.

Within a few months, she had met Rudy at a Saturday night dance, and in front of Irma's reproving stare, Ana followed the lead of Rudy's smooth, confident steps, responded to the press of his hand at the small of her back as he steered her left or right, answered the cue of his fingertips as they spun her away and then reeled her back in.

In between dances Ana learned more about this dashing young man because Rudolfo Luis Borrego spoke as charmingly as he danced. First of all, he liked to be called Rudy, as in Rudy Vallée, and he crooned an imitation of the singer. He didn't mind being called Rudolph, though, as in Valentino, and he struck a swashbuckling stance. He said he was a painter, and Ana imagined canvasses filled with passionate strokes of color until Rudy laughed and said, no, he painted buildings—tall ones. But his real profession was boxing, and he bounced back and forth on the balls of his feet to demonstrate and then gracefully slid into a foxtrot because, he explained, dancing was an extension of his athletic training. Then he winked, adding that dancing was also romantic, especially with a partner as beautiful as Ana, and he took her in his arms and guided her effortlessly, in command of the music, in command of the other dancers who yielded the floor, in command of the onlookers who watched with both envy and appreciation—and in command of Ana herself who surrendered to the fast-slow-fast-slow sway of Rudy's foxtrot.

As he dressed, Rudy hummed the popular songs of the day, inserting words here and there to display the progress of his American accent to Ana, who held onto her Spanish as if it were a shawl cloaking her from the cold. Rudy wriggled into his jacket to the beat of the song he hummed and then executed a few dance steps, again with his reflection, this time in the window, the neon blue of the diner sign flashing on his strutting figure.

"I can come if you'd like," Ana offered, though her clothes felt untidy and the pull of Carmela's mouth draining her breast made her drowsy.

"But Ana," Rudy scolded only half playfully, "you don't like the fights."

He took it personally that she didn't like boxing, didn't see the art in it.

"And besides, what about the baby?"

She held Carmela up as if to say *our baby*. Rudy stepped up, cooed at Carmela.

He delighted in her squirming, the way she threw her tiny

fists at him and worked her mouth in circles bubbly with saliva. "A fighter," Rudy laughed. "Just like me."

She pulled Carmela back. He dropped a kiss on the braid wound in a knot at the back of Ana's head.

"Who's fighting tonight?" she asked, as if it mattered to her.

"Jimenez and the Turk."

It was not Jimenez and the Turk for whom he dressed so fancy. It was for himself. But as long as he was dressed so prettily, it should not go to waste after the fights, and Ana knew he would stop at the dance hall afterward.

"What time will you be home?"

"Late. Get your rest," he told her. As if it mattered to him, she thought. He disappeared behind the flimsy door of their one-room apartment. But the smell of him lingered on—a bouquet of hair cream, mouthwash, and cologne. Ana dispersed it momentarily with a sigh.

She listened as his footsteps faded down the stairs, heard the slam of the street door shut them out completely.

She remembered the pound of her own footsteps the day she ran to meet him.

The South City Athletic Club, he had said importantly, as if it were a famous landmark. Nevertheless, he drew a map on the inside of a matchbook.

When she arrived, she was breathless from the walk, the distance longer than she had counted on. Sweat dampened her temples and the nape of her neck, places Rudy's fingers had grazed as they danced the night before. She dabbed at the moisture on her face with the back of her wrist, lifted her long hair and fanned herself with her hand. She worried about her appearance, how her ruffled hair and damp skin could make her seem careless.

She paused at the door to the gym. There was a sign that she couldn't read, except for the word *NO*, and this was enough to stop her. She didn't know what to do next. She took the matchbook out of her pocket and looked at it again.

NO had seldom stopped her before. But *NO* surrounded by as yet mysterious English words made her shy, even with a door. She backed away to look for another entrance that might not have *NO* on it. But once she turned the corner and started down the alley, she had to look no further. She came upon a small yard, an outdoor extension of the gym where several young men were engaged in various boxing exercises—punching a bag or sparring with an invisible opponent. Against a low brick wall a collection of women lounged attractively to admire the sleek fighters intent on their workout.

Ana understood that was where she was supposed to go, to sit with the other spectators, but she would not do it. She had not come to this country to be a spectator to someone else's life. Still she watched. Saw him dance, lithe and quick, evasive when necessary, attacking when he saw an advantage. She waited for Rudy to notice her, and when he didn't, she both fumed and felt forlorn as she turned to walk away. She had just rounded the corner when she heard Rudy call her name. It was almost a bark. And yet she did turn around because of the pleading inside his gruff command. She watched him trot toward her in his singlet and shorts, his hands fixed in boxing gloves, the bare portions of his body—arms and legs and a swath of chest—gleaming.

"Why are you running away from me?" he called.

Ana, who believed her life was not about running away but running toward something, did not answer, because she also did not believe in raising her voice in public. Rudy, however, was not concerned with the eyes that followed him down the street. *He's a spectacle,* she thought. A beautiful spectacle of a man. So when he asked his question again, instead of saying proudly, *I'm not running, I'm walking away,* she told him. "You were occupied." It came out apologetic instead of reproachful as she meant it to be. But it sent Rudy to his knee and Ana's will on a gentle gust of wind.

She didn't like the actual fights though. Fighting as sport didn't make sense to her. The first time Rudy took her, it was to watch a fighter whom he would face in the ring the following Saturday. As Rudy pointed out his soon-to-be opponent's strengths and flaws, Ana could feel the energy of his body, the intensity in his eyes, the readiness in his fists.

Ana closed her eyes each time a fist made contact. She wanted to cover her ears against the urgings of the crowd, through which an occasional grunt or groan from one of the fighters could be heard.

"Next week, you'll see me in there," Rudy said.

He said it as a certainty, and Ana wondered how he knew she would come.

He saved a place for her in the second row, just to the right of his corner, so she would always see him at least in profile. She covered her face at the bell.

She found herself trying to defend the sport to Irma and her husband, Donald.

"It's an art," Ana told them. "There is beauty in the movements." She had rehearsed the words that Rudy had so often given her, and though she could say them without error at Irma's dinner table where English was the rule, they sounded flimsy. Weightless.

Weightless was how Ana felt as she sat in the rocking chair

alone in the one-room apartment above the corner market, Carmela asleep in her crib. Here in this California city, the limits of her world were fixed by newspapers that she did not read because the English headlines baffled her, by street signs that were unfamiliar beyond a few blocks, and by conversations that rushed past her undecoded in the aisles of the market downstairs—sounds that were bland and indifferent, like the bread she bought there.

Ana stood up and paced the room slowly, stopping now and then at the window to look beyond the blue sign of the diner to the community hall. All she could see was the roof, but she knew that the windows blazed yellow with light, and inside, sweating couples danced as if their lives depended on it. And she knew that Rudy was there, dancing with first one and then another of the partnerless women that lined the wall near the punch table, fingering the glass beads at their necks, gazing with practiced nonchalance at the pairs of lilting bodies on the dance floor. As she paced, Ana heard Rudy's voice remind her that dancing was essential to his profession in the ring. It kept his reflexes responsive, rehearsed him for a fight.

She continued to trace the perimeter of the room, and with each turn she quickened her step. As the room began to shrink, she remembered how she used to walk the plaza in San Blas until, finally, she resisted those boundaries, making her way north on a slow, crowded train to end up here in Kimball Park in this apartment above the corner market. And the memory of why she came made the disturbance she felt in her stomach disperse to her limbs. It clenched her fists, made her feet jittery with energy.

Ana lifted the sleeping Carmela from her crib, descended the stairs, let the door slam shut behind her. She tucked the ends of her shawl around Carmela, though outside the night was warm and embracing. She crossed the street, passed under the cool, blue wink of the diner sign, and as she turned the corner to the community hall, she could already hear the music. She entered the hall and paused, let her eyes take in the pair of potted palms that curved dreamily at each end of the stage where the band, its members dressed in matching powder-blue jackets, delivered brassy jazz. She scanned the dance floor, restless with the undulations of entwined pairs, and in the middle was Rudy, limbering his muscles, timing his reflexes for his next fight, swirling an orange-chiffoned brunette, and not seeing Ana until she was within an arm's length of him and his partner.

He looked at her with alarm and tried to chase her away with his eyebrows, bushy, expressive caterpillars that, no matter what their message, seemed to Ana terribly persuasive. But the bundle in her arms squirmed and Ana was emboldened. She stood her ground. Rudy took his rumba in the opposite direction. He was ignoring her now, wanting to avoid a scene by pretending he didn't know her. He had guided his partner so deftly that she was so far unaware of Ana and the baby she held. But now Ana inserted herself in the space between Rudy and the chiffon lady. Before the chiffon lady could react, Ana was thrusting her arms out, displaying the swaddled Carmela who was awake now, her black eyes quizzical, a spit bubble emphasizing the O of her mouth. The chiffon lady recoiled and receded into the crowd around them, which had stopped dancing though the music continued. Ana was glad for the music, for the blare of the horns and the crash of the drums, making it difficult for any words to be heard. But words were unnecessary. She turned to Rudy who was smoothing his mustache, trying to hide his astonishment at her trespass into his territory. Yet she didn't claim her dance. Instead she carefully laid Carmela at his feet, at his shoes with their high sheen. Through the parting, gaping crowd, she walked away, trusting, knowing Rudy would follow.

RUDY ALWAYS SLEPT late on Sundays. He slept heavily. There was barely a trace of the cologne he'd slapped on himself last night before he left, barely a trace of the smells of crowded places— gin, sweat, cigarettes, chiffon-clad ladies. It was obscured by the apartment's stale air. By the odor of Ana's own skin.

Ana sat in the rocking chair, Carmela in her arms, and watched Rudy. His hair, still oiled from the night before, gave off a dull sheen, blotted the pillowcase that she would wash that morning. Outside, the diner sign was unblinking in the daylight. She closed her eyes, alert to the slightest noise, the merest change in temperature, the tempo of breathing.

Irma the Practical

———————— ❖ ————————

IRMA CLAMPED HER mouth so that the pins pressed into her lips and the tiny metal heads tilted toward the roof of her mouth. She had never swallowed any pins, but she thought of what it might feel like if she did. She removed them one by one, slipping them into the satin to hold the hem.

She smoothed the wedding dress that was spread across the bed and considered the different opportunities she would have that day to tell Donald she wanted a divorce—or rather, that she *would* have a divorce. Despite the church, despite the social stigma, it was an American thing to do, and she had been an American for nearly thirteen years now. She basted the hem of the dress in place, and with each pull of the needle, she recited one of the options—*when he comes home from work, after dinner, at bedtime.* When she had one stitch left to complete the hem, she was on the third option—*at bedtime*—but decided to add an extra stitch so that she ended up on *when he comes home from work.* And these were the words that filled her head like a broken record as she readied the dress for Louise Mitchell, who was coming for her final fitting this afternoon with that cow of a mother.

Irma carefully gathered up the dress from the bed, one arm beneath the bodice, the other cradling the skirt, the sleeves dangling free so that she appeared to be lifting a limp and senseless bride. Before placing the dress on the dressmaker's dummy, Irma held it against herself and stood in front of the mirror. It wasn't her size. She was tall and thin, while Louise Mitchell promised to assume the bovine bulk of her mother. Louise's current robustness notwithstanding, Irma had snipped and tucked at Mrs. Mitchell's instructions, and Irma could only hope that on the day of the wedding Louise had no plans to eat, sneeze, or laugh. Irma had done all these things on her wedding day nearly thirteen years ago in the Iglesia de Santa Cruz, the tiny church in Colonia Real.

She did not, however, have her own wedding dress. It was a dress that was shared among the family, traveling up the coast to be worn by one cousin or to the interior for the vows of another. Even as she pleaded with her mother to allow her to alter the neckline to suit her elongate frame and to add new lace at the sleeves, she was reminded that the dress must be preserved for her young cousin Ana. Irma shook her head now at the thought of Ana, who never did wear the dress, leaving Mexico without being married, arriving at Irma's door one day, tired and dusty but with a shine in her black eyes when she announced she had come to the United States for a better life, as if it were an original idea. As if her way was better than Irma's.

Perhaps if she had not worn a used wedding dress, perhaps if she had not celebrated with such uncharacteristic behavior—eating pan dulce until her stomach cramped, inhaling the scent of her bouquet until she showered it with a vigorous sneeze, laughing at the old and silly jokes about wedding nights that her male cousins delivered with a sly wink—perhaps things would have gone differently.

Idiota, she scolded herself now. She was too reasonable to succumb to such foolish explanations. Still, they were sometimes easier to accept than the truth—that she had married the wrong man.

As Irma positioned Louise Mitchell's wedding dress over the dummy, she remembered how she had thought her own wedding day would never happen, how she had made it happen.

Donald O'Hare had come to Mexico from *el norte* in 1917. The first time Irma saw him, she was behind the reception desk for the Bustamantes, a family of lawyers known in San Blas for their prodigious triumphs in the courts, the fruits of which did not improve the parsimonious wages paid to their office help. Irma greeted the *norteamericano* with her businesslike smile and accepted with a solemn nod the card he handed her. She motioned for him to sit down, and though the chairs in the Bustamante office were plush and comfortable, the *norteamericano* perched rigidly on the edge, his fingers quietly drumming the large black case at his side. He was a salesman, and Irma knew the Bustamantes kept such people waiting. As she busied herself with minor paperwork, she stole glances at the lanky American with thinning blond hair and pale blue eyes that reminded her of endless sky.

Ilusiones, thought Irma with both scorn and regret. She went to her sewing table and found the box of beads Mrs. Mitchell had left at the previous fitting. She winced as she wondered what that woman would bring today. At each of the last few fittings, Irma had watched Mrs. Mitchell open up her voluminous handbag and pull out a tendril of lace or a set of opalescent buttons or a tiny silver cross, saying, "This should add a bit of elegance." So Irma had affixed them all, the lace in a small bow at the waist, the buttons to accent the cuffs, the silver cross embedded at the throat in her skillful stitching. She congratulated

herself on her ability to incorporate these extraneous adorn-
ments without ruining the line of the dress. But these beads, she
thought as she rattled them in their box, could only be trouble.
"Ilusiones," Irma said aloud this time.

"It's a busy schedule today," she said to the American, who
answered with a polite smile that told of patience and endur-
ance. Irma looked at the card he had given her since already
she had forgotten his name, such was the impression made by
this quiet and pale man.

"Mr. O'Hare, would you like a cool glass of water?" she
asked, and the man answered in slow but proficient Spanish
with a pretty speech about the hospitality and beautiful people
of Mexico.

Irma blushed because she knew she wasn't beautiful, knew
also that this man was speaking about manners and customs,
which seemed to matter more to him than looks. A sentiment
she would have found noble had he himself not been so lacking
in physical beauty. And yet this man's very appearance—the
long and not entirely inelegant limbs; the kind, if docile, mouth;
the steady hope in his eyes—triggered something in Irma, an
impulse at first and then something much more calculated.

Knowing that it would be a half hour or more before one
of the Bustamantes deigned to receive the salesman, Irma sat
down next to Donald O'Hare, who took appreciative sips from
his water glass. She knew some English, an important skill for
someone like her who expected to move up in the world, who
was meant for someplace larger than San Blas. Though her
English was far from the fluency of Mr. O'Hare's Spanish, she
wanted to put it on display.

"And from where is it that you come, sir?"

He smiled to acknowledge her words as if they were something genial and gracious, and Irma flinched inwardly at her self-serving motives.

He gave a brief answer back in English. "From California. San Diego. Kimball Park, really."

But then, as if accepting Irma's linguistic offering for what it was—a gesture—he reverted to his slow but nimble Spanish.

He was in Mexico, he said, to satisfy a need for travel and adventure and, he added, to escape the persistent inquiries regarding his absence from the Great War. Asthma was not something conspicuous like a limp, was not regarded with the same consideration as other conditions or infirmities, he explained without rancor, though with a slight air of injury. Irma nodded in understanding, allowing a judicious pause before a casually phrased question about his return to Kimball Park.

It was here that Donald O'Hare was transformed, his body less rigid, his pale blue eyes more focused. He leaned forward and spoke in a confidential tone and immediately disappointed Irma by a wandering explanation of his job selling typewriters in Mexico, how his employer based in Guadalajara had assigned him to travel the smaller towns out toward the coast, how in his travels he had been struck by the variety of crafts, by the rainbow colors and the graceful designs painted on or woven into them.

Irma had nearly decided to leave the gringo to his ramblings and return to her desk when Donald O'Hare finally came to the point. He would start his own business in Kimball Park, selling authentic Mexican handmade goods. He had already accumulated an array of serapes, sombreros, ollas, obsidian sculptures of frogs and birds and Aztec gods, and clay replicas of pyramids. Within a few months he would be back in Kimball Park, no longer a traveling salesman. He would set up a shop and people would come to him. Irma nodded her head in approval. A marvelous idea, she agreed. She settled a gaze on him that conveyed how deeply sincere she was, and he responded with a smile and an invitation to dinner.

It was a small café, inexpensive and without intimacy. However, the candlelight flattered and the scratchy music from a radio filled the more than occasional silence between them. An agreeable silence, Irma thought and even ventured to say out loud.

"Yes," Donald said.

"It's as if words are not necessary between us."

Donald nodded, and Irma placed her hand on the table, the easier for him to take it in his own.

The wedding six weeks later was a simple and hurried affair, squeezed between a town procession in the morning and an evening fiesta in the church plaza to mark the start of the fishing season. This resulted in some additional and unexpected guests at the nuptials, morning stragglers or early fiesta-goers supposing them to be part of the daylong fishing celebration, and Donald O'Hare was seen embracing perfect strangers, supposing them to be the friends and family of his bride.

Herself a bit giddy, Irma excused this blunder, smug as she was about starting a new life in *el norte*. No longer would she answer to the Bustamantes or their clients in exchange for the slim wages she earned and the condescending looks she didn't. She would instead be a witness to her husband's business venture, an idea that never failed to produce a light in his pale blue eyes and a hope in Irma's dispassionate heart. It was this promise of a future for their thin, plain daughter with the stern face that persuaded her parents to so readily consent to her marriage to a foreigner. And so the wedding dress was brought out, sent down from the hills of Copala where it was last worn by a cousin of a cousin. Irma wore hyacinths woven in her hair and pinned at her throat because the flowers camouflaged her long neck and the reddish hue made up for the fact that her skin lacked the rich cinnamon tone of the other women of the region and was instead the color of corn tortillas.

The day after the wedding, Irma packed her modest belongings into Donald's car, already crammed with a final shipment of authentic Mexican crafts that would complete the inventory for the opening of the shop that Donald intended to call La Perla del Mar. While she agreed the name was romantic, Irma suggested something more straightforward and in English such as Treasures of Mexico or simply Treasures. But Donald's mind was made up, and Irma only shrugged, knowing that marriage was a compromise. Irma settled in the front seat of Donald's American car, and the overflow from the back seat of blankets, pottery, huaraches in every size, and miniature piñatas gave a feeling of festive abundance.

Before starting up the engine, Donald reached in his shirt pocket, withdrew a small box, and presented it to Irma, his eyes alive with the pleasure of giving. When she opened it, she emitted a quiet gasp of delight. She slipped the string of pearls around her neck and admired the way it swung down her chest as the light played on the beads like some congenial spirit.

Donald and Irma O'Hare drove through the dusty streets of San Blas, and with the cheers as well as her parents' sighs of relief behind them, they headed north on the highway. Through the mangroves of Sinaloa and the deserts of Sonora, skirting the border of Arizona and then California, the car took on sand and heat and the oppressive weight of the silence that had inserted itself between Donald and Irma from that first candle-light dinner.

"The strain of traveling," Donald said as they drove through Tijuana, trying to ignore the clothes laid out to dry, disembod-ied and abandoned on the roofs in the shanty towns.

"Exhausting," Irma added.

"Almost there," Donald said as the border gate came into view.

Irma leaned forward to look and her string of pearls that she had worn from the start of the trip looped around the gearshift. Before she had a chance to extricate herself, Donald downshifted, yanking the necklace loose and sending the beads to bounce and roll like the contents of a broken piñata. Her hands flew to her neck as if she could somehow restore the beads there intact. But even though Donald pulled the car over and they gathered the pieces into Irma's lap, even though they measured the number of beads they found against the length of the string to verify they had collected them all, they never restrung them.

Irma stirred Mrs. Mitchell's beads with her fingers. Best to anchor each one separately, she decided. Stringing the beads to loop at the waist would be a quicker solution, but the te-diousness of sewing each individual bead in place somehow ap-pealed to her. She threaded her needle and began her task, po-sitioning the first bead and then the next, marking a trail of the events in her life. The grand opening of La Perla del Mar, cel-ebrated with bunting and bright paper flowers that drew only a handful of people who fingered the merchandise curiously and then let it fall back to the shelf; the quiet closing of La Perla a few months later, the piles of unsold items moved to their tiny house to be stored under the bed, stacked in the closet, thrown across furniture, and crowded onto tables; Donald's return to a traveling sales job, this time door-to-door in the neighborhoods of Kimball Park, not the towns of west central Mexico; Irma's job in a sewing factory where the work was unimaginative, but Irma was not, finishing extra pieces to earn bonuses and eventually saving enough to buy her own Singer.

Throughout all of this, Donald and Irma did their duty by each other as husband and wife, producing a daughter who resembled her mother in every way and a son who was also a near replica of Irma except for the pale blue eyes. It was the passing on of this trait that left Donald completely bereft of the light in his own eyes that had once kindled with the dream of La Perla del Mar. As the years went by, it was Irma's sewing business that flourished. The concentration in her sharp face and the nimbleness of her thin fingers could swiftly yield uniforms, costumes, evening dresses, wedding gowns, whatever the customer desired.

Irma was nearly finished now with fulfilling Mrs. Mitchell's desire for beads on her daughter's wedding gown. She stepped back to examine the effect and was pleased again at how skillfully she had rendered a bad idea. She had sewn the beads into the folds of the skirt so that they were not immediately obvious, but a glint here, a gleam there, gave a hint of something to be disclosed. She stitched in the few remaining beads and as she drew the needle through the last one, the doorbell rang. Irma knotted the thread and broke the extra length with a practiced yank. She passed a final look of stern approval over her handiwork, then pulled her face into an agreeable expression for Mrs. Mitchell and Louise.

At the door, Mrs. Mitchell prodded Louise across the threshold and greeted Irma with a brisk, "And how is it looking today?"

"Elegant," Irma replied as she led the way to the dress.

Mrs. Mitchell confirmed this assessment with a deep, satisfied inhale. She breathed out slowly to savor her creation. "I knew it was a good idea!" she exclaimed. She looked to Louise who nodded dumbly.

"Louise," Mrs. Mitchell groaned in irritation. "Show some appreciation, dear." She steered her daughter closer to the dummy on which the dress was displayed. She cupped Louise's face in her hands, shook it slightly as she whispered urgently, "Honey, it's all for you."

Louise's round face went splotchy with a sudden onset of tears. "Oh, dear," Mrs. Mitchell sighed, pulling a handkerchief from her purse and mopping at her daughter's face with the same motion Irma had seen her use when wiping a spill from her teacup. "Louise has the bridal jitters," Mrs. Mitchell explained to Irma.

"It's perfectly normal," Irma remarked, though she offered this more from hearsay than from experience. Her own wedding day emotions arose not from second thoughts about her acceptance of Donald's polite and proper proposal, but from gratitude that it had been spoken at all.

"It just doesn't feel right," wailed Louise, who nonetheless yielded to her mother's hands, which busily unfastened belt, buttons, and hooks until she stood exposed in stockings and slip.

Irma removed the wedding dress from the dummy and held it out to Mrs. Mitchell, who stroked it like a favorite pet before helping her daughter into it. As Louise stood silent and stone-faced, Mrs. Mitchell smoothed the sleeves, fluffed the gathers at her daughter's thick waist, spread the skirt evenly around her feet, and carried on a vigorous monologue.

"Louise is marrying a dentist. She'll have a house, over on Clover Street, where so many of the best families have lived for years. It's a very good match for Louise."

Irma remained silent, her throat prickly as if small pins lodged there after all. She wished for the fitting to be over, wanting them out of her own house here on Fig Street, her home since her marriage to Donald.

Mrs. Mitchell was directing Louise to walk the length of the small room made smaller by their presence. She indicated with a twirling finger when Louise should pirouette left or right. Then she held up her hand to halt Louise, who was perched on the balls of her feet, her hands hovering at her sides, fingertips brushing the shiny white fabric of her dress.

"It just doesn't feel right," Louise said again, more quietly this time, but with no less conviction than before.

Mrs. Mitchell was more sympathetic now. Her voice was gently conspiratorial. "There's no shame in it, Louise. It's the way of things."

She motioned Louise forward. "Come, dear." She swayed her hand back and forth to set the tempo of her march. As Louise walked steadily toward them, Mrs. Mitchell nodded her head with encouragement while Irma watched the wink of the beads in the folds of the dress.

As Mrs. Mitchell and Louise left, Irma's children came home from school. They ducked from Mrs. Mitchell, whose hand found only air to pat. She laughed, and the sound made Irma think of the shrill chuckle of the mangrove cuckoo she used to hear as a girl in San Blas. The thought of her hometown made her nostalgic, not for the life she had there, but for the life she had counted on having here.

She revised the thought she'd had earlier about having married the wrong man. Who would she have married if not Donald? She went to the bedroom closet, and from beneath a pile of serapes and woven blankets filmy with age, she withdrew a cloth pouch. She didn't open it, just pressed it between her hands, felt the hard, knobby contents. She shook the pouch to hear the soft clack of small objects, then put it in the pocket of her sewing smock. The weight of it hit her in her stomach.

She heard the front door open and a clank of metal in the hall as Donald dragged in the model Hoover he demonstrated to housewives in their homes. She remembered the decision she'd made earlier in the day—*when he comes home from work*. She spied the check Mrs. Mitchell wrote out to her before she left, exclaiming something about taking care of business. "After all, marriage is a practical matter. Isn't that right, Irma?"

Donald's footsteps sounded in the hall, and she knew that when he entered the room she would see in his eyes the resignation and the faint, faint hope of a dream. Instead of greeting him, she headed to the kitchen to heat the stew for dinner. *After dinner*, she told herself.

Donald came in as she stirred the pot on the stove. He put his thin, barely puckered lips to her temple.

"How was your day?" she asked. She knew he took it as an inquiry into the number of vacuum cleaners he sold that day, which is, after all, how she meant it.

"Two," he answered. "Maybe."

She waited for him to explain.

"One customer isn't sure. She wants a second demonstration."

Irma wondered if when he was demonstrating his vacuum

cleaner a housewife might unbutton her housecoat, let it drop in a heap at her feet. She saw the handle of the vacuum cleaner slip from his grip, and while he satisfied his desire, the Hoover roared on its own, suctioning the same piece of carpet over and over. She wondered, but she knew better.

"Be forceful," she told him. "Show that you believe in your product."

"I am. I do."

Irma sighed into the pot, bubbling now.

At the dinner table, there was little conversation, the children as taciturn as their parents. It was the way they were, a quiet family, Irma reasoned. There was nothing wrong in it. And yet, she wanted to prod them in some way.

"Sit up straight," she said.

Her blue-eyed son complied. Her daughter did too, but in an exaggerated way, sitting stiff and tall, her shoulders at her ears, her chin tilted upward. It was a posture that was both cartoonish and familiar, and Irma was suddenly seized with the suspicion that her daughter was imitating her. But then she saw the earnest look on her face and knew she was sincere, which made Irma feel worse than if her daughter had been mocking her.

After dinner, Irma released the children from their kitchen chores and sent them off to play in their rooms. Donald went to the living room to watch the evening programs. Irma sat at the uncleared kitchen table with a bottle of beer. *At bedtime,* she thought. She got up and took a second bottle from the refrigerator and carried it into the living room. She set it on the coffee table in front of Donald and left quickly so that he had to call out his thanks to her retreating back.

She still had the hem of Louise Mitchell's dress to finish. The dress was on the headless dressmaker's dummy. She knelt at

the hem, lifted and let fall the folds, eyed the bottom for even-
ness. Her work was faultless. She removed the dress from the
dummy, laid it across the bed just as she had done earlier in the
day, and sewed the hem in place with a permanent stitch.

At least that girl was starting out with a dress of her very
own. It was one more in a long line of wedding dresses Irma
had made. Tomorrow she would begin another.

Tomorrow Donald would show another housewife a vacuum
cleaner.

The Last Canasta

———— ❖ ————

1. Toby barked

Maybe, Rosa thought later, it was just time for things to collapse, like an old shed whose supports had been gradually removed, like an old dog with arthritic limbs.

The first thing that was wrong was the order of arrival, Irma spanking the screen door before rather than after the others, as if she were there to get it over with. Ana, less dreamy-eyed than usual, came next, and Rosa was outnumbered by the cousins, whose constant quibbling belied their allegiance to each other. And Lupita, who should have been there first, arrived after the lemonade was poured. What's more, she came with her apron on, as if Rosa's living room was just an extension of the Camacho residence.

Rosa's house was in Lupita's backyard, shoved up against the alley so when she exited through her backdoor, she lurched into the ruts in the dirt road. When she sat on her front porch, Lupita's wash waved at her in lazy, offhand ripples. At least the curtain of sheets, towels, and trousers obscured Sergio's shed, a rotting plywood and tar paper igloo that sheltered a lawnmower and some seldom used fishing rods, but mostly pyramids of canned dog food that Rosa suspected were what really propped up the makeshift building. A stake in the dusty ground at the shed's entrance held the twenty-foot chain that kept Toby from ranging beyond the fan of dirt that he had beaten clear of grass with his stiff but obstinate limbs. Toby usually lay at the center of the fan, directly in the flight of the wooden swing that hung from a misshapen tree nearby. No one used the swing anymore, but sometimes Rosa imagined her bulk in the hard narrowness of the seat, pushing off with both feet and aiming her high heels at the old dog's soft center.

This morning as she passed Lupita's rose garden, Rosa plucked a large, fleshy bloom, shielded it with her body as she scuttled past the shed, past Toby, past the swing to the tiny house that she and Camilo rented from Lupita and Sergio Camacho. She trimmed the stem of the rose and slipped it into the narrow vase of blue glass whose edges curled like wavelets of water. The petals slouched upon the hard blue curls because she had trimmed the stem too close. She put the vase and its stolen rose in the usual place atop her bedroom dresser where visitors were not likely to see it, a place where she herself often forgot about it, so that days later she found dried petals had floated into corners, fallen inside her drawer and mingled among the itchy fake lace of her underwear, or glided inside the bedsheets where her toes met their soft crackle instead of Camilo's calluses.

It was Rosa's house where the four women met each Saturday afternoon for a game of canasta. They met here because Rosa was the only one who didn't have children to interrupt their game and their gossip. She liked having the women at her house. But she would rather have had children. Maybe. At least she would've liked to have had the possibility.

She entertained her guests first in her living room, despite its cramped dimensions, because the chattiness that occurred and the *canciones* they sang when they weren't preoccupied with making a canasta were the most enjoyable parts of the afternoon. There were shelled peanuts in little ceramic dishes on either end of the scarred coffee table that she had covered with a throng of doilies, and in the middle a pitcher of lemonade, three matching clear glass tumblers, and a golden-tinted one, though Irma called it amber. Rosa rotated the gold glass among her guests as consolation to the one who had to have her as a partner. Besides, it hid the fact that she didn't have a full set of matching glasses. Later they would move to the kitchen table, Rosa reluctantly, since card games bored her and she found herself attentive only to Irma's constant intake of *galletas*, expensive ones that she felt obliged as hostess to offer.

Though everything was the same as usual—the refreshments, the arrangement of pillows on the sofa, the two decks of cards side-by-side in trim stacks on the kitchen table—Rosa couldn't help but feel that today was different from all the previous Saturdays. Maybe it was Toby's barking at some phantom enemy, or the way the wind gusted suddenly off the alley bringing the odor of garbage cans and the dust of dandelions, or the column of ants she had seen drag away a twitching beetle when she had gone outside earlier to sweep the porch.

She held a glass of lemonade out to Lupita, who made herself at home in the yielding old sofa. Rosa herself was still standing, and she felt a moment of separation from the three who were sitting—Lupita getting the best of the tired springs beneath her, Ana already daydreaming in the chirping rocker, and Irma in the stiff wingback with which her long thin frame had formed some sort of alliance.

2. Irma asked a question

There was no give to the cushion, and her spine and tailbone meeting the chair's hardness produced a bracing friction, but

Irma liked the angle it gave her of the room and its occupants. It was a meek little house, and Rosa's attempts at interior decorating were as accomplished as her exertions with face powder and eyebrow pencil, a regretful encounter between cheap cosmetics and a faded facade. They all pitied Rosa for her bids at glamour, Irma most of all, who long ago had reconciled herself to the uninspiring cast of her own face.

"Who shall we listen to?" asked Rosa, chirping like Ana's chair. She pointed to a selection of records, the four that she owned and the six on loan from Lupita. Irma considered the two friends, how Lupita invariably tipped the balance, not extravagantly, but unmistakably. Six records to Rosa's four, a rose garden to Rosa's potted geraniums, a full set of glassware to Rosa's mismatched four. Small things. Then there was the fact of Lupita's house and seven children, and this tiny rental that Rosa inhabited with just Camilo.

"Pedro Infante," Ana said.

But Irma said Jorge Negrete.

Rosa's sigh was like the swish of a broom as she looked to Lupita to defuse the standoff. But Lupita was studying the ice in her glass. Rosa wanted everyone to behave in her house, but only Lupita could make that happen. And today she was indifferent, perhaps resigned, which amused Irma, but also made her watchful.

Rosa's house was too small for disharmony, and the four of them through their years of friendship had adjusted their passions to its size. So Irma said, "Pedro Infante. Why not?" She saw, not regretfully, that she had confused Rosa because Ana was the one who always gave in. When Rosa set the phonograph playing, it was Negrete after all whose warble displaced the stuffy air.

Rosa offered Ana a silent apology, that funny pucker in her

forehead, which nearly closed the space between her penciled brows. Ana replied with a shrug, and Irma absently filled her mouth with peanuts as she now studied Ana's preoccupation.

Lupita began to sing along to "Cuando Quiere un Mexicano." Her eyes were closed, and her hands, still in the pockets of her apron, marked the rhythm. Soon they all began to sing, mouths wide with the words of love. Irma didn't care that she misted peanut particles into her lap with each syllable of song.

"Look at us," she said when they had protracted the last note even past Negrete's lavish achievement. "Braying like donkeys."

"Speak for yourself," Ana said. She was the only one among them who could carry a tune, but she was always drowned out by the others.

Irma could still feel the echo of their song in the walls of the house. "Why do we always listen to Mexican music?"

The others sat a moment looking at Irma, and she welcomed their silence, their contemplation of the question.

"Because we do," Rosa said finally, looking at the record cover in her hands as if that explained it all. "We sing along."

"And who would you rather have us bray like donkeys to?" Lupita asked.

"Maybe Perry Como." Irma wasn't just showing off that she listened to American music. She really did like the patterns and resonance of English. Her ear was habituated to its hard sounds, her face to its mouth-stretching vowels.

"We don't know the words," Rosa said.

"You could learn." *As I have*, Irma thought.

3. Ana sang

"Ana knows American songs. Sing one," Irma prodded.

Ana was annoyed whenever Irma gave her orders. *Sing a song,*

Ana. As if she were her cousin's parrot. Yet Ana did want to sing. Not to please Irma or to show off her American vowels. She wanted to sing the song from the radio, the one Rudy sang all the time, when he shaved, when he dressed, when he took the stairs two at a time from their apartment to meet his friends and the words stayed behind in her head—words about an enchanted evening, about finding your true love. She wanted to get them out, to expel them like some bad germ. She didn't stop rocking her chair to sing. In fact, she sped up the lurch of it, the chirp became a screech to accompany her voice, both so insistent that even she didn't know what emotion was driving the sounds.

4. Lupita didn't laugh

Lupita sank deeper into the sofa, not seeking its comfort. It had none to offer. It was Ana's singing from which she shied. Lupita knew this song from the radio. It was a love song. Wistful. Hopeful. Like youth, which had deserted her. But Ana performed it like a joke that was only funny to the one who was telling it.

5. Rosa roused them all

Rosa was dismayed by her guests. "Let's play canasta," she announced, clapping her hands the way she did when she chased pigeons that roosted on her flower box.

"As always," Irma said.

6. A salesman knocked

They moved to the kitchen and took their places at the table. This week Irma and Lupita were partners. They sat opposite each other and Ana and Rosa did the same. Ana dealt and Irma watched her smooth hand flit across the table, the cards radiating from her long fingers. Irma thought it unnecessary to be so graceful at such an ordinary task as this. She picked up her cards and slapped a red three faceup in front of her, drew a replacement from the deck. The others discarded and drew as well, Rosa wielding her cards even more sharply than Irma. Not intentionally, though. Rosa was an elephant in eye shadow and lipstick, her thick movements were true to her lumpish and ponderous body. Irma felt no guilt in thinking such thoughts, knowing how the others looked upon her. She thrust her face further into their disagreeable contours.

Irma looked over her cards at Lupita. She wondered if Lupita liked having her as a partner, if she would miss the way her points snaked down the score sheet when the columns were tallied.

Before Irma took the next turn, there was a knock. It jarred them, so unused were they to having someone come to the door. Rosa's house was not completely hidden from the street, but its size and color gave it a dollhouse quality and so it was usually ignored.

Lupita raised her eyebrows at Rosa, but Rosa's own eyebrows were already arched like cathedral doors as she dropped her cards at Irma's elbow and skidded her chair back from the table with the fullness of her buttocks. Lupita's eyes followed Rosa as she scurried to the door, wending her hips though the narrow spaces between the furniture. She leaned from her chair to see Rosa reach the door, but she straightened when Irma pretended to cough.

"How curious for Rosa to have a visitor," Irma commented after sipping some lemonade and pretending its tartness caused her pursed lips. "A peddler, probably."

"There's a sign at the front that says No Peddlers," Lupita said.

"At your front door," Irma pointed out. "This is Rosa's front door."

"And I'm the landlady. And her best friend."

"Yes," Irma said and dabbed a napkin at the corners of her mouth.

They listened to the voices at the door. The salesman spoke Spanish. Lately, companies had been sending Spanish-speaking salesmen into their neighborhood with the result that more residents were buying encyclopedias, clocks, magazine subscriptions, backscratchers, and other items of vague importance to their lives. Lupita confessed that just last week she herself had spent money meant for a new pair of shoes on a set of wind chimes, which only triggered barking from Toby. Now a salesman was interrupting their canasta game.

"Rosa," Lupita called, "No pierdas el tiempo."

"Un momentito." She sang it like a radio jingle.

Lupita tapped her cards on the table, Irma helped herself to another galleta, and Ana excused herself to go to the bathroom. Finally, Lupita threw down her cards and marched to the front door.

7. *Ana looked in the mirror*
Ana rid herself of the watery lemonade with a sigh. There was something about being in Rosa's house that made her thirsty, made her drink the near-colorless lemonade in alarming quantities. Maybe it was the heavy scent of living—the nicotine that laminated the walls, the aged ammonia preserved in the linoleum, the lard that sat white and waxy in an open jar next to the stove, and Rosa herself, a panic of hair spray and cologne.

As Ana held her hands beneath the faucet, she checked herself in the mirror. She was the youngest of the four women and, without any trace of conceit, she recognized that she was the prettiest. When would her features turn hard like Irma's, tired like Lupita's? Would she one day camouflage her deficiencies with impervious cosmetics? She looked for Rosa's makeup in the bathroom but saw only soaps, powders, and mouthwash in the cabinet and on the counter.

In the years they'd been playing canasta, Ana had never been inside Rosa's bedroom, though she had glanced inside on occasion and caught a glimpse of the silver satin bedspread that Rosa claimed was an exact duplicate of the one Rita Hayworth reclined on in her famous pinup pose. Ana had always honored the privacy of this woman, simply because there was no mystery about her. Everything about her was conspicuous. Nothing to be revealed.

But today, Ana paused at the door to Rosa's bedroom. It was dim inside since the shades were drawn at the window to the alley. She crossed the threshold. The air smelled different here than the rest of the house, still burdened, but less so. Ana ran her hand along the bedspread, discovered that, of course, it wasn't really satin. She fingered a frayed edge, imagined Rosa and Camilo side by side beneath the sheets, her large breasts billowing out from his cupped palms. Was he a gentle lover? Was he faithful? Was she?

She thought of Rudy last night, his ex-boxer's body above her, his elbows making deep wells in the mattress on either side of her, and how she had felt herself sinking. Rudy was passionate as ever, but she knew she couldn't absorb it all. The intensity that he once reserved for an opponent in the ring was now at large and undirected. He was back painting again—houses, storefronts, bowling alleys. He had recently taken up bowling, and on Friday and Saturday nights he rattled down pins with the black balls that he hurtled down the lanes with the force and speed of a right hook. That was where some of that extra energy went, to the Bayside Lanes, and when he came home his shirts carried the smell of beer and sweat and cigarettes. And sometimes perfume.

Ana saw Rosa's small vanity table in the corner and seated herself on its small stool, wondering how it accommodated Rosa's generous bottom. She examined the dime-store perfumes, their peeling labels, cloying scents. She looked in the mirror and saw Rosa penciling her eyebrows, stroking rouge onto her cheeks, tracing her mouth in red, coloring her face the way Ana's daughters drew hers with crayons on paper.

8. Lupita's hands were in her apron pockets
She was making fists.

9. Rosa examined the merchandise
Rosa heard Lupita approaching and quickly invited the salesman inside. The display case he had been balancing on his knee now rested on the coffee table, and the sheen of the door knockers that glinted in the sunlight seemed diminished in the stingy space of the living room.

"Mira, qué bonito," she said, waving her hand across the display as if she herself were the seller and Lupita the customer. "A choice of gold, silver, or bronze." She repeated the pitch of the salesman who stood beside her nodding and smiling. But Lupita waved her own hand to dismiss the salesman and his merchandise.

"We don't need any," she said, poking a finger at the open case. The salesman rescued his collection of door knockers, snapping the case shut and safeguarding it under his arm as he lunged out the door, down the walk past Toby and the shed and the flapping laundry.

Rosa wanted to run after him, to tell him to come back tomorrow, but Lupita was shaking her fist at the trespasser. She wanted to shout at Lupita that this was her house, that she had the right to have a salesman in her living room, that she should decide whether she needed something, that, in fact, she did need a door knocker and Lupita as landlady should buy it for her. It would improve the appearance of this comfortless house, and it would save a person's knuckles on the wood where the paint was starting to crack. But she only watched as Lupita shut the door, muttered something about fools and scoundrels, and stalked back to the kitchen. Rosa followed, her molars compressed against each other, and wondered if she could ever get even.

"Where's Ana?" she asked as she sat down.

"Bathroom," said Irma. Rosa looked down the short hallway to see Ana emerge from her bedroom. She studied Ana's face to see what she had discovered, but Ana's faraway stare swept right past Rosa's questioning glare.

Ana took her seat, "Shall we play?"

10. Irma was the only one holding her cards

She made a black canasta, placing the wild card at right angles to the others. She preferred it to a red canasta, the natural or pure meld of cards. She liked having a string of queens or tens or eights interrupted by a deuce. Or a Joker.

11. Ana wanted to pass

Why did they play as partners? Ana wondered. Why did everyone have to have a turn? Why did Irma have to be the one to make a canasta?

12. Lupita took stock

As play progressed around the table, each snap of a card being drawn or discarded increased the weariness Lupita carried inside her, clustered like the hardened scraps of dough and other crumbs furry with lint in her apron pocket, the residue of a morning's work. Sometimes she forgot to empty her pocket and the detritus was washed and ironed with the apron, making her pocket bumpy with the dense flat nodules. There was a certain comfort in running her thick fingertips over the uneven shape of them, in peeling them away from the fabric, loosening them so they jiggled in her palm. But tossing them away seemed almost a denial of her strength and purpose, which was to toil and nurture even when nobody seemed to notice or care.

When her children were little, they held her hand, followed her around, demanded a kiss at bedtime. It was reflexive, unwilled. Now, just as instinctively, they overlooked her, passed through the kitchen with a nod more at the food she was cooking than at her. She had become a joke to them. When she tried to break up a fight that morning between Milagros and Alicia Carmen, they ignored her remonstrations to release each other's throat. Armed with the broom she had been using to coax a spider from her pantry, she charged at her daughters, aiming for the hip-level gap between them. But it was not the broom that separated them. They were each overcome with laughter at the ranting spectacle of her, which spurred her on to chase Milagros around the dining room table while Alicia Carmen cheered with shouts of *olé* and *toro*. When Milagros had completed two laps of the table, she ducked behind Alicia Carmen, and Lupita had them both down the barrel of her broom, ready to dispense a little discipline. But Milagros yelled "Afuera!" and they took off in opposite directions, Milagros scampering out the back and Alicia Carmen through the front and over the porch railing in a dancer's leap. Lupita was left alone, her broom swaying in her hands like a sorry foxtrotter as she looked out the dining room window at her daughters intercepting each other in the side garden of pink hibiscus, clutching shoulders as they collapsed together, kicking the air in hysteria at their victory. She clutched her broom tighter as she realized how little control over her children a mother really had.

She couldn't be a mother to these women. Of course not. Not all of them anyway. Especially Irma, who was so aloof and mocking and who flaunted her preferences for American things the way a butcher brandishes his knives.

Once it had been easy to count all the things they had in common. Now their list of differences was longer. Now it was a catalog of complaints. Lupita named one silently each time a card was drawn or discarded.

– Irma's ear had been retuned for American harmonies.

– Irma ate more than her share of Rosa's galletas.

– Irma spoke English without hesitation or unease.

– Irma sneered with her potato face at Rosa's makeup.

– Irma's laughter happened by itself, a vibration apart from theirs.

– Irma played cards as if it were a duty instead of a game.

– Irma was winning the game.

13. Four women . . .

Rosa insisted on making conversation during the game once she realized her team was irredeemably behind. "Toby was barking this morning."

"I looked out the window, but nothing was there," she continued when nobody answered. "Barking at nothing."

"Qué perrito loco," Ana said lazily.

Toby was Sergio's dog, a decaying bowlegged mutt. Still, Lupita defended him. "He barks for a reason."

"Squirrels," Ana suggested.

"Boredom," Irma declared, then reconsidered. "A thief, maybe."

"Out to ransack Sergio's shed," giggled Rosa. But then she also revised her theory. "Or steal the laundry," she sputtered, her cheeks shedding powder as they agitated with laughter.

"Or Lupita's roses." Irma lifted her eyes from her cards for a moment.

Rosa's throat clogged with the reined-in laughter. She changed the subject abruptly to door knockers. "What kind do you have?" she asked Irma and Ana.

"You've been to our homes," Irma said. "You notice everything."

"Yes," Rosa admitted. "Let's see, you have a doorbell, Ana has a wooden door knocker . . ."

"Oak," Ana said, though it was only a veneer.

"Oak," repeated Rosa as if it was a salient point in her argument. "Lupita has a doorbell *and* a door knocker, and I . . ."

"Rosa," Irma interrupted, "who comes to your door except for us? Besides," she added, "it's Lupita's house."

"And Rosa's hospitality," Lupita said, coming to her defense as she had Toby's a few minutes earlier.

Irma sighed, a whoosh that made everyone motionless with yearning.

"May I go out?" Irma asked, using the phrase to end the game. As her partner, Lupita had to answer yes or no. The answer was binding.

But Irma didn't wait. She discarded her final card. Play stopped and Lupita dutifully scored the round. But no one was paying attention to the numbers her pencil rasped onto the sheet of scented stationery Rosa always provided for the reckoning of points. Ana wandered off to inspect a spot of yellow color on the kitchen floor that turned out to be a stray rose petal. Irma finished off the last of the galletas. Rosa scraped crumbs from the table into her hand.

2

Ambition

Natalie Wood's Fake Puerto Rican Accent

---------------- ❖ ----------------

WHEN LYLA MARRIED Vin at age sixteen, her belly three months swollen, she still believed she would dance again and kept the photo from Lupita's Brownie camera framed on her dresser as insurance. When she divorced Vin the year the twins turned eight, she put the photo away in her underwear drawer, face down among the tangle of panties and push-up bras. Even Lupita (her mother) and Rosa (her mother's best friend), who in their irksome, scolding way had long nurtured her dream of stardom, by that time had ceased their clink of Saturday night Coronas in fervent toasts to her *destino*.

Now, two years later, Lyla removes the photo from the mesh of lace and straps, frees it from its frame, and holds a lighter just below the scalloped border of the black-and-white glossy. But the heat has barely curled the corner when she suddenly releases the photo, lets it fall to the floor, and lights a cigarette instead. She leans into the mirror and watches herself smoke, exaggerating her cheekbones as she sucks in nicotine. Her exhale flattens her too-broad nose, a feature to which she has never been reconciled. Her attention turns to the cigarette burning between her fingers, the smoke coming between her own face and her mirrored one. She is careless with the ashes, whisking them off the dresser with the edge of her pinkie.

She retrieves the photo, its corner limp, shoves it back into the frame, and is about to stash it back in her drawer when she thunks it atop the dresser instead. She changes out of her slacks and paisley tunic into a lime-green polyester mini-dress and go-go boots, and as she checks herself in the mirror, she mimics the pose in the photo—a victory arabesque as she reaches for the trophy that her once-upon-a-time dance partner Ricky holds above his head. *Ricky*, she sighs, as she heads to her daughters' room.

Ofelia is buttoning Norma into a ruffled dress just like her own, gifts from Vin who hasn't an ounce of taste, a trait Lyla fears has been passed to their daughters. They stand side by side for Lyla's inspection. She smiles encouragement as she removes the clip-on bows they have affixed to one another's heads. "What movie are we going to see?" they ask together, grimacing at each other's unadorned hair.

She is always a bit disconcerted whenever her daughters speak in unison. "A modern tale of Romeo and Juliet," she tells them, failing to hide her irritation that they can't remember the name of this Broadway hit brought to the big screen. Hasn't she sung them her repertoire of musicals from *Gentlemen Marry Brunettes* to *The King and I* to *South Pacific*? Hasn't she insisted they sing along with her to "I Feel Pretty?"

She kisses the tops of their heads and tries not to care that her daughters are not delicately made like she is, but large-boned and thickly built like Vin. *Vin*, she sighs.

WHEN THEY WERE still together, Vin would come home from his job as a car salesman to find her cueing their curled and crinoline-clad daughters to step lightly to "Good Ship Lolli-pop," while dinner sat still packaged on the kitchen counter. So they went to the twenty-four-hour pancake house, and while Vin allowed the girls to order the large stack, Lyla put her foot down when it came to the bacon.

She had sent them to dance lessons when they were old enough, but the sight of them packed in sequined leotards or tiny, flared dance skirts had been too much for her. Instead she took them shopping or to the movies.

In the movie theater, she sits between her daughters to mon-itor their intake of popcorn and bonbons, but as soon as the Jets start snapping their fingers, start kicking and leaping and landing in cool-guy arabesques, Lyla is caught up in the jazzy rhythms that signal danger and daring and ultimately despair. She gasps when the Sharks come on the scene and one of them is a dead ringer for Ricky, her old dance partner. She claps her hands over her mouth to stifle a shout of delight when Rita Moreno, authentically brown, sashays onto the screen and ex-claims, "I like to be in Amerrri-ca!" and Lyla feels a long-held regret thump in her chest.

But it's the sight and sound of Natalie Wood opening her mouth in a preposterous imitation of a Puerto Rican's English that makes her choke, anguish clogging her windpipe along with some inhaled popcorn. Even Ofelia and Norma giggle at Na-talie Wood's fake accent. Lyla thinks it should have been her up there emoting through the dialogue, mouthing the words to "I Feel Pretty," dancing with Richard Beymer, kissing him with passion, walking away, noble and good, from his bullet-pierced body. She should have been Maria. She—Lyla Castillo, neé Alicia Carmen Camacho, the youngest daughter of Ser-gio and Lupita, Mexican immigrants and now proud, though

barely English-speaking Americans—she could have played a
Puerto Rican!

And why not? There was Ricky, a Filipino, for heaven's sake,
playing a *puertoriqueño*. Her face burns and her hands clench as
she recalls Vin's gentle but laughing admonition to her when she
was Alicia Carmen, fifteen years old and, yes, full of herself, but
also full of hope, which he so lovingly dashed. "Mexicans don't
become movie stars in Hollywood," he whispered, as he ran his
lips along the side of her face. Though Vin's hushed tone was
romantic and beguiling as if he were paying her compliments,
the words were little spasms against her cheek. She waited for
their prickling chill to dissipate. He was wrong. Wasn't he? And
how much did she believe him when he said everything was
going to be fine as his hand traveled up her thigh?

After the Sharks and the Jets come together to carry Tony's
body away, she studies the credits but doesn't find Ricky's name.
It doesn't matter. Even if that wasn't Ricky up on the screen, it
could've been, and that seems to count just as much.

When the credits cease to roll, when the lights go up, she
wipes her face of tears. She knows her daughters are staring at
her. Her large-boned daughters, who can barely differentiate
their left foot from their right, whose fingers shine with popcorn
residue, each pat one of her hands.

"It was a sad movie, wasn't it, Mama?" they ask.

Lyla wipes her hands, greasy from her daughters' touch, with
the crumpled napkin she has used for her tears. "Life can be
tragic," she sniffles through the nose she has never managed to
have fixed.

She follows her daughters out of the movie theater into the
glare of the afternoon. In the parking lot, she has an urge to

grab her daughters and spin them in circles. To wave her skirt and stomp her feet, toss her head like Rita Moreno and sing a piercing "I like to be in Amerrr-ica."

But her daughters are already at the car, and she watches them squeeze themselves into the back seat. On the drive home, her daughters start humming the theme song, bouncing in their seats and snapping their fingers, each to her own clumsy rhythm. Lyla focuses on the road in front of her, but it tugs at her—who she used to be, who she might have been.

And just like that, as if God or the universe or Jerome Robbins were telling her there *are* second chances, the idea comes to her.

At home, while Ofelia and Norma snack on carrots and brownies, Lyla calls Frannie and, with hardly a greeting, demands of her sister, "Ricky Bayla. Whatever happened to him?"

Frannie, the girl who sat on the sidelines in high school, nevertheless has managed to track the whereabouts and goings-on of their classmates, whereas when Lyla, the popular one, dropped out of school, it was as if she had been resettled to another planet, with Vin and the twins the only other living beings.

"Ricky? That cute dance partner of yours who had a crush tan gigantesco on you? The one whose advances you scorned and exploited? Ese?"

Lyla remembers the afternoon she hurried away from dance practice, away from tiny Lola clapping her hands to her own choreography, away from Ricky and his big ears and lovestruck eyes, his shy swagger as he mumbled, endearing as a puppy, "Hey, Alicia, wanna go for a Coke?" She had declined, politely, and as consolation she caressed his shoulder lightly the way she did when they danced. Then with the smell of Ricky's sweat-stained shirt still in her nostrils and Lola's admonition of *más ánimo* in her ears, she went purposefully and ardently to the Hotel Ritz to meet Vin.

"Yes, Frannie, that one."

"Well, I thought you knew."

Lyla wonders how Frannie has come to have the upper hand. It was she, Lyla, who used to bully Frannie and sweet-talk Ricky into cutting school to go to the movies to see Fred and Ginger or Gene Kelly and Cyd Charisse. On the way home, she tried the steps herself and made Ricky do the same, and they danced around lampposts and dodged pedestrians. She made Frannie dance, too, and Frannie laughed at the absurdity of a gimpy girl like herself wiggling her hips in a jazzy swing move until a misstep sent her stumbling, and then shame over her polio-shrunken leg turned her giggles to tears.

Lyla sighs her impatience. "Knew what?" she asks.

"Ricky and his wife have a dance studio in the valley. They teach little muñecas how to dance. Big ones, too. Housewives and secretaries and store clerks. They put on shows. Ted Mack's Amateur Hour." Frannie is all cackles.

THE FOLLOWING WEEKEND Lyla is jittery as she sits at the breakfast table with her daughters. Under the table her legs are crossed and the vigorous swing of her top leg makes the milk dance in the cereal bowls.

"Mama, stop," Ofelia says, circling her bowl with a protective arm.

"Don't whine," Lyla tells her. She gives a few more bounces to the table before she settles both feet to the floor and takes a last sip of coffee, adding one more smear of lipstick to the rim. "Well, finish your breakfast. Your dad should be here soon."

Norma eyes her over her buttery toast. "Why is he coming so early?"

"So you can have a little extra time together this weekend." Lyla goes to the sink and drops her cup into a tub of suds, then turns around and leans against the counter, arms crossed, waiting.

"What are you going to do while we're gone?" Norma asks through her chewing.

"What I always do when you're with your father," Lyla says. "I'll be missing you."

Norma snorts, spraying bits of toast.

Normally she would scold such impertinence, but today she dismisses it, turning back to the sink to wring a sponge, ready to wipe down the table as soon as her daughters swallow the last of their breakfast. But her daughters seem particularly bent on making a siege of it, so Lyla runs the sponge along the bread box, cookie jar, toaster.

She lingers at the toaster, at her distorted reflection in the chrome, at her wide nose made wider. When she was young, she told herself it was a minor shortcoming, that nose of hers, because the movies offered larger-than-life color proof of what was possible if you could demonstrate all the major emotions while keeping a rhythm. The day she left rehearsal, ditching Ricky to meet Vin, was a day when the possibilities for change seemed infinite and reachable. She had stopped on the way to gaze at the poster in front of the Roxy. It was *Summer Stock* with Judy Garland and Gene Kelly. She had seen it three times already, had practiced "Get Happy" on the front porch in full view of passing traffic, in the kitchen for Lupita and Rosa, naked in the bathroom. She stood there, a sassy and sure Alicia Carmen, fixed on the poster that had a head shot of Judy and a full body shot of Gene in mid-jeté. She imagined it was her there on the poster with a remodeled nose adorning her face and a new name, Lyla, splashed across the page. She caught her reflection in the display glass, its polish distorting her hopeful gaze to a wondering gape. Startled at this insinuation of doubt, she hurried off to the hotel for her rendezvous with Vin.

Lyla swipes the toaster with her sponge, then turns around to an empty table. Her daughters have vacated without clearing their dishes, and she is debating the advisability of yelling at the top of her lungs for them to get their butts back in the damned kitchen, when they reappear, steering Vin as if delivering him to her. He greets her with a kiss the way he seldom did when they were married, though she has told him not to as it encourages the girls' hopes that they will marry again, which they certainly will not, Lyla always tells them to no avail. But the kiss is always respectful and platonic and today even more so. In fact, it's downright distracted, and Vin appears almost as jittery as she feels—as if he is the one with some bold, life-changing design.

Her daughters start to clear their breakfast dishes, but she shoos them off. "Just go," she tells them. "Go on and get ready."

They're quick to comply, happy to abandon their kitchen chores but even more eager to leave Lyla and Vin alone together, and she shakes her head at their childish delusion.

Though she does not want to prolong Vin's stay, she offers him a cup of coffee.

"No, thanks," he says, not in that mumbling, laid-back way of his, but like a timid schoolboy, something he has never been.

She stares at him, her ever-handsome ex-husband, all-occasion sharp dresser in his sport coat and open-necked shirt, from which dark hairs sprung dense and curly just below his collarbone. "Anything the matter?" The question seems to rouse him from his oddly diffident demeanor. "No, no, nothing's the matter." As if to prove it, he slouches against the counter, and she wonders if he's being deliberately sexy.

She remembers him in high school—no man-about-campus since he didn't play any sports, wasn't a member of any club, and couldn't claim any academic success beyond showing up for class. But he sure could lounge sexily against the fender of his Chevy lowrider or his seldom opened locker, which she made sure to pass each morning.

"Mornin', Alicia Carmen," he would say. It slid out the side of his mouth, like a blade of grass from Montgomery Clift's lips in *A Place in the Sun.*

Sometimes she returned the greeting, sometimes she just smiled as she walked by in the straight skirt that outlined her hips and accentuated her dancer's legs. And if she wasn't brainy like June Allyson's character in "Varsity Drag" and lacked her pert nose, she could burn up the dance floor in a mean jitterbug. And she had a full, pouty mouth and could affect a June Allyson innocence, a perfect match for Vin's closed-mouth smile that made Alicia Carmen wonder at secrets he might have, and made her want to reveal her own.

Despite her anxiousness to have Vin and the girls out the door, Lyla sits at the table still cluttered with dirty dishes. "Vin, do you remember my dance partner, Ricky?"

Vin scoffs. "How can I forget? The skinny, big-eared, hip wiggler? Yeah. I hear he has a dance studio out in the valley."

She leans back in her chair, crosses her legs and swings the top one madly. Why, she wonders, does everyone know this about Ricky but her?

Vin raises his Victor Mature eyebrows at her. "Why do you ask?"

She sighs. "Nothing to get jealous over. There's someone in *West Side Story* who looks just like him."

Vin laughs. "You mean the way he used to look or the way he looks now?"

She stops swinging her leg. "You mean you've seen him?"

"Ran into him a few months back. But Lyla—" Here Vin is back to mumbling.

"But what?" She is getting impatient with Vin and the sexy swooniness he seems unable to control in her presence. He should be saving it all for Vera, whom he is far too handsome for—her with that tumbleweed hair and crow's feet eyes.

"Lyla, I'm not jealous."

There is something new in this denial that makes her both curious for and resistant to an explanation. Giving into the latter, she suddenly busies herself, noisily gathering up cereal bowls, spoons, and juice glasses. Vin doesn't raise his voice through the clatter, but she hears his words as clearly as if they had been shouted in her ear.

"Lyla, I'm getting married."

She does not drop the dishes into the sink but sets them down as if they are fine china and then proceeds to arrange them as if they are pieces of a puzzle.

"I need to tell the girls this weekend," Vin continues. "And actually, to tell the truth, I wasn't quite ready to come and get them this early. I had everything planned out."

She whirls around, a spoon in her hand, which shakes of its own accord. "The world does not revolve around your plans,

Vin." Or your silly Vera, she thinks. By all rights, it should re-volve around her plans, which she can hardly recall, what with Vin's news.

The girls' lumbering footsteps sound in the hallway.

She looks at the spoon in her hand, shakes it at him. "Our little girls," she says. "You'll break their hearts."

The girls are there in front of them, their abundant, pre-pubescent bodies straining at their Annette Funicello Mouse-keteer T-shirts, their overnight bags clutched in hands that could palm a basketball. Lyla kisses each one, hardly needing to bend, so near to her height are they and growing. "Be good," she tells them. "Have a nice time," she says, shooting a warning at Vin, but he is engulfed by the twins as they head out the door.

"I feel pretty," sings Norma.

"Oh, so pretty," sings Ofelia.

They mimic Natalie Wood's fake Spanish accent and break into giggles.

Vin shuts the door behind them, and Lyla is left holding the spoon, which she slams into the sink with an exceptionally fine clatter.

She gathers her keys and counts to ten to give Vin's car time to turn the corner. Then she's in her own car, driving east to the valley, checking her lipstick in the mirror, "I Feel Pretty" stuck in her head.

She sits in her car across the street from the little box of a building, watching small girls file out while bigger girls file in, some with their mothers and trailing siblings. The bigger girls are not as big as Norma and Ofelia, though they appear to be about the same age. She wonders now if she should've brought her daughters instead of insisting that Vin come by early to pick them up. She does not want to think about Vin getting married, nor their daughters' reaction to such a ridiculous notion. She does not want to think about that wrinkly faced, frothy-haired Vera as stepmother to Ofelia and Norma.

No, she's satisfied that she ruined Vin's plans. She has plans of her own, even if she's not entirely sure what they are exactly.

The sign on the building makes her pulse flutter. City Champion Dance Studio—surely a reference to the title she and Ricky won just over ten years ago. She feels she has a stake in it, this square, yellow building with a pair of dancing silhouettes on the sign, which she is sure is the exact image of her and Ricky when they were preparing for the championship dance.

They had rehearsed all that afternoon with tiny Lola, their fiery dance instructor, clapping her hands to keep the beat, running alongside them to hiss *más ánimo*, or to shout *eso es* as she stamped her heel in approval. "¡Demuestren al mundo!" she would shout. "Show the world that Mexicans can jeeterbug!"

Lola had choreographed it just for them, her star pupils—Ricky with the wicked hips and Alicia Carmen with the slinky shoulders. They swiveled and gyrated, arms and legs fluid as octopuses. When Ricky threw her, it was as if her limbs were rubber bands, springy and supple. She landed in splits, her arms reaching for sky, her fingers jitterbugging on their own until he slid over in his polished two-tone oxfords to lift her for their final, show-stopping combination.

When they were done, Lola assessed them with narrowed eyes, perspiration feathering her pencilled brows. "Vamos a ganar. The city championship is ours." Except that Lola said "seedy shampionship," which made Alicia Carmen snort.

It was true, though. They were the real thing. They—of the treeless neighborhoods and small, low-slung houses fronted by crab grass lawns and backed up against dirt alleys—would dance the pants off the competition. Their closest rivals came from across town, a lithe blond and her matching partner whose signature dance was a tango performed in gaudy, red-sequined torero costumes. But their moves were no match for the rhythm that resided in Ricky's hips or the undulations that rode Alicia Carmen's upper body from the inside out. It was pure dance chemistry. "¡Qué mágico!" Lola purred.

Lyla checks herself in the mirror one last time, adjusts the scarf knotted at her throat á la Audrey Hepburn, then briskly jaywalks across the street, feeling the warm asphalt through her flat-soled ballerina shoes. The shoes are an accident, merely a fitting accessory to her Laura Petrie capri slacks and sleeveless shell top, but now as she approaches the dance studio, her feet itch for the smooth polished floor. As she crosses the threshold, she does a barely perceptible glissade. Her body has not forgotten.

She's in an anteroom, and for all the gaggles of girls and mothers she had seen pass through the door while sitting in her car, there is an alarming emptiness. Except for recorded piano music and a voice giving instructions and encouragement in some deeper recess of the building, the room is quiet. The walls are lined with photos of little dancers in costumes, posed or in performance. She thinks of the photo on her dresser that shows her hand reaching high for the trophy, raising the hem on her homemade dance skirt.

Lupita had sewn her costume, but Alicia Carmen had raised the hem the night before the competition by flashlight on the back porch. In the warm-up room, Ricky combed his hair, and as Alicia Carmen adjusted her dance skirt, she realized that the ruffled border slanted visibly left to right.

Lola, who had been pacing while scrutinizing the competition going through their routines, trotted over to them. "Es cierto," she told them. "Vamos a ganar." But then the lithe blond and her matching partner swept past them, the spangles on their professionally made costumes flashing boldly. "Perfecto," Lola muttered, but then added, frowning at the couple's precise but ardorless moves, "les falta ánimo." Her frown increased as she noticed Alicia Carmen's hem. "What's wrong with your skirt?"

"Nothing," Alicia Carmen said, slouching on one side to correct the slope of the hem.

Lola placed her hand under Alicia Carmen's chin, lifted her erect and then grabbed the elastic waistband and shifted it until the side seams ran down the front and back, giving the flawed skirt a sudden grace.

"Así es mejor," she said.

Then Lola led them through their routine, clapping a quiet beat with her small, hard hands and whispering instructions. Left, right. Feel the music. One, two, three, four. Live the dance. Although Alicia Carmen could see the lithe blond and her partner in their impeccable outfits out of the corner of her eye, Lola's exhortations made her forget that she was wearing her skirt sideways. This small woman who hissed like a cat and moved like a chimp, who could once dance like a showgirl, was leading her to the championship and who knew what possibilities beyond. The future gleamed as brightly as Ricky's slicked-back hair.

Lyla is aware that she is no longer alone. She turns slowly, a half-pirouette, and sees herself. Well, no, not exactly herself, because the woman in front of her is blond and, if Lyla is to be completely honest, trimmer. But they are dressed nearly alike, though the blond woman wears a slinky tunic rather than a clingy shell over her black dancer's pants. Beyond the clothes, there is something familiar about the woman in front of her tugging at a strand of her gleaming pageboy, a look of concentration pinching her pert nose. Lyla feels her own face screw in thought as her memory grasps for a name that won't come. When the blond suddenly snaps her fingers and shouts, "You're Alicia Carmen!" Lyla exclaims back at her "Yes!" not in agreement, because she is no longer Alicia Carmen, hasn't been her in ages, but because now she recognizes the blond, the female half of the tango-dancing toreros who came in second in the city dance championships all those years ago.

"It's me. Suzanne."

She makes a question out of it as if to invite confirmation from Lyla, and Lyla says, "Of course," though she has only ever known her as the blond torero. Now Lyla wonders what Suzanne is doing in Ricky's dance studio.

"It's been ages!"

Suzanne is a gusher, which Lyla would never have imagined. She had always seemed so demure and antiseptically packaged in her sleek costumes and tightly coifed hair. But then that was ages ago.

"A lifetime," Lyla says.

"Well," Suzanne says, "you look terrific."

Lyla, never one for false modesty, accepts the compliment, but then Suzanne can afford to give it since she, too, looks terrific, even more so than Lyla herself, a realization that makes her suddenly angry at Vin.

"What brings you here, Alicia Carmen?"

Lyla decides not to correct her. She wonders if Ricky remembers that she changed her name.

"I'm looking for dance lessons." Then remembering Frannie's comment about housewives and secretaries and store clerks and Ted Mack's Amateur Hour, she clarifies, "for my daughters."

Suzanne looks at her as if she's expecting her to produce the daughters as proof.

"What a coincidence that you ended up here."

"Yes," Lyla says, smiling.

"Well, we offer lessons for all ages, all levels, all styles."

All sizes? Lyla wonders. All categories of awkwardness? She remembers how she enrolled the twins when they were young and how they showed little talent, but serious effort. She thinks that maybe she didn't give them a chance to develop as dancers.

"Maybe I could sit and watch a class. See if it's right for my girls."

"Of course. We encourage it. Usually mothers bring their daughters to observe, but really, it's fine."

She leads Lyla to a set of swinging doors, and Lyla finds herself imitating Suzanne's bouncy walk as she follows behind. "Won't Ricky be surprised," Suzanne says. She points to a viewing area with risers where mothers are smiling upon their children as they practice jazz squares.

Lyla sits down among these dowdy mothers with thick waists and ugly shoes, aware that for a moment she has shifted their attention away from their hip-swaying moppets. Muñecas, Frannie said. A quick glance tells her they're a few years younger than Ofelia and Norma and, she can't help but register, many pounds lighter. But her real focus is on Ricky, who is still long and lean, though with a little more muscle than before. The only real difference is that he is nearly bald, which makes his ears more prominent than ever, but which strangely gives him a more youthful look, sexy even. He's a good teacher, cheerful and patient, encouraging. The way he was when they were partners and she was too busy chasing after Vin to notice or care. She can't help but think about Vin's still-thick, wavy hair. But look at him now, his dream of being a big-shot hotel manager reduced to being the manager for some rickety apartments, pool or no pool. And here's Ricky, true to his art, after having a short career on stage and screen (at least she supposed this was so, having just days ago seen his look-alike in *West Side Story*), now passing on his experience to the next generation. The muñequitas—cute, precocious. The way she was at that age and then at fifteen, her precocity at its peak, when she spent an afternoon with Vin in a supply closet of the Ritz hotel where he was a bellboy, and then had her day of triumph with Ricky and the world watched—well, maybe not the whole world. But her world.

When contestants lined up to enter the competition room, Alicia knew the blond toreros were behind her and Ricky. But she didn't look back, only forward, and when she paraded in with the rest of the dancers, she looked for her family in the audience. There was her father, Sergio, in a tie, his shoes polished, one foot tapping though the music hadn't begun. Lupita wore a new dress, and in her lap sat a Brownie camera, its big silver flashbulb a giant gleaming eye. Rosa in her new lipstick sat beside her, and there was Frannie flirting with Ricky's cousin. Frannie's good leg was crossed provocatively over her bad one, which was tucked toward the back of her chair. It was a precarious posture, and Alicia Carmen gritted her teeth, fearful that Frannie would topple forward and ruin the afternoon. Even the sight of Vin in the back of the room, propped against a pillar, hands in pockets, did not entirely loosen the clench of her molars.

Lyla studies the little dancers. She can pick out the ones who show promise. The tall one on the end exactly on count. The one center front whose isolation moves signal a natural gift. Ricky and his little dancers are oblivious to their audience of doting mothers and restless siblings until Ricky puts them through their final combination and they all turn to the risers and bow to hearty applause. She waits for Ricky to catch sight of her among the dumpy mothers. When she sees his nonspecific, all-purpose, for-public-consumption grin suddenly flash wide with recognition and pleasure, she imagines them both in the scene in *West Side Story* when Tony and Maria spot each other at the dance as if they are the only ones in the room despite all those Jets and Sharks and their tough-talking girlfriends—a moment undefiled by Natalie Wood's fake accent.

But her own moment is broken by the rumble of mothers gathering themselves, their purses, and their assorted children and smothering Ricky from her view with their thank-yous and questions and compliments, and she sits on the stiff bench, one leg crossed over the other, swinging furiously to some fast, hard tempo in her head.

When the room finally clears, there is one little *muñeca* left— the one with the natural jazz hips—and it hits Lyla like someone tap-dancing on her face that this is Ricky's little girl. Ricky's and Suzanne's little girl.

Ricky is calling out "Alicia Carmen," and at first Lyla thinks he's talking to his daughter until she realizes that it's her, Lyla, that he means. For some reason she thinks it's better not to tell him that she changed her name, that it's better to be Alicia Carmen today.

She steps down onto the dance floor and skims in her ballet flats toward a grinning Ricky. As soon as their hands touch, he spins her into the sweetheart position, her back to him, his arm above her chest, his hand caressing her shoulder. It lasts only a moment before he reverses the move and she is face-to-face with him again, and he's still grinning to his big ears, and she would like to kiss him the way she failed to do so many times back when they were partners, but Suzanne is standing next to him now and the little *muñeca*, too, and a small sound comes out of Lyla's mouth like the whimper of a lost puppy, which she tries to cover up with an exclamation about the enormous talent of such a tiny dancer.

Ricky lifts his daughter in the air and she raises her arms above her head like a little pro, and Lyla thinks how impossible it would be for anyone to lift her daughters that way.

"This is Roxie," Ricky says as he holds the *muñeca* up for all to see. He puts her down and she curtsies as if at the end of a performance. She is all charm and delight and Lyla hates her and hates her name and is glad when she runs off to the other end of the studio to dance alone in the corner.

"And you remember Suzanne."

"Of course," she says, stepping back slightly, trying to put some distance between their look-alike outfits.

"What brings you here?" he asks, grinning his big old grin that is recognizable and yet unfamiliar now. "I haven't seen you since . . ."

"We won the title," she blurts. "City champions." She feels the hiss of air through her teeth.

Ricky seems not to notice her pluralizing the name of his studio.

"She's looking for lessons for her daughters," Suzanne tells him.

Ricky looks around for her daughters as if they might appear from behind her legs.

"They're with their dad," she explains. "You know. Vin."

"Yeah, big Vin." He says it almost fondly, as if they had been one big happy family. "Bring the girls in for a free trial," he says. "Bring the whole family."

"I'll get you a brochure and a class schedule," Suzanne says, and bounces her pageboy out of the room.

Lyla does not check the surprise, the near-accusation in her voice. "I never imagined that you two would end up together."

"Kinda like the movies, eh? From dance rivals to dance partners for life." Ricky can't hide his pleasure, and she wants to shout, *It's me you had a big fat crush on,* and to remind him for good measure it was her, Alicia Carmen, who had won the championship with him, not the blond torero in the fancy costume. And that was kinda like the movies, too.

But she says nothing, though Ricky doesn't notice and is already bubbling over with a question. "Guess what I teach all my students?"

She is afraid that he's going to say something cheesy like *they can all be champions in their hearts.* But then when he doesn't, she is disappointed.

Ricky slides over to the phonograph, flips through some 45s and sets one on the spindle. It's "Come Go with Me" by the Del Vikings, the song they jitterbugged all the way to the championship. She is already moving to the music when Ricky takes her hands.

The city championships were held in a hotel ballroom, not the Ritz, but one closer to the bay with a terrace that looked onto the tuna fleet and swooping seagulls. The water was blue and the sky bright. The brilliance of the day muted the dancers' glitter and made their makeup look garish. As each couple took its turn in the sunlight's glare, Alicia Carmen knew that none of them were as good as she and Ricky.

She could feel her heartbeat in her red-glazed fingertips, against the inside of her soft-toed dance shoes, and when Ricky led her to the dance floor, her body quivered with readiness like the greyhounds Sergio bet on at the racetrack. She and Ricky struck their opening pose—a half-embrace to the audience, his free arm on his slim hip, hers sassily behind her head—a flirtatious overture to the crowd. When the music started, it was as if a switch had been thrown to set them in motion, so tuned were their reflexes to the jitterbug beat. She felt the energy radiating from their torsos to their arms and legs, meeting the floor, skimming the air, touching everything in the room.

When they were done, the applause was jet-plane loud, expansive as the bay beyond the window, and though it eventually died down, she felt its boom in her temples even as the blond toreros strutted through their tango. As she watched their perfect limbs navigate the sunlit dance floor, their perfect noses point in twin profile, their perfect blondness catch a sprinkle of dust motes like haloes, her heart beat to the hope of an MGM musical.

When the last contestants had danced, all ten couples promenaded the dance floor for a final turn and then lined up to face the audience and the judges. The girls stood a half-step in front of their partners, and Alicia Carmen felt Ricky's hand rest on her behind. She didn't slap it like she normally would have. She saw a future with Ricky onstage and a future with Vin offstage. She looked for Vin now and saw him still leaning into the pillar the way she leaned into Ricky's long, skinny hand.

Lyla finds herself stumbling, her feet somehow off the beat, her mind suddenly blank, and all of her trying to recover, but nothing working in unison. Then even as her body regains its balance and hint of the lost rhythm, she realizes that the choreography that once oozed from her cells, dwelled in her bone and muscle, is completely and undeniably lost to her. She stands, alarmed, one foot raised behind her, not knowing whether to step back or forward, frozen in disbelief. She thought it would always be there, waiting for her—the dance.

Then Roxie is jumping up and down, uncontainable in her glee, the words she is shouting barely discernible in her eagerness to lay bare the facts of the matter. "Mommy knows how, Mommy knows how."

Suzanne is shushing their daughter, and Lyla hates her for considering her feelings, hates her for knowing her dance. She refuses to look at Ricky. She's not sure how she makes her way to the car, not sure what words, if any, were exchanged, not even sure when the music stopped.

The next evening she waits by the window, watches Vin's car pull up, sees Vera ensconced in the front seat, watches her daughters spill out from either side of the car. Vin says something to them, but they are already on their way up the walk, thighs a gentle wobble, feet splayed outward to carry the weight of hips and torso. Lyla studies their faces. They are grim, but not heartbroken.

She goes to the door to meet them.

Ambition

————— ❖ —————

IF SHE WERE to place blame, Millie would say it was the June 1965 issue of the *Ladies' Home Journal* that began it all—Gil's remodeling of the house, her grooming of the children, home improvement projects that never quite met expectations. Even now, ten years later, the roof leaks, making the tiles in the ceiling curl at the edges like old toenails. Even now, Rica slouches her way into a room despite the Wendy Ward Charm School lessons to "lead with your breasts," and Bonita scoops snot from her nose with the long polished curve of her ringed pinkie when she thinks no one is looking. Mario she has left to his own devices, reasoning that a boy needs more freedom to stretch and swell into his manhood. When he reads girlie magazines at the breakfast table, she pretends not to notice and sips her coffee as if naked women were the appropriate complement to the Fruit Loops her son still prefers. She does venture to advise him that it feeds his acne.

"The cereal, I mean," she says.

"It's an old wives' tale," he says behind the picture of the uncovered cover model.

She sighs. Boys will be boys. But girls will be women, and Rica and Bonita will one day marry, someone tall, maybe, and manage a house, larger than this one, for sure, and with the latest gadgets and accessories in style-setting colors. It's natural for her to wish a life for her daughters better than her own. Hadn't her mother wished that for her? Or had she? Well, even if Lupita hadn't, Millie nurtured her own sense of ambition. And yet, some obstacles just can't be overcome, especially when your husband is one of those obstacles. Not that she has held a grudge since 1965, back when she was younger, slimmer, and, despite being the mother of three children, almost glamorous-looking. Not that anyone cared.

THEY WERE BEING particular nuisances at naptime, Rica and Bonita in their room encouraging Mario in his room across the hall to blow farts on his arm. She lost her temper, like all mothers will often do, cooped up all day through the hot and monotonous summer with three demanding children. If pressed, she would admit to wielding a brush, perhaps even making contact with Rica's backside, maybe Bonita's too. And the looks of terror on their faces—they were at least partly an act. Children could be so cunning.

And now she could even think that the whole thing was planned, their running from her straight into her and Gil's bedroom. The master bedroom with the adjoining bathroom and its built-in, wall-to-wall vanity was the only room in the house with a lock on the door. They slammed the door shut on her threats and on the other side there was a sudden silence, and even though Millie had continued with her screams, all indications that her children existed had disappeared behind the door. She stayed there a moment listening, her blouse sticky more from the exertion than the heat, her temples throbbing, her jaw tight. She made her muscles go slack, heeding what her mother had always told her when she was a girl and what she now told her own children—that if she made an ugly face it would stiffen and she would look that way forever. Of course, she knew her face wouldn't freeze instantaneously. It would happen gradually, over the years of dealing with peevish children.

She slapped the door with the palm of her hand. "If you know what's good for you, you won't come out until naptime is over."

"Niños traviesos," she muttered. She used her Spanish when she was angry at them or when she talked about them to her sisters or her mother. She used it at them or over them, never to them, so they never learned to speak it. She hated that about them.

They were wiggly, fidgety children who wouldn't stay down for a nap. But Millie needed *her* rest. She had for a while threatened them with every conceivable punishment and deprivation. *I'm going to spank you so hard you won't know what happened to you. No snacks for a month.* She had spanked, too. Justifiably. She had withheld snacks. Gleefully helping herself to the cupcake they had forfeited through their disobedience. But even though they deserved such consequences, it all took so much energy.

She waited again, finally heard the rustle of the bed, smiled with a grim satisfaction at the picture of the three of them down for a nap. She had won.

She went to the living room to lie down and smoke a cigarette. As she withdrew the cigarette from her mouth, she could see a residue of lipstick at the tip and she started crying. She continued to smoke and cry and at the same time used the fingers of her free hand to massage away the wrinkles that she knew were distorting her forehead.

Soon she pulled herself together, reminding herself of the aging effects of stress she had read about in a magazine article.

She went to the hall bathroom and washed her face, checked it briefly for damage. Ten years of marriage and three children had aged her very little. To prove it, she went to the living room and brought back the picture of her and Gil on their wedding day. She held the airbrushed photo next to her face. Her cheeks had been pinker then, her skin smoother, her hair thicker. But all of that could be attributed to the studio touch-ups. The difference between then and now was microscopic. Not so for Gil. But that was to be expected. It was a happy coincidence that the man she fell in love with was twelve years older than she was. She would always look young by comparison.

Feeling better, she carried the photo back to the living room, burnished the glass with her sleeve, and positioned it to avoid the midday glare. She smiled at the contrivance that showed Gil's head above hers when in fact she was a full two inches taller.

She reached over to flick on the radio and then the portable fan. She kicked off her flats and settled into the couch for a nap, belly down, her arms underneath her, pressing against her breasts. Tom Jones sang "What's New Pussycat?" She burrowed deeper into the couch and slept.

A HALF HOUR later, she lay with her arm over her eyes waiting to hear the bedroom door being hurled open, her children bolting free. Instead, she heard a slow creak and then soft careful steps, and from under her arm she peeked at them making their way past her like munchkin burglars.

"Hungry after your nap?" she asked. The three jumped, and Bonita shrieked and then stifled a giggle.

"What's wrong with you kids?"

"Can we go out and play?" Rica asked. "We're not hungry."

"Yeah, we're not hungry," Bonita echoed.

Millie surveyed her children. "What about you, Mario? You want some cookies?"

Mario shook his head, and that's when Millie noticed the pink, scrubbed look on all their faces. For once they had washed up without warnings, threats, or bribes. They were atoning for their nasty behavior earlier. She smiled at them. "Go out and play then. You can have a snack when you come back in."

These were the moments when parenting was the way Dr. Spock described it in his book, though she hardly referred to it anymore, so often annoyed was she at the gap between theory and real life. To encourage continued obedience, she knew she had to reward this instance of correct behavior. She hadn't gone to college, but she'd read enough articles in *Ladies' Home Journal* to practically qualify her as an authority on the psychology of child-rearing. No one had to tell *her* twice about positive reinforcement.

She went to the kitchen and opened the doors to her pantry, an eternal source of satisfaction for her with its floor-to-ceiling shelves that she stocked weekly with cereals, canned soups, condiments, paper napkins, and snacks for the children. During the Cuban missile crisis, it had bulged with beans, sardines, Spam, and other unpleasant foods that would withstand nuclear attack. When the crisis had passed, she donated it all to the soup kitchen downtown.

She located a package of angel food cake, a can of fruit cocktail, and the whipped cream in a can. When she had assembled three Jeweled Mountains like the ones in the holiday issue of *LHJ*, she looked out the window for her children. They were huddled near the swing set Gil had insisted on building rather than buying. She never knew whether the huddle meant they were playing together nicely as she constantly scolded them to do or if they were plotting some forbidden act. Sometimes, with Gil at work during the day, she felt so alone, just her against the children. They were laughing at something now, the braids down Rica's and Bonita's backs jiggling like snakes.

She tapped on the window and they turned their laughing faces to her. It struck her how much they resembled her, the radiance of her wedding picture, even her reflection in the bathroom mirror just moments ago. They were a part of her. They would live on after her, replace her. She gritted her teeth at the responsibility of showing them how. She beckoned them inside and met them at the kitchen door. She was pleased with herself when Rica led the way to the sink to wash up. She was even more pleased when her children saw the treat she had concocted. She took their wide-eyed hesitation to be gratitude.

"Go ahead," she said. "You deserve it."

They moved shyly, inching toward the table, but once seated, they set upon their Jeweled Mountains with frenzied spoons, hacking hollows into the plushy cake. She clapped her hands loudly once, and the spoons dropped in an answering rattle.

"How do we eat?" she reminded them.

"Mouths closed," they said like ventriloquists.

She watched them for a few minutes, smiling and nodding as they trimmed off properly sized portions that fit neatly in their spoons and chewed slowly, mouths closed. She went to the living room and turned on *General Hospital*.

Later, just after putting the Swanson's Fish Sticks in the oven for dinner, Millie went into the master bathroom to freshen up. Though there was nothing obviously out of the ordinary in the pink-tiled room, she had a nagging sensation that something had been disturbed. Her mind immediately flashed to the laughing faces of her children, their mouths swelling with chunks of Jeweled Mountain. Her eyes swept the counter lined with bottles of facial moisturizers, body lotions, and colognes. Nothing out of order there. So she yanked open each drawer, nearly bouncing the contents onto the floor and making it impossible for her to detect any trespass by small hands. She looked up, saw herself in the mirror, was annoyed at the worry lines striping her forehead and the corners of her mouth. She yawned widely to oxygenate her pores, dug in a drawer for her rouge, and patted a glow onto her cheeks. Her fingers scrabbled among a litter of lipstick tubes, scooped one out and uncapped it, and there in the squashed tip of Romantic Red was the unmistakable handiwork of her children. One by one she examined the tubes of mashed color, her displeasure accumulating with each wrenched and wounded stick.

But when she had screwed the cap back on the last of the mutilated lipsticks, she grasped her dilemma. Confronting her children with the evidence of their little crime after she had lavished whipped cream and cake on them would make her look foolish. But letting them get away with it was unthinkable. She was about to dump the drawer of lipsticks into the wastebasket with one furious shake when she remembered how quiet it had been during naptime. She rattled the drawer and the lipsticks clacked. Then she pushed the drawer closed gently so that the lipsticks only nudged against each other. There was certainly nothing wrong with quiet play at naptime.

After that she kept her good lipsticks in a zippered pouch tucked at the back of another drawer, and each afternoon she led her children to her bedroom. "It's naptime. Be very quiet," she told them. Sometimes she stood by the door and listened, waited for whispers, the brush of feet against the carpet, the stealthy breach of a drawer.

"THESE ARE TURBULENT times," she told Connie on the phone, repeating what she had heard Walter Cronkite say on the news last night, except that she said "troublent."

"Yes," agreed Connie, who couldn't resist telling her sister that she had mispronounced "troubling." They commiserated a while. Nothing was the same since Kennedy died. So they hung up and Millie picked up the latest *Ladies' Home Journal*.

The *Journal* came in her mailbox each month. It was a dignified title that signaled culture and quality and taste, and the sight of the mailing label that read Mrs. Millie Mejia on the front was like membership in a club. And Millie loved to belong.

But when she saw the avocado kitchen appliances featured in the six-page spread of the current issue, she knew absolutely she could not belong to this trend. Such things would never be suitable for her home. They would have to be installed in a brand-new house, larger and in a better neighborhood, like the ones in the hills to the south or near the beach communities up north, the ones with sunken living rooms, combined fan-chandelier fixtures, backyard swimming pools in eggplant shapes, as Gil called them.

"Kidney," she would always correct him.

But Gil was a gardener, not one of those "-ologists" that looked after kidneys. If Gil *were* one of those "-ologists," they would already be living in a large bungalow near the beach or a split-level in the hills, not here in this barrio of square stucco houses and dead lawns.

Where was his ambition? Why was it left to her to be the striver?

After high school Millie enrolled in typing classes at the secretarial school. She wore white blouses and dark skirts, low-heeled pumps that she kept flat to the floor as she sat, back straight, eyes hard on the copy, fingers tapping the keys. Millie was fast. She was made for fast. Her limbs were long and slim and in a constant state of readiness, not for something to do, but for something to happen, because Millie expected that life was like that—waiting around the next corner poised to spring or be stumbled upon. She walked fast and talked fast, always the first to arrive someplace, often the first to assert her opinion on something. And she knew when to abandon the typewriter posture, such as on the day she met Gil.

She sat with two classmates, Sylvia, a mediocre typist, and Ramona, who was competent but had thick ankles. They sat on a park bench sipping Coca-Colas. Millie's legs were not only crossed, but the shoe on her raised foot dangled jauntily in the direction of the sailors at the next bench. She pulled a Lucky Strike from her purse, and when she looked up, one of the sailors stood before her to offer his lighter.

He walked her back to class with Sylvia and Ramona trailing behind like bridesmaids. At first he carried his hat under his arm, his elbow crooked to hold it in place, but she asked him to put it on. She liked the complete uniform, plus the hat on his head brought him nearer her height. And she imagined how he would rise in the ranks with her there beside him.

Later, when Gil left the navy, he said he felt a sense of freedom, and Millie tried to imagine this, too.

WITH HER SELF-MANICURED nail, she traced the coils of the burner on the avocado range that filled the left side of the page. As her finger spiraled, she felt again that her life was running in tight circles. She had yet to live up to her name. Milagros. Not that she believed she could perform miracles. But she could make things happen, whip the uninspired into shape, produce results. Her last public opportunities, though, had been in high school when she had organized the pep club's homecoming rally and when she took over as chair of the dance committee after Darlene McPherson got pregnant and was sent to an aunt who owned an almond farm in Modesto. She and her friend Alma Rosas had managed to maneuver their way into these elite groups dominated by the blond, pony-tailed Darlenes of Lincoln High. Alma had married Russ Munger, a skinny white boy with a silly grin who turned out to be a genius at selling high-priced cars. Alma and Russ lived in a new development with a golf course and a man-made lake. Sometimes Alma appeared in Russ's car commercials, posing next to a convertible, her arms sweeping the length of it in a ballerina flourish. Alma probably had an avocado kitchen.

Millie left the magazine open at its centerfold, the chic greenish-yellow refrigerator gleaming off its pages, and walked over to her own standard white Amana. She lifted out the Tupperware pitcher of Kool-Aid, filled three tumblers, and set them on the kitchen table. She sat down, the glossy pages of avocado kitchen appliances in front of her, and thought about how to make Gil see the need for a new house.

The children were sprawled in the living room playing Candyland. Bonita's shorts were too small and she fidgeted with the crotch. The strap on Rica's sunsuit hung off her shoulder. Sweat matted Mario's hair at the nape and forehead. How little they matched the neat, perspirationless children pictured in the pages of *LHJ*.

The fan was off to keep the playing pieces from blowing off the board, but the room still buzzed from the flies at the screen door. The children added a hum of their own as they whispered among themselves.

"Who's winning?" Millie asked.

The children went silent so only the flies fretted.

"Mario's winning," Rica called out.

"Yeah, Mario," Bonita agreed.

"Finish your game and have something to drink," Millie told them, turning back to her magazine.

An old house and three children needing room to grow, she thought as she watched them stain their mouths red with Kool-Aid. They were the reasons a bigger, better house was essential. She closed the magazine, but she marked the page with her finger and stroked its enamel feel as she imagined the avocado kitchen she would stock with matching potholders and dishtowels, ruffled curtains at the window lined with red geraniums, a wooden fruit bowl on the counter with real avocados in it.

Mario wiped his mouth. "Mom, can we have a pool?"

"Of course not. We can't build a pool here." She wasn't thinking of the logistical impossibilities, but of the incongruity of such a luxury in their neighborhood. "People don't have pools here," she scolded.

"Not build one," Mario argued, exasperated. "Buy one."

He handed her the advertising insert from the Sunday paper. "Like this one."

Millie looked at the picture of a large inflatable pool in which a family of four frolicked. A boy floated on his back in the middle, a girl prepared to toss a beach ball over him to her father, and the mother was reaching for a glass of something pink on a table at the edge of the twenty-five-foot diameter, three-and-a-half-foot-deep plastic pool.

"Please, Mom."

Millie was skeptical of the source of the request. The girls always made Mario ask Millie for things, certain that she could not refuse her only son. Millie would not be manipulated.

"We can practice putting our heads underwater," Mario said.

She had taken them to the city pool last summer, bought them new bathing suits in the most becoming styles. The girls were thin but had good lines, and she expected them to fill out nicely, unlike Connie's daughters who were hopelessly bony. She regretted that Mario was not athletic, but at least he would never suffer the humiliation of being chubby or knock-kneed like the boy in his swimming class whose bathing trunks hung precariously at his hips. It was alongside this boy that Mario and the girls flailed, swallowed water, and cried. Millie could not watch after the first few lessons. She dropped them off, went to have coffee and a slice of cream pie at the Bob's Big Boy, and returned later to pick them up, steeped in chlorine and exhausted from a half-hour of agitating in the water like broken propeller blades. She didn't sign them up for the second session.

"Well, can we?" Mario demanded.

"I'll think about it."

Rica rolled her eyes and pulled Mario out of the room. Bonita sat rattling the ice in her cup. "What are we going to have for dinner?" she asked.

Millie found herself chafing at Bonita's question. It was Gil who did most of the cooking. He liked to and was good at it. And while Millie gladly relinquished the chore, she felt the loss of jurisdiction in her tending and nurturing role. It's what she attributed Bonita's question to—an uncertainty about what Millie could promise and deliver.

"Bonita, you clean these up," Millie said firmly, handing off a task she normally did to her daughter.

"Not like that," she told Bonita who was stuffing the tumblers one inside the other. Millie reached over and separated the tumblers, popping the seal that had formed from the force of Bonita's fidgety wrists. "Go take those to the sink," she told her.

"I am."

"Don't talk back." Millie watched Bonita's back for any signs of insolence, a movement of her scalp caused by a sneer, muscles tightening in her neck from sticking out her tongue. The last thing she needed was opposition.

"Bonita," she said sweetly, "what's the best thing and the worst thing for you about this house?"

"The worst, that's easy. There's no good hiding places."

"Oh, for playing hide-and-seek?" Millie asked, flicking a stray crumb from the table.

"No," Bonita said. "Just for hiding."

Millie looked up and studied her daughter's face. "You're very right," she said. "This house is too small." She rose, clapping her hands together to end the discussion and send Bonita out of the room.

"And the best thing," Bonita said backing out of the kitchen, "is that it has a backyard with *egg* plants." She left the room shrieking with laughter.

Millie shook her head. Ever since she'd been told the name of the purple vegetable Gil grew in his garden, Bonita went into hysterics over the mention of it, as if it were something unbelievable or a joke that improved with the telling. But she did have a point about the backyard. It was large, and with the exception of the swing set, it was given over to the vegetable garden. It had the look of a farm, with its crop of eggplant, zucchini, tomatoes, beets, and chili peppers planted in long rows. Millie wanted a flower garden, profuse and rambling, but balanced—the kind in magazines. She wanted to hire a professional landscaper, had in fact tried to once, but Gil came home early that day and chased him off, shaking a limp coil of hose in threat. Now Millie added a large flower garden to her mental list of requirements for a new home.

AT DINNER THAT night as they ate the *chuletas* Gil had marinated and cooked, Millie ate hurriedly, setting the pace for the others so that the clink of forks against plates and the rap of drinking glasses on the tablecloth made a clamorous meal, so that the lack of conversation was barely noticeable. Dessert was a scoop of ice cream with a vanilla wafer on the side, and once the remains of these were cleared from the table, Millie shooed the children from the room and set a cup of coffee in front of Gil.

"Do I get to drink it?"

"Of course you can," Millie said, impatient at Gil's sarcasm. She sat down across from him, stirred sugar and milk into first her cup then his, then sat back in her chair, sighing into a serene position.

"So how was your day?" she asked. "We never get to really talk, discuss things, you know." She gripped her cup, then let go, watched Gil test his with a tentative slurp. "Here," she said, stirring more milk into his coffee.

"We never discuss things," Gil said, looking into the muddy waters of his cup, "because you decide things on your own and I find out about it later."

"That's not true," she chided him, though with a smile. Sometimes he could be as contrary as the children. His face was set as hard as the leftover breakfast biscuits that still sat on the counter. "Not on the big things," she said.

Gil said nothing.

And Millie couldn't help herself then. "It's because you never want to change anything. I want to make things better for us."

"We have everything we need," Gil said.

"Gil," Millie heard herself shriek. "What do you know about what we need?" She obeyed his gesture to lower her voice. It was a knob-turning motion he made with his thumb and forefinger and a twisting wrist. The words whistled through her teeth. "Just ask Bonita."

"Ask her what?"

Millie was composed now and issued her words slowly to feel their weight in her mouth. "About how there's no room to grow in this house."

"Is that true?"

"Yes," she said, struck by her own certainty.

Gil sipped at his coffee. "Okay," he said, nodding at her. "Leave it to me."

She nodded back at him, in agreement, in approval, in anticipation, nodding still as he took his cup to the sink, then headed to the living room to turn on the TV.

THE NEXT MORNING when Gil came in for breakfast, she was throwing away yesterday's biscuits, enjoying the sound of the stale thuds as she skidded them off the corner of the counter into the garbage can like billiard balls. As he sat down to his toast and eggs, Millie lined up the last biscuit for disposal. "Where should we move to? The beach or the hills?"

Gil's mouth was full of egg and toast, but he spoke anyway. "What?" she asked. "The hills?"

He swallowed. "Stay here." A piece of toast clung to his lip. "I said stay here."

"What?" Her palm covered the biscuit, pressed it down.

"We'll remodel."

Millie looked at her husband, at his mild features. It was at times like this that she despised him for being short.

"Don't you want to live in a better neighborhood?"

"Mil, this is a good place to live." Gil rubbed his chin, knocking the piece of toast free. "I don't want to live in the white neighborhoods."

Millie looked out the kitchen window, at the broad leaves of the eggplant, the feathery ends of the tomato plants. "I don't want to live on a farm."

"It's a garden, Millie." Gil carried his plate to the garbage can and scraped yolk and bread crumbs. "I'll put in some flowers. A lily pond, too." He picked up his lunch box and left.

Millie, who was not going anywhere, ground the biscuit under her palm.

IT TOOK A half-hour to fill the pool.

While the children pretended to nap, Millie ran the hose, measuring the progress of the water with the start and finish of *As the World Turns*. When the announcer said, "Tune in tomorrow," the children bolted from the bedroom. They were already in their swimsuits and on Millie's heels as she led the way out the back door, a glass of iced tea and a magazine in hand. Rowena was waiting at the back gate. The children had become popular with the neighborhood kids since getting the pool, but Millie's rule was one friend at a time, and today it was the girl with the funny name who brought licorice whips. Millie helped herself to one before settling herself in the shade of the patio to sip her tea, flip through the pages of her magazine, and occasionally look up to see that no one was drowning.

For a while they just splashed around, bending at the knees so the water came to their chins. But Rica soon had Rowena at the side of the pool making licorice bracelets. Bonita stood apart from them, her arms waving back and forth beneath the surface, making eddies. Mario, the only one of them still trying to make good on the promise to practice their swimming, threw himself on the surface in a face float. He came up for air and shook the water from his face, and Bonita turned her head to avoid the spray. Then he sucked in a deep breath and launched himself again onto the water, his arms stretched over his head, his feet inches from Bonita. She grabbed them and held on. Mario's head shot out of the water and his feet struggled for the bottom. Bonita held on. Mario's head flopped back up, then down, up and down again as he gasped for air. Bonita held on.

"You're drowning him!"

Even as Millie screamed at her from the patio, Bonita couldn't let go, her eyes scared and amazed.

Just as Rica splashed over to loosen Bonita's grip, Mario's frantic gasps calmed to a rhythm, his face turning to the side the way they had all been shown in swimming class. Bonita let go and Mario did two more cycles before bringing his feet underneath him to touch bottom. He was panting, speechless.

Millie was in the yard by now, one foot bare, the other partially trapped in a house slipper. "Why did you do that?"

"Bonita made Mario swim, Mrs. Mejia," Rowena said, a licorice whip dangling from the side of her mouth.

Bonita nodded and Mario demonstrated. Millie opened her mouth, then closed it and rubbed her face as if to remove her glower. She shrugged her shoulders, and then applauded. "At least someone around here can swim. Rowena, no food allowed in the pool." She turned and headed back to the house, her gait lopsided from her one bare foot.

GIL AND HIS friend Oscar were framing the patio. It was going to be a family room with an alcove at the back, a private corner to fulfill Bonita's request for a place to hide. It would have a sunken floor owing to the lower level of the patio relative to the rest of the house, and Gil intended to install a fan-chandelier combo fixture to meet Millie's hankering for the latest interior fashions. He called the project a remodel. But Millie vehemently disputed the claim. They were enclosing the patio with walls, gluing linoleum to its cement floor, replacing the green plastic sheeting with roof tiles. "Same house, same neighborhood," she shouted over the hammering. "Yes," he shouted back, a nail catapulting from the corner of his mouth.

Millie would not be defeated. She would show him. She would mold the children into the kind who lived in the real new houses in the new and elegant neighborhoods. They would rise above their circumstances.

At the moment, though, the children were enthralled with their circumstances, at the construction rising up around them, the raw beams of wood that invited crayon markings, the wadding of insulation that pulled apart like cotton candy, the smooth flatness of the drywall that could be punched through with a screwdriver when no one was looking. Millie overlooked these little misdeeds. It was the final outward appearance that mattered after all.

And so at the same time that she chose curtains and Indian throw rugs, Barcaloungers, lamps, and ashtrays for the family room, she picked out ribbons and bracelets, taffeta skirts, patent leather shoes with velvet bows or rhinestone buckles for the girls. Sometimes she tilted a beret on Rica's head or hung a bolero on Bonita's thin frame for a European look. She curled, braided, or swept into a chignon—to her credit she knew it was French, though she pronounced it *chig-yawn*—their not-quite-thick-enough hair. Later when they were old enough, she would teach them to properly apply the lipstick they had played with during naptime.

MILLIE SMEARED COLD cream on her face and neck, wiped the excess from her fingers, then adjusted the net on her curlers. The tedium of her bedtime ritual was relieved by the comfort and size of the master bathroom. When she was growing up with four sisters in a two-bedroom house, five minutes alone in the bathroom was a foolish hope. They stood two and three at a time at the sink to brush their teeth, their elbows bumped as they combed their hair, heads butted as they applied mascara, and the single light bulb that swung from the ceiling never flattered.

Millie switched off the mirror lights first so that she was lit just by the glow of the overhead lights. Then she turned these off, too, and headed for bed.

Gil was already there. He always went to bed early, but usually to read the paper and smoke. Since the remodel began, he just went to sleep. Millie slipped in on her side, tucking her nightgown between her legs to keep it from rumpling to her waist when she slept. She leaned over Gil and quashed the cigarette he had left languishing in the ashtray bearing the name of a bar in Singapore. It was a souvenir from his time in the navy. There were other things—a pair of Japanese prints, a seascape and a mountainscape that hung above the bed, teak carvings of a caribou herd from the Philippines that graced the dresser, a conch from Hawaiian waters that separated the Dr. Spock childcare book from the Bible in the small bookcase in the corner.

Millie turned out the light in the one room in the house that Gil had decorated with any of his belongings.

WHEN THE FAMILY room was done, when the beams had been sanded and varnished, when the ceiling and floor tiles had all been laid, curtains hung, rugs thrown, and bolsters arranged on the sofa, the family sat in front of the TV watching the *Ed Sullivan Show*. In the commercial break between a blind-folded acrobat act and a medley by the Kim sisters, those Korean beauties sheathed in spangled Mandarin-collared tunics slit to reveal shapely calves, Millie announced her plan. "Rica and Bonita will have the master bedroom."

She smiled at her squealing daughters as she bestowed this gift and then faced Gil, or rather his big toe, which pushed through a hole in the sock on his foot resting on the vinyl ottoman. Gil's toe, looking unusually large relative to his face from Millie's angle, twitched slightly. She spoke at it as if it might be a microphone she was testing with staccato vocal patterns. "It's a *small* sacrifice. For the sake of the children. They'll outgrow *this* house soon. Even *with* a new family room."

Gil brought his other foot up onto the ottoman so that now he was sighting Millie between his two big toes, sizing her up. "Okay," he answered. Then the Kim sisters came on, blowing on sax, trumpet, trombone, and they all turned their attention back to the TV.

It was not the solution she had wanted, but life was full of sacrifices. She watched the Kim sisters, the rhythm of their hips, the flash of their shiny instruments. Rica and Bonita should really learn to play.

NOW RICA'S ALMOST sixteen, and the French horn Millie bought and polished for her has been stowed in a corner of the family room for years. Sometimes when she's dusting, Millie picks it up, traces the whorl of the metal, clicks the buttons, wonders at its mysteries. Rica couldn't get the hang of reading music. Millie feared that her constant squinting at the page of black notes would give her migraines. She encouraged her to play by ear, but nothing Rica played sounded like anything Millie or anybody else had ever heard.

At least Bonita still strums the guitar, though she knows only a few chords. Millie catches her sometimes seated on a stool in the family room or cross-legged on the braided throw rug, the fingers of her left hand white against the frets, her right thumb and forefinger clasping the pick above the strings. Millie watches her hum softly against the repetition of the chords, and there is something discordant in the sounds she is making and the look of rapture she wears. Nevertheless, if Bonita happens to drop out of her trance, Millie nods encouragement. "Practice makes perfect."

But the only thing they're practiced at is their appearance, thanks to Millie's attention to detail. Waxed legs, painted nails, curled eyelashes, glossy lips, and doses of amoxicillin to keep their skin free of blackheads are the daily standard. She's proud of her achievement—her beautiful daughters. And proud of Mario, too. He's permed his hair and shaped his eyebrows.

She tries not to care that the children's grades are average, that they're disinclined to join the yearbook staff, run for student council, organize the dance committee (things she had done), or try out for cheerleader or at least the drill team (things she hadn't done since they remained the domain of the Darlene McPhersons of the world back then), or that they never really learned to swim after all, Mario never having advanced beyond that one performance.

Some days Millie walks right past her children, past their demands, their failings, their insolence, their needs, and she heads through the master bedroom, which belongs now to Rica and Bonita, and locks herself in the master bathroom, now also Rica's and Bonita's. She applies the makeup that belongs to her daughters. Bonne Bell and Cover Girl. Brands that speak of innocence and youth. Eventually, there's a knock on the door, loud and protesting. "Mom, you're in our bathroom."

Millie doesn't answer, dabs the lipstick on her mouth with a tissue. They call for Gil. She sits on the toilet seat and watches herself in the mirror as she lights a cigarette. She narrows her eyes at her image through the smoke, and looks away before it clears.

When Danny Got Married

———————— ✤ ————————

MISUNDERSTANDING WAS THE rule in my family. While I did my part to contribute, I mostly observed—the misheard words, the misread signals, the misremembered moments that were supposed to have been unforgettable.

When the call came that Danny was finally coming back to Kimball Park, I anticipated the miscommunication that was bound to ensue, even welcomed it in a way, because I believed with my thirteen-year-old heart that I was destined to escape it. It was Danny himself who led me to believe such a thing. Hadn't he singled me out the last time he visited? Somehow, though, I overlooked the fact that the reason Danny was coming was to bring his new bride across the ocean to meet us, our large, loud family that took up so much of the dry air in the dozy confines of Kimball Park.

The news that Danny was married had crackled long-distance from Germany in Lupita's old ear.

"No me lo digas," she wailed, even as she begged him to repeat his message after each wave of static, hoping it would reshape itself into something ordinary and unobjectionable.

Danny was my uncle, and Lupita my grandmother. I referred to all adults by their first name—just not to their faces. I communicated my adolescent rebellion by not communicating. I harbored an unoriginal catalog of unspoken impertinences.

My looks of derision were directed at people's retreating backs. Only my sighs, heaved with the force of Connie's late-model Hoover upright, were obvious. Connie was my mother and the most frequent recipient of my noisy exhalations.

But with the news of Danny's marriage, my sighs were lost in the collective moan. Danny was ours no longer. Lupita lamented the loss of her youngest. Connie and my aunts shook their perms at the intrusion of Teutonic stock into our family. He should marry his own kind, they grumbled of their only brother, their fingers twanging the telephone cord as they called each other over morning coffee. None of the sisters, though, had married her own kind, having introduced Filipino, Polish, Irish, and Caribbean genotypes into Lupita and Sergio's Yaqui-dominated Mexican bloodline. Lupita liked to emphasize the fierceness of the Yaquis, their resistance to enslavement by other tribes, even their murderous attacks on trains when they sliced the wrists and ears of passengers for speedy acquisition of a silver bracelet or pearl earring. Then they were crushed like the rest, Sergio always added as epilogue, the heel of one hand grinding into the palm of the other. Let's face it, even at thirteen I knew my family was a hodgepodge of conquered peoples.

But then there was our Danny, conqueror and hero. Since Danny had been stationed in Europe, we had boasted to our friends of his sampling of the culture. That he had carried baguettes under his arm in France, clinked steins of beer in Frankfurt with the locals, revved mopeds around fountains in Italy. Only Danny had ventured so far from our corner of the world. From Lupita and Sergio's modest one-story on Palm Street, the clearinghouse for news of Danny's adventures, we celebrated his triumphs, invested him with hero status even before he became one. The commendation and scarred hand he received for saving his buddy in a barracks fire proved his place in the world and in our family. Until we learned the news.

While there was no mistaking the fact that Danny had a bride, details about her suffered in the transmission. "She stands stiff as a salute, you know," reported my aunt Lyla, who had relayed the tidings of that first phone call to Petra. By the time Connie got the call from Millie, Danny's wife was antiseptically clean and carried germicidal sprays in her purse. She was obsessively nationalistic and concealed a tattoo of the German flag between her vast breasts. She was brawny, a former athlete who handled a steak knife as if it were a javelin. She smoked cigars.

"I hate to say this," said my mother who strove to maintain a semblance of fairness in the midst of such satisfying gossip, "but your uncle seems to have married a . . ."

"Visigoth?" I offered.

Connie thought I was making the word up and ignored me. "An invader," she shouted in triumph. "Magda is an invader."

But Magda was not the invader.

What we gradually sorted out from a spate of phone calls was that Magda was Mercedes, Spanish not German. "Well, he was calling from Germany," Lyla said to defend her initial dissemination of the particulars about her new sister-in-law's origins. As for the details of the tattoo, javelin, and cigars, there was silence all around.

The truth was less exotic but more intimidating.

"She speaks Spanish," Millie pointed out. "We have that in common."

"It's different, though," Petra said.

"Castilian," confirmed Lyla darkly. "With a lisp."

The women were seated around the dining room table, talking across the dregs of Sunday dinner before them, the tripe curling in the last of the menudo, tortillas stiffening in the uncovered basket, the gnawed corncobs becoming skeletal as they withered under the bulbs of Lupita's cracked chandelier. The men played poker in the living room, scowling at their cards through eddies of cigarette smoke. My cousins and sisters were in the bedroom playing records. The Supremes were *ooh oohing* through the plaster walls, and I knew my cousins Bonita and Rica, the pretty ones who already had boyfriends, were taking turns being Diana Ross. I should have been in there lip-synching backup. But I sat in the corner of the dining room and listened to the meditations on Mercedes and the plans for a homecoming reception, wondering what they would get wrong and who would be blamed.

Rosa, Lupita's old friend and so much a fixture in the house she was often mistaken for furniture, cleared her throat. When she was still ignored, she stirred the air with her napkin.

"¿Qué quieres, Rosa?" Millie said, probing a molar with a toothpick for some impacted hominy.

"The Spanish look down on Mexicans because we eat corn." Rosa leaned toward Lupita as if she were telling a secret, although she spoke in her normal baritone. "You should feed that daughter-in-law masa."

Lupita was silent as the women turned to look at her. "We'll have duck," she said firmly. And we knew we were to treat Mercedes the way we had always treated Danny—like royalty.

So the preparations began. Connie and my aunts did the shopping and cleaning and, in the process, some refurbishing as well. Whenever they dropped by with a bag of groceries or to take their turn at scraping crust from the kitchen tiles or sweeping cobwebs from the porch ceiling, they also settled some new accessory onto the faded decor of Lupita's house. Petra planted freshly crocheted doilies under ashtrays, Lyla draped serapes over the backs of chairs, which clashed with the floral pillows Millie artistically tossed against the worn seats. Connie donated a large plastic fuchsia, and Frannie sprinkled knickknacks like confetti.

My mother and my aunts had a common decorating scheme —nouveau kitsch—a blend of Early American and 1960s colored glass doodad ornamentation. They coveted patchwork quilt cushions on maple rockers, as if they had crossed the plains themselves on Ward Bond's *Wagon Train* with their heirlooms, muslin skirts, and Calamity Jane spunk. They accented their colonial trestle leg tables with Montgomery Ward accessories— ashtrays and vases blown from purple, green, or orange glass in sleek shapes that lifted upward like flower petals or curled like ocean waves.

Even with this shared decor, my relatives' living rooms were distinguished one from the other by some particular detail— Grecian statues for Millie, stained glass coasters for Petra, cuckoo clocks for Frannie, mirrors for Lyla, and for Connie a profusion of artificial plants. My mother cultivated a plastic garden of ivy and fern—not from pots or vases, but from the heads of shepherdesses or the bellies of trolls, various body parts of ceramic figurines she painted and glazed herself at the community center adult craft classes.

When I was young, I was completely taken with this world my mother had created of fake greenery springing from fake waterfowl, gnomes, or other creatures of the woodland. My sisters and I rotated dusting and vacuuming chores, and every third Saturday it was my turn to take a rag to the week's accumulation of dust on the imitation flora and fauna. My aversion to housework found an exception in this chore. I was meticulous in the grooming of each plastic leaf, each ceramic curve, and when my mother said, "Good work, Julia" and slipped an extra quarter in my hand, the callused tips of her fingers in my palm were as good as the hugs she so rarely dispensed.

"Woolworth's in Tijuana" was my cousin Leonard's assessment of the aunts' embellishments of Lupita's living room. He was in high school, a cheerleader, on the spirit committee responsible for festooning hallways with posters and streamers prior to football games. He had credentials, and so when he recruited us kids to make decorations for the reception, we placed ourselves in his apprenticeship.

We met at Lupita's house every day after school, which annoyed me. I had been in the habit of spending afternoons alone at Lupita's, biking over after lying to Connie that I had no homework. I wasn't fitting in at school, stymied as I was by the social rules and customs of junior high, and at home Connie misinterpreted my every grunt and glare. So it was relaxing to be with Lupita, where it was clear why we didn't understand each other.

Lupita didn't speak English, even after more than forty years in this country. The only Spanish I knew came either from the elementary textbooks at school or the pejoratives, endearments, or exclamations that flecked my aunts' conversations. So aside from a trite comment on the weather, I had little to say to Lupita, since a context for bursting out with *¡Ay! qué pendejo, maldito sea*, or some other insult or curse seldom presented itself.

I generally just shadowed her at whatever she happened to be doing. Sometimes I sat with her on the couch, she watching a telenovela and I watching her twist her knuckles over the black-and-white melodrama until Sergio came in to claim the TV for the news or the fights. Sometimes I leaned against the kitchen sink while she slapped tortillas between her rough palms, or I trailed her around her rose bushes as we both pinched off brown petals, massaging the scent into our fingertips. Throughout, Lupita chatted in Spanish, a soothing murmur. Perhaps she was talking to herself. Still I responded, simulating conversation as I alternated nods and small laughs with something mumbled and incoherent.

But now, because of Mercedes, my afternoons alone with Lupita had turned into a quilting bee of sorts with many of my cousins showing up and Rosa and Leonard vying for queen bee status. Rosa was teaching us to make paper flowers, and we were piecing them together to make assorted frills and flourishes—bouquets, trellises, window hangings—supposedly to offset the Woolworth effect. Rosa demonstrated the technique she had learned as a girl in Mexico, though it was hard for us to imagine this plump, mustached woman could ever have been a *niñita.* "Se hace así en Acaponeta," she instructed us, her fat hands threatening the tissue paper into shape.

But most of us imitated Leonard as he experimented with shapes and sizes, and Rosa paid us false compliments on our reckless handiwork to show that she didn't care. We paid her back by stealing drags from her cigarette when she wasn't looking. She would wobble on chubby legs to the bathroom and return to find her Camel smoked to the butt.

"Ay, qué molesto," she would scold the smoldering stub.

We took turns lighting a fresh cigarette for her.

Once, Tony, the budding family Romeo, nearly set fire to Bonita, who had the habit of trying on all the flowers she made. They adorned her hair, hung at her throat, twined around her wrists, crisscrossed her newly sprouted breasts.

"You look like a piñata," Tony told her. We always laughed at Tony's jokes because he was handsome and we could practice our flirting with him. But then Bonita almost went up in flames, and he had to douse her with Rosa's tamarind water. Besides Bonita, well over a dozen flowers were among the casualties.

"You could have killed me," Bonita screamed, flinging bleeding tissue paper from her drenched blouse and running to tell Lupita. It didn't matter that Lupita understood little of Bonita's hiccupping denunciation. She understood tears and within seconds came her sharp, "Ven aquí, Antonio."

Tony picked his way around the ruined flowers to face Lupita's reprimanding finger and the cannonade of Spanish negatives. Being scolded in Spanish was always comical to us. We tittered among ourselves at the table, and when Tony came back in wearing a grin, Rosa pronounced us *veddy bad shildren*, which completely broke us up.

Leonard recovered first, sputtering a final guffaw that gusted some unfastened flowers off the table, reminding us of the work yet to be done. We started up again, and because we were tired—of paper flowers and each other—the only sound in the room was the rumpling of tissue paper and an occasional belch from Rosa as we crimped and creased blossoms for Danny and his bride.

After a while Bonita said, "I wonder what Mercedes thinks of his hand."

Our hand, we all thought, possessively. Our heroic Danny's hand, its deformity something only we could rightly cherish.

Tony made a claw with his hand as he reached for a piece of

tissue paper, and we let escape an appreciative giggle or two. But Rosa shushed us, having decided to take credit for and maintain the quiet that had slumped on us before, and we obliged her.

DANNY WAS OUR favorite uncle, though we rarely saw him. We knew him from pictures and from the scant memories of his visits on leave from the army. He was trim and athletic, performing push-ups on our command, and his laugh resembled a riot of crows. But the best thing about him was his burnt hand, which we learned about the summer I was seven.

We were at the dinner table when Millie called with the news of Danny's deed. My father always made us ignore a ringing phone at meals, and we all dutifully continued chewing until the caller gave up. But when the ringing persisted, my father leaned over and grabbed the receiver from the wall with the intention of slapping it back on the hook. But Millie's voice could already be heard calling for Connie who, though frowning at the interruption, hurried to the phone.

Now we all stopped chewing so we could hear better.

My mother's two-word exclamations gave us the story in abbreviated form.

"A fire? His hand? A medal?"

But it would all be embellished as the story was retold over Sunday dinner at Lupita's, and when we finally read the account in the *Stars and Stripes* that Danny sent, we were appalled that they hadn't gotten the details right.

"That's the military for you," Millie said.

And everyone nodded, confident of the truth.

Danny earned leave for his heroics and we got to see the fresh scars. The women fussed over him and the men patted him on the back, hesitant to shake the newly healed hand. For us kids, he would contract the tendons and then offer the deformed pincers to one of us. "Wanna kiss it?" he'd hiss. And we'd scream, even though we always felt honored to have the ugly hand thrust in our direction.

But none of us was so favored when Danny came home this time, his arms for once empty of the European chocolate we always expected, too full were they with Mercedes, whom he carried over the threshold of the Sunset Inn. A misunderstanding about the flight schedule resulted in no one meeting the newlyweds at the airport. Their arrival apparently unheralded, Danny hailed a taxi that delivered them to the best Kimball Park could offer: a two-star motel by the bay. So Mercedes could be awakened by the sound of *gaviotas*, explained Millie with a laugh to Connie and Lyla as they sipped lemonade on our front porch the day before the reception.

"What are gaviotas?" I asked from inside the screen door.

Lyla made a squawking sound.

"Seagulls," Millie translated.

"Did you do your homework?" Connie asked, squinting to see me through the screen.

I opened the door and joined them on the steps. "I think the sound of gaviotas is romantic," I said. I meant the word and not the actual bird, but I knew they would get it wrong.

"Listen to the expert," Lyla said, winking over her cigarette at Millie. This affront allowed me to rise and stalk off. Performing my adolescent tantrums in front of an audience served both me and my mother. Her admonitions were more subdued when subjected to the arched eyebrows of her sisters. But at least my huffy stomping exit left her with sympathetic company.

I took my bike and headed to Lupita's. On the way I thought

of Mercedes's fondness for seagulls and twice aimed my bike at a *gaviota* roosting by the side of the road. I sprinted the last few blocks and arrived in Lupita's living room with my hair in a snarl and sweat sucking my shirt to my armpits. I was about to flap the hem of my shirt for ventilation when I noticed the man on the couch grinning at me, a familiar sight, altered, though, by the fact of the woman next to him.

"Hey, stranger," Danny said, getting up to hug me. He smelled like limes and cigarettes and something else, something new and foreign. Then Mercedes stood and Danny introduced us. She was small, her streaked-blond bun level with my nose. Though I knew the Magda image had been a figment of our imaginations and ill will, I felt that somehow Mercedes was an impostor in her petite frame and mousy face.

"Mucho gusto," she said, which I mumbled back at her.

They sat back down on the couch, and I perched on the arm of Sergio's easy chair. I watched Mercedes cross her legs so that her sandal showing her painted toenails touched Danny's ankle. Danny draped his right arm around her shoulder, and he fingered the strap of her sundress with his burnt hand. Or what was supposed to be his burnt hand. Confused, I checked his left hand for signs of damage, but it was unblemished. My eyes went back to his right hand and I realized the scars had faded. The mottling and discoloration, the ridged skin were still there, but now barely noticeable, and in a certain light, at a certain angle, nearly invisible.

"Well, what do you think? I'm a married man now."

"Great," I said, studying the daisies on Mercedes's dress, which were overly large and bright, an annoyingly welcome distraction from Danny's practically normal hand. "Congratulations." I looked at Mercedes, who answered, "Grathias."

"Did you hear that?" said Danny. "It's Castilian." Then he talked in his jaunty and meandering speech about how they had met. He was on leave in Madrid, buying a round for his buddies when Mercedes began her shift at the sidewalk café.

Mercedes interjected something in her high-speed Spanish.

"You could see the opera house across the street," Danny explained. "A Puccini opera was running."

As Mercedes nodded to confirm, I wondered when Puccini had become part of Danny's vocabulary.

"I had a bet with the guys that I could get a date with her," Danny said. "She didn't like Americans. But I surprised her when I spoke Spanish to her. That won her over."

He patted Mercedes's leg with his once-burnt hand, and her toes arched inside her sandal.

We sat there smiling at each other for a minute until Danny excused himself to go to the bathroom. Then it was just me and Mercedes smiling. When our smiles went slack I could see that she had an overbite. She was on the cusp between pretty and plain. I pictured her serving tapas to my uncle and his buddies on a Madrid sidewalk, their leering faces lit by neon and all of them ignorant of the baroque opera house across the street bathed by golden lamps, strains of Puccini issuing from its stone walls, and it occurred to me that maybe Danny had not necessarily conquered worlds—only Mercedes.

Mercedes gave a little sigh and we both looked in the direction of the bathroom. I searched the ceiling for something to say. "Las gaviotas," I began stupidly. Mercedes smiled, waited. "Son interesantes," I concluded lamely.

"Sí," nodded Mercedes as if I'd said something original and profound.

Now I wondered if she was the stupid one. Or was she being

nice? Either way, her response embarrassed me. I folded my arms and, still balanced on the side of my grandfather's chair, I swung a leg back and forth, the heel of my sneaker banging the frame beneath the worn upholstery. I resumed my study of the daisies on Mercedes's dress, wordlessly daring her to make conversation. After a few moments, satisfied that I had bullied Mercedes into silence, I stole a glance at her, and found her occupied the same way I was—absorbed in the daisies on her dress. I could tell her preoccupation was different from mine, though, and I looked away, not wanting to feel sorry for her.

Lupita came in wiping her hands on her apron. It was time for her telenovela and even her new daughter-in-law could not prevent her from her daily episode of *Amor de Mi Vida*. She turned on the set and adjusted the antenna for the best reception of the Tijuana station. Mercedes had stood up when Lupita came into the room, and I stood up now, too, and greeted my grandmother with a kiss, laying claim to her and to my place in the family.

But *Amor* was about to begin, so Lupita patted me aside and took a seat on the couch, motioning for Mercedes to join her. I dropped back into my chair and placed myself at its edge to demonstrate my interest in the wretched life of the beautiful Gabriela de los Santos. I watched Gabriela's perfect eyebrows rise in disbelief, her full mouth inflate with denial as the treacherous Ramón planted rumors of her lover's betrayal.

"Mentiroso," denounced Lupita under her breath.

"No le creas," Mercedes warned Gabriela.

I felt my feigned anxiety for the soap opera characters turn to real concern as I realized their wretched lives were bringing Lupita and Mercedes together.

During the commercial break, Lupita filled Mercedes in on

previous episodes and Mercedes gasped at the perfidy, clucked at the misery, and they patted each other's hands in commiseration.

Danny came in with a beer and stood by my chair. I looked up at him, ready to exchange looks of friendly exasperation. "Ramón is scheming to win Gabriela," I informed him with a roll of my eyes.

"Oh, yeah?" he laughed. But then he sat down on the couch with Mercedes and Lupita.

I left them to their soap opera, to fret over the passionate and impulsive lives of others. I went to the kitchen and scanned the refrigerator, considered swiping a beer but instead took one of the bottles of orange soda bought especially for Mercedes. Out on the back porch I tossed the bottle cap in Lupita's rose bushes and surveyed the yard. There was Sergio's dilapidated shed that, though officially off-limits to us kids, once served as our secret clubhouse. There was the rectangle of crabgrass where my cousins and I had spent so many Sundays playing Red Rover and tag. There was the cracked sidewalk that led to the rental that had housed Rosa and her husband Camilo since the beginning of time. And there from the gnarled branches of the lone tree hung the long undisturbed wooden swing that we used to fight for turns on. I went over, sat on its worn plank, and pushed off gently. I could feel that it was only a matter of time before the swing broke loose.

When I got home I told Connie that I had met Mercedes.

"What did you think?"

"Nothing special," I said, but then I realized how satisfying my answer was to my mother, so I added, "Just one more member of this whole entire stupid family." And I was on my way to my room before Connie could send me there herself.

A FEW YEARS after the burnt hand incident we saw Danny again. He had been assigned for special training stateside at Fort Huachuca in Arizona, and when he finished he hitched a ride on the back of a buddy's Harley-Davidson to Kimball Park, where he arrived dusty and helmetless. Lupita fussed and scolded, chastised the buddy who, after depositing Danny and his duffel in my grandmother's geranium bed, revved his motor and roared off, popping a wheelie before turning the corner. Danny waved with his scarred hand until the Harley was out of sight and Lupita, clutching his other hand, pulled him inside the house. We would have him for only a few days before he headed back to Europe for missions he only alluded to with tight lips and lidded eyes.

When the family gathered for Sunday dinner, Danny laughingly recounted the journey on the Harley, its wheels skimming the westward ribbon of asphalt, the desert spreading out on either side, then the climb up the mountains, the twists and turns and the race down again. Finally, there was the stretch of highway pockmarked with warehouses, dying shopping plazas, and used car dealerships that led to Kimball Park and us.

After dinner we kids played tag in the backyard, louder and giddier than normal because Danny was home. We still thought of him as being home, even though he didn't live here anymore, hadn't for a long time, and wouldn't ever again, we knew. When Danny came out to the back porch for a break from the poker game, I went to sit beside him. I was sweaty and out of breath. Danny lit a cigarette, and in the twilight the flame from his match made the scars on his hand dance. He wasn't talkative, so I stayed quiet too.

Every so often, Danny would be called upon to resolve a dispute over whether or not someone had been tagged.

"I'm neutral," he would say. "Like Switzerland."

Just his reference to a foreign country made us respect Danny. And I liked the word *neutral*, as if he was above the commotion and strife of the world and the squabbles of our family.

I didn't know anything about Switzerland, except that it was the home of Heidi and it was famous for its clocks, and though neither of these things interested me, I wanted to go to Switzerland because Danny had been there.

"What should I see first when I go to Switzerland?" I asked as if my trip were imminent.

Danny leaned back on his elbows, the cigarette in his scarred hand growing a long cylinder of ash. He thought a long moment, looking up into the darkening Kimball Park sky. "You should see Berne. It's medieval."

I nodded, picturing serfs and plague from the pages of our encyclopedia at home, and I heard in those words *you should see* an invitation, and I answered, "I will."

He handed me his spent cigarette, and I stamped it out for him.

WHEN I CAME out of my room for dinner, the table was not set and my mother was lying on the couch. "What's wrong?" I asked, wondering more about the lack of food on the table than about my mother's well-being. She had an arm draped over her forehead, which she lifted halfway to peek at me with one eye.

"Your father took you kids out for Kentucky Fried Chicken."

I gaped at her, waiting for her to acknowledge that I was there in front of her and not feasting on a drumstick and slaw.

Connie sighed heavily. "Julia, why are you here? Why didn't you go, for heaven's sake?"

"No one told me," I fumed. "What am I, invisible?"

"Well, you're very moody."

"I'm very hungry."

"You'll have to make yourself something. I have a terrible headache."

Connie sank back into the couch, and I sulked to the kitchen to make a peanut butter sandwich. The peanut butter was too stiff and the bread too soft, so my meal resembled a child's art project. More fuel for my resentment.

The phone rang and I grabbed the receiver off the kitchen wall. Millie's voice reached my ear before the receiver did.

"Is your mother there?"

"Yes, Auntie, but she has a terrible headache." I probably shouldn't have put such an emphasis on *terrible*, but it went entirely unnoticed as both my aunt and my mother seemed anxious to talk to each other.

My mother called from the couch, "I'll be right there."

While I waited for Connie to shuffle her headache to the phone, I attempted small talk with my aunt.

"What's new?" I chirped.

"Well, that Mercedes, I tell you. You just won't believe—"

"What?" I prodded. But Connie was next to me now and I had to surrender the phone.

I sat down at the table and tore bite-size pieces off my sandwich, chewing them slowly as I listened to my mother's half of the conversation. Even though Connie was primarily the listener in any conversation with Millie, I knew she would repeat enough of Millie's annunciations to suggest the gist and spirit of the story.

This was something that was baffling about my mother and her sisters. They never talked behind closed doors or in whispers, yet they harbored a delusion that their conversations were private and confidential. In a matter of minutes, I had pieced together that Mercedes and Danny had had an argument, after which Mercedes had gone for a walk and not yet returned. Connie and Millie were speculating on which one of Mercedes's shortcomings was responsible for the fight.

I abandoned any further pretense of eating my sorry sandwich. I mimed to Connie that I was going to take a bike ride, and she nodded, absentmindedly, her face and body attuned, despite her headache, to the trill of Millie's voice on the line.

I pedaled quickly, as if on a mission. I actually felt that I *was* on a mission, though it wasn't clear to me what sort.

When I arrived I could see through the screen door that Danny was in the living room watching *Perry Mason*. As usual, Millie and Connie seemed to have got it wrong. If Mercedes were missing, Danny would not be sitting in front of the TV.

Danny motioned for me to come in. I stood just inside the door, where I could see through the dining room and beyond into the kitchen.

"I'm alone," Danny said.

The words sounded sad to me the way he said them, but, oh, so familiar.

"Where's Mercedes?" I asked.

Danny shrugged. "Aw, she'll turn up," he said, as if she were a misplaced sock. He explained that Lupita had gone around the block and Sergio to the corner grocery in search of Mercedes.

I didn't say anything, just stood there. Finally, he took his eyes from *Perry Mason* and I could see embarrassment and confusion, too. "We had a little fight," he said. And then he looked around at the decorations tacked to the walls and streaming from the ceiling and gave me a feeble grin.

Leonard had come by earlier and worked his magic with the paper flowers we had made. The reception for Danny and Mercedes was tomorrow.

"What about?" I asked.

"Aw, married people stuff."

"I'm never getting married," I vowed. As I said this, I realized I saw Danny's marriage as a betrayal, that Connie and my aunts did, too, and knew I didn't want to be aligned with them. I sat down next to Danny on the couch.

He lit a cigarette. "You're still young," he said. "You don't have to worry about any of this stuff yet." He sucked in some smoke and then released it to the ceiling where it curled itself around some paper flowers. His words felt dismissive. We sat in silence while he smoked.

When he was done, he held out the smoldering butt to me for old times' sake, but I got up, leaving Danny to put out his own cigarette. I headed to the back porch, stopping at the freezer where Sergio kept a stash of Eskimo Pies. I claimed one for the rest of my dinner. I went outside and sat in the old swing, rocking gently back and forth, lightly skimming my feet against the ground so as not to stir up any dirt into my ice cream. I was facing the back of the old shed, staring at its sun-bleached planks, its sagging roof, thinking about Lupita knocking on neighbors' doors in search of her Spanish daughter-in-law, and Sergio at the corner grocery checking the aisles for Mercedes and picking up a box of cigars and a bag of saltwater taffy while he was at it. I couldn't imagine Mercedes from Madrid roaming the streets of Kimball Park.

I was down to the last bite of Eskimo Pie when I suddenly stood up, the swing thumping the back of my knees as if prodding me toward the shed. I rounded the corner to the front and saw the door slightly ajar. I pushed it open and came face-to-face with Mercedes. Though she sat precariously on the edge of an old wooden chair to avoid too much contact with the dust around her, her posture was prim, her arms were crossed, and her chin firm with determination. But her eyes were scared, and I was sure that I was not entirely the cause of that.

"Hola," I said. For some reason I whispered it.

"So," Mercedes said. "You find me."

"Sí," I told her, suddenly finding my little Spanish words ridiculous, and her efforts at English touching.

I persisted in this bilingual communication and, trying not to sound like a cartoon, I said, "¿Qué pasa?"

"Oh, we have a fight." Mercedes's eyes began to leak tears and a reflex I was unaware I owned made me want to dab at them, but all I had was the ice cream wrapper in my hand. Another reflex took over, and I told Mercedes to wait, stay there, and I put my fingers to my lips to indicate a secrecy between us. I ran back into the house and grabbed an Eskimo Pie from the freezer and ran back to the shed, breathless with this gift of solace, and I was relieved when it made her smile.

I sat cross-legged on an old trunk, and we talked, our conversation fractured and hobbling, a mixture of my elementary, unconjugated Spanish and her travel dictionary English. I learned that Mercedes loved Madrid and missed it fiercely, as she pressed her hand to her heart in case her English did not properly convey her meaning. I wondered what it would be like to be in love with the place where you lived, thinking fiercely that I could never miss Kimball Park.

Then Mercedes said she was afraid no one here liked her.

"Not true," I told her. "No es verdad," I said, a phrase I had heard too often on *Amor de mi Vida*. I was concerned it had a melodramatic ring.

"Sí, es true."

"No, ees not," I countered, and we laughed at the muddle we had made of our languages.

After a while, Mercedes asked, "Why you no ehspeak ehspanish?"

The words stung. I wanted to ask back why she didn't speak English. But then I saw there was no malice in her face, only curiosity.

"Only the grown-ups speak it," I said, which was no explanation at all, merely an anthropological fact, but Mercedes seemed to accept it. Or she didn't know how to question it further.

"Mañana, tomorrow," she said, "I want say something in English. Words to Danny."

"Like a vow?" I didn't know the Spanish word. "Una promesa?" I ventured.

"Maybe, un poema," Mercedes said, hopeful, suddenly taken with the idea.

I didn't know any poems except for the refrain from "The Midnight Ride of Paul Revere," which we had been required to memorize at school. I did know songs, having spent countless Sundays lip-synching backup to my destined-for-stardom cousins, Rica and Bonita. We were the Supremes, the Marvelettes, Martha and the Vandellas. I had the perfect song—one that admitted confusion and confessed love.

Mercedes was a quick study, memorizing the lines I gave her in minutes. Then we scrounged around the shed and found a dirty crayon and a bit of paper, and I wrote the words down so she could practice on her own.

"Grathias," Mercedes said.

"Grathias a ti," I said, saying the word back at her, replicating her Castilian accent, pleased at how nearly authentic I sounded.

I walked her to the back porch and then ran off to round up Lupita and Sergio.

THE NEXT DAY the family assembled in the house on Palm Street for the blessing of the couple. Father Silvio, a nearly deaf, retired priest who lived down the street, positioned Danny and Mercedes at the wide threshold that separated the living room and dining room and from which garlands of paper flowers cascaded. Lupita and Sergio and my mother and aunts formed a semi-circle behind the newlyweds, close enough to touch the couple if they wanted, or to push them apart. The rest of us stood behind Father Silvio, me and my sisters and cousins jostling with Rosa for the best view. My father and uncles hung back, restless for the poker game that would follow the ceremony and meal. Leonard, holding a clunky, important-looking camera, darted in and out among us all.

Mercedes stood composed in an ivory A-line chiffon shift with a hemline that invited go-go boots but was instead coordinated with matching stockings and pumps that lifted her to my height. Her coral lips were closed against her overbite, which gave her a demure, flattering look. Danny was solemn and confident in his suit and his military posture. He was not a tall man, though he had always seemed larger than life to us. Now with Mercedes at his side, he was both more and less familiar. More and less ours.

I saw Bonita stare at Danny's hand hanging at his side, the faint mottling a pretty abstraction against the dark of his trousers. I stared, too, and I tried to remember if we had really been scared or if we had just pretended to be when Danny used to thrust it out and hiss at us to kiss his hand. Father Silvio took Danny's once-burnt hand and put it in the small white hand of Mercedes. He delivered a blessing, his Spanish made more unintelligible by the scouring thickness of his voice, adding to the mystery of his words.

When Father Silvio finished, we clapped almost as much for the newly blessed couple as for the end to the old priest's droning, but he held up his hand to shush us and we obeyed, embarrassed at our blunder.

"First," Father Silvio said, "Señora Camacho—Mercedes," he clarified, lest we all thought he was referring to Lupita, "has a few words to say." He beamed at Mercedes, though there was a hint of uncertainty at the corners of his large smile.

We stood still and silent, and it was possible to hear the rustle of the paper flowers caused by our breathing. My hands were sweating as I watched Mercedes take both of Danny's hands in hers. She looked at him shyly and began, lisping that she "couldn't ethplain it," didn't understand it, that she "never ain't felt like thees before."

It was the word *ain't* that set off the twitter. Where had she picked up that word? That bad grammar?

Mercedes seemed more intent on getting out her full declaration than on the reaction that was beginning to make a low whine around her, the way a mosquito sounds as it swoops in search of exposed flesh. She seemed oblivious even to Danny's puzzled expression. I felt my face and neck go hot, and I closed my eyes as Mercedes continued about the funny feeling that was so amazing she didn't know what to do. She pushed her side bangs further aside and said that her "ed" was in a "aze."

"Is she all right?" one of my aunts whispered loudly.

"¿Qué dijo?" Lupita asked.

"It's the excitement. She might be feeling faint," said another one of my aunts.

Mercedes, determined to finish, spoke louder, more emphatically, her accent more pronounced. "Ees like a eat wave," she proclaimed, "burning in my art."

With these last few lines, Mercedes had dropped Danny's hands and placed both of her own at her heart, which prompted Millie to shriek, "Get some water, quick!"

Millie's outburst, rather than spur us to action, brought us all to a standstill as Mercedes turned to stare in confusion at all of us. I felt that I should say something since, after all, I had been the one to put those words in Mercedes's innocent lisping mouth, words that had seemed perfect for the occasion, but which I now realized had only been perfect for me and my befuddlement with the world and the hope to one day be out in it. But I kept quiet. I looked around at the faces straining at the silence, teeth on edge.

But then suddenly everything clicked, a collective light bulb radiated understanding above the heads of my hyperventilating family. Danny grinned his big grin, let loose the crows in his laugh and wrapped Mercedes in his arms, accepting the gift she had made him, of English words spoken by heart, from the heart—a noble and sweet intent, never mind that she had little clue of the meaning. Bonita and Rica, having finally discovered one of their favorite songs lurking beneath Mercedes's accent, began to warble, one of them assuming the role of Martha and the other channeling a Vandella.

In the commotion that followed, I tried to catch Mercedes's eye to exchange winks or a thumbs-up or some other sign of team spirit, but she was engulfed by family. Lupita and Sergio hugged their new daughter-in-law and clung a moment to Danny, then the other grown-ups crowded behind to do the same.

Lyla and Millie handed around champagne in stemware redeemed with S&H Green Stamps and poured Dixie cups of Fresca for the minors. We raised our glasses and cups over and over toasting the couple's happiness, their health and prosperity, their fecundity, Puccini, sidewalk cafés, Danny's burnt hand, Mercedes's Castilian lisp, *gaviotas* (my toast), America the beautiful, *España para siempre* (Mercedes's toast). And then a reluctant final toast—a safe trip back to Europe. Our glasses were empty now and we were reminded that a taxi would take Danny and Mercedes to the airport in a few hours.

"Pues, vamos a comer," said Lupita, herding the couple to the buffet laid out in the dining room. We set upon it greedily, as if it were our last. Still there were leftovers. Duck meat glistened in its gelled fat, rice fastened in perfect mounds to serving bowls, *carnitas* lay unskewered next to a brimming bowl of salsa. Though we wanted to, we couldn't eat any more, couldn't hoard against future hungers. There was a brief lethargy when forks ceased to rasp against plates, when conversation lacked the shrill one-upmanship of my aunts, when we were in danger of saying something cruel or stupid simply to avoid descending into silence.

Frank Sinatra saved us, or rather Father Silvio did when he

set the phonograph spinning. It was Mercedes who coaxed Danny to his feet, but then he took over, steering her left or right, back and forth, then finishing by dipping his new wife to a daring angle as Frank warbled the last notes of "The Way You Look Tonight." Mercedes's squeal was matched by our applause. Then Sergio and Lupita danced to Pedro Infante, Leonard led Lyla in a cha cha, and soon we all wriggled to the Beatles.

Enlivened by the music, we faced Danny's departure like overworked puppies, jostling one another as we slapped his back a little too hard, rumpled his thinning hair, shook his once-burnt hand. We kissed Mercedes European style, bumping noses as we moved from cheek to cheek, and even then it seemed I was lost to her amid the blur of faces. We formed a gauntlet down the porch steps and heaved paper flowers as they ran for the curb to escape in the taxi. I aimed especially for Mercedes and saw my flower catch in the crook of her arm.

I stood on the front lawn next to Connie, who closed ranks with Lupita to wave goodbye as our Danny left home again. They were silent, but I understood them both perfectly. Before the taxi pulled away, Mercedes leaned her head out the window, and even though I was in the crowd of my family, I knew it was me her eyes searched for, me to whom she blew a kiss. For minutes after the taxi disappeared around the corner, we stood there watching the traffic pass. Then we all went back into Lupita's house, no one willing to go home right away.

I sat in the kitchen for a while listening to Lupita and Rosa converse in Spanish, not trying to understand, not pretending to.

I walked through the dining room where my mother and aunts were dividing the leftovers and trading gossip.

Then I joined my cousins in the bedroom just as Leonard was sliding a stack of 45s on the record player. When the needle hit the groove, I was already in place beside Rica and Bonita to sing backup—not for the last time, but not forever.

Fleeing Fat Allen

———— ❖ ————

IT'S MY IDEA—THE solo trip down the coast. I tell my husband he doesn't have to come. But he hears it in my voice—that I don't want him to come. That's not quite it though. Wanting to go alone and not wanting him to come are not really the same thing.

Besides, it's not a pleasure trip, I tell him. It's family stuff.

Ed is not keen on my family. It's too large and loud and gossipy, he thinks, though he's only met them a scant few times during our ten-year marriage. He comes by his opinion largely as a result of my own very vocal grievances—the feuding aunts, the one-upsmanship among the cousins, my mother's maddening indifference. Not that he has much sympathy. He can't understand why I don't just detach myself from them. "You're a grown-up, Julia," he says. As if that has anything to do with it.

"It's family stuff," I say again.

"Why don't you fly?" he asks.

"Driving helps me think," I tell him.

He doesn't ask me what I need to think about, just observes, "It's a long drive."

FOR THE FIRST six hours out of Seattle, I hardly think at all. I just drive. I'm a steady sixty-mile-an-hour driver, an unchang-

ing occupant of the slow lane, trying not to be pressured outside of my comfort zone by the velocity around me.

Ed and I had driven this route ten years ago when we were
not yet married, and the possibility for marriage was up in the
air where I had thrown it that first night when we stopped in
Ashland. I thought he would agree with me—that our decision to marry was too sudden, that maybe we should take more
time to think about it. "*I* don't need to think about it," he said,
staring hard at me, his eyes showing hurt and disbelief, but also
a kind of condescension. The weight of his pronoun, the con-
ceited pitch of that "*I*," made me livid while at the same time
fueling my congenital need to please.

I drive past Ashland, not even stopping for gas until crossing
into California where I fill up, first the tank and then my bag of
depleted provisions—nuts, granola bars, fruit leather, bananas,
Gatorade. I would like to treat myself to dinner, but I remind
myself this is not a pleasure trip. Still, when I open the door to
my Comfort Inn room to the queen-size bed and the TV that
will be all mine, I feel a twinge of satisfaction. I eat in bed and
watch *The Love Boat.*

The second night I bypass the turn-off to Berkeley where
we had stayed with a friend of a friend of Ed's—a young phi-
losophy professor who captivated us both with her wacky wit.
Maybe it's because we fell in love with her on the spot that we
made up with each other—me retracting my retraction and he
benevolently accepting my apology for having qualms about
marrying.

I stop instead in San Jose, check into a Rodeway, and allow
myself the Blue Plate at Denny's.

The next day I finally focus on my destination, a pilgrimage
really. I'm driving to see my Aunt Lyla. She lives in a moun-

tain town east of San Diego called Descanso. Descanso means
rest, and that's why my aunt has moved there. To rest. Perma-
nently, she says. It's really a theatrical gesture on her part, if my
mother and my other aunts are to be believed. They say that
if she had found a town called Muerte, she would have moved
there. What about Death Valley, I suggest. Too obvious, they
reply. They're right. Lyla scorns cliché, not to mention sand
and cactus.

My pilgrimage from Seattle has followed the roller coaster
precipices of the Pacific Coast Highway down to its trendy
beach communities where the smell of coconut oil settles like
fog. Because a pilgrimage should be arduous, I stop in Kimball
Park to visit my mother. I ask, "How are you?" and she answers,
"Life is a bowl of spaghetti—." I wait for the rest, for the punch
line, the part about the meatball. But I realize she has finished
her sentence. There is no meatball for my mother.

She invites me to stay for coffee. She never remembers that I
don't drink coffee, never have. "No, thank you," I say. I look at
my watch as if time is an issue. "I should be on the road," I say.
"Lyla is expecting me," I add, though she isn't really, at least
not at any particular time. I invite my mother to come along,
but she declines. Briefly, I reconsider coffee, but she is already
waving goodbye to me.

She will go in a few weeks, when she and my Aunt Milagros head to the Barona Reservation to play the slot machines.
"Kill two birds with one bone," she calls out with a yawn. "One
stone," I tell her. I decide not to point out that Barona and
Descanso are on different highways.

I drive east. As the road winds into the Cuyamaca Mountains, I slow down to look for my turn to Descanso, and the traffic collects behind me. For a moment, I am leading a procession

to see my aunt. But then the honking starts. I refuse to pull to the side, refuse to be bullied—as I once was by Lyla, as I felt I was by Ed, as sometimes I am by my own desire to play along, to not rock the boat, to be liked.

I never thought to call what my aunt did to us bullying. But that's what it was. And despite it all, I used to wonder what it would be like to be her daughter instead of my mother's.

On Saturday afternoons, we sat on my grandmother Lupita's front porch because her house faced the street, unlike our own, which sat behind my grandmother's like a plaything—a little rental, shaped like a box and painted gumball blue. On my grandmother's porch, my sisters and I could sit side by side and watch the people who had places to go drive by in cars, and my Aunt Lyla could call out to the ones without cars strolling past on the sidewalk.

Those she knew and liked she greeted by name; those she didn't, she gave a name. "Look at that pendejo," she would say. "Eh, zonzo," she would call, "your fly is open." She said this even when it wasn't, even when she couldn't see his fly. My mother would shake her head without looking up from her magazine.

My aunt didn't even live in the neighborhood. She lived in a better part of town on a tree-lined street with my Uncle Vin and my large-boned twin cousins. Those were my Aunt Lyla's words, *large-boned*, and she would cross her slim legs, lean forward on her elbows so that her breasts bunched together in the scoop of her blouse, and sigh, "That's genetics for you. That's what happens when you let a big guy with charm and a wallet kiss you."

Aunt Lyla came almost every Saturday to sit with us on the porch. She always came alone. "It's my day off from kids," she would tell us as she blew smoke through puckered lips. My sisters and I, who were not large-boned but skinny as pencils, stood looking at our toes sticking out of our sandals, not knowing what to do. Then she would hold her cigarette away from her body and beckon to us with her free hand. "Give your Aunt Lyla a kiss."

I let my sisters go first, and when it was my turn, I lingered at my aunt's side until she laughed at my shyness and thrust her cheek at me. I smelled her cigarette and lipstick and rose petal perfume, and after I kissed her, I sat as close to her as I dared without eliciting a sharp reprimand from my mother to move away from Lyla's lit cigarette. "Do you want to get burned?" she would ask. I would scoot away and Lyla would wink at me.

Did I mention that Lyla is not her real name? My mother said her name was Alicia Carmen, but that when she was eighteen she declared herself to be Lyla. Her name had never been legally changed, but that was Aunt Lyla. She could decide something, say it was so, and it was.

So when she said Fat Allen was coming to kiss us, we believed her and we ran for our lives. It wasn't just that apparently objectionable thing called genetics or the disgraceful consequence of large bones that sent us screaming and scrambling underneath my grandmother's bed to avoid Fat Allen's kiss. Mixed with the panic that we felt at an unwelcome kiss from a giant boy whose fist seemed always wrapped around some drippy, smeary snack was another source of confusion.

It was my aunt's husky laugh as we cringed in the musty dimness that made us jockey for the farthest corner below the bed. "Here comes Fat Allen," she sang. "He's coming to kiss you."

"Really, Lyla," my mother would scold. Then she called to us, "It's all right. Come on out now." She said it as if it were our fault that we were scared, as if we should've known better in the first place.

Rosalie, since she was the oldest, edged her way out first. We dusted off our knees and straightened each other's braids, then went out the back door where there was no traffic to count, no passersby to watch, just a circle of dirt where my grandfather's mean and mangy bulldog, Toby, ranged on a leash.

This happened most Saturdays. Fat Allen would appear down the street, my aunt sang her song, we ran for cover, eventually taking refuge in the neglected backyard with Toby. But one Saturday Aunt Lyla didn't come and it was just me and my sisters on the front porch and my mother and her magazine— my mother who could take a day off from her kids without leaving home. Without my aunt to yell greetings or insults, people just passed by hardly noticing us. I had just lost my turn at jacks and Lucy was next, which meant coaching from Rosalie and extra chances, so I shifted my attention to the street just in time to see Fat Allen round the corner and head our way. I stood, ready to run, more out of habit than from fear this time. Without Aunt Lyla there to sing her song, the threat of Fat Allen seemed removed—improbable even, and this emboldened me. Like a reflex, the song came loud and chanting from my throat, "Here comes Fat Allen."

Immediately, I was yanked off my feet, my butt slapping the cement step, my head jarring as my mother's clenched whisper scorched my ear. "No candy money for you today." Fat Allen passed, a wavering blob through my watery eyes.

"Aunt Lyla says it," I muttered, not quite to myself.

"You are not Aunt Lyla," my mother said angrily. "Do you hear me?"

Later, to make her point and enforce my punishment, my

mother allowed me and my sisters to go to the store at the corner. But while Rosalie and Lucy each had a nickel and a jangle of pennies, my pockets were empty, my mother having confiscated the coins my grandfather had dropped in my hand after his morning at the dog track.

While Rosalie and Lucy browsed the candy counter, I stood near the comic book rack. It was the kind that rotated, but Mr. Felix didn't like us to touch anything unless we were going to buy it. So I circled the rack, hands behind my back, reading the front covers of all the comic books. It was all I could do to keep my hands off the latest issue of *Nancy* to find out what new mischief she had done and how nice her Aunt Fritzi still was to her. I must have made some involuntary movement toward *Nancy* because as Mr. Felix rang up Rosalie's candy cigarettes and Lucy's Tootsie Pop, he warned in his billy goat's gruff, "No dime, no read."

I held up my hands to show my innocence and began to follow my sisters out the door. Just then the telephone rang in the back of the store and Mr. Felix rushed to answer it. As soon as he was out of sight behind the shelf of dog food, I ran back in just to touch the comic book, to lift it from the rack and tickle its pages and put it back just for the sake of it. I had just completed this quiet act of defiance when I heard my sisters outside, Lucy squealing like a pig and Rosalie letting loose with a *Hi Ho Silver*, and then the sounds of their footsteps in a panicked retreat.

I turned to see Fat Allen in the doorway, his lumpy bulk spreading a wide shadow on the green-tiled floor. There was no escape and nowhere to hide, though I couldn't have moved if there had been. I heard Lyla's singsong in my head. *Here comes Fat Allen.* I longed for the dusty underneath of my grandmother's bed. I wanted my mother to come and save me, or at least to hear her sigh impatiently that "It's all right."

Fat Allen was moving down the aisle where I stood. I was too scared to close my eyes, so I just watched him come nearer. He wore untied sneakers with no socks, baggy shorts, and a T-shirt with stripes whose symmetry was distorted by the breadth of his belly. A halfway-picked scab hung at one knee and dried beads of orange sherbet traced a path down his right forearm and picked up again on his shin and the toe of his shoe. My heart beat loud in my ears, my throat clogged with unswallowed saliva. He walked right by, looking at me only briefly, the expression in his small brown eyes and slack mouth barely registering a change. I watched him lumber over to the soda case, scan the selection, and then reach with both hands, the left seizing a root beer, the right an Orange Crush. As I watched Fat Allen clutch those soda bottles so protectively, I began to feel the anger rise in me: At Aunt Lyla for chasing us under the bed with her terrorizing taunt. At my mother and her stupid magazines. At Fat Allen.

I waited for him to walk back down the aisle toward the cash register. He turned in my direction, his cheeks flushed but his face expressionless. And that's what struck me—the innocent blankness of his face behind the sticky residue of sherbet. Yet it didn't move me to sympathy. As soon as his fleshy, impenetrable self was within inches of me, I stuck my foot out to trap a loose shoelace. It was enough to throw him off balance and send him sprawling to the floor. His soda bottles shattered with the impact, and Orange Crush and root beer ran and puddled around him. It was the broken glass and spilled liquid, so irretrievable, that scared me, and maybe Fat Allen, too, because he began to cry. I stood staring at the big blubbering bulk of him.

Mr. Felix came running out of the back room. "What are you doing? What have you done?"

"He fell down," I said. "He made a big mess." I pointed.

Mr. Felix shooed me with his apron. "Go on, get out of here."

I ran. As hard as when I used to flee Fat Allen. When I got home, Rosalie and Lucy were sitting safely on our little front porch, not our grandmother's that was exposed to the street, but our own, tucked away from the world. They were eating their candy.

"What happened?" Rosalie asked, a candy cigarette dangling from her lips.

Lucy removed the Tootsie Pop from her mouth. "Did Fat Allen kiss you?" There was fear and excitement in her eyes.

"Really, Lucy," I said, imitating my mother. And then I added, "Don't be stupid."

"I'm telling," Rosalie said, and I knew she would.

My mother's magazine lay on the porch, and I stepped on it as I ran inside and scooted under my own bed to hide. I was safe. Free of Fat Allen, I told myself, though even then I knew it wasn't true.

The next Saturday Aunt Lyla didn't come or any other Saturdays after that. We learned that she left my Uncle Vin. Later she would move to Las Vegas where she loved the neon glitter amid the desolation of the desert. Sometimes as we sat on my grandmother's porch, Fat Allen would pass by. My mother might look up from her magazine for a moment, my sisters would exchange glances, but I would always turn away, my aunt's cruel, merry singsong in my head.

WHEN I ARRIVE at the crumbling red A-frame, Henry, Lyla's third husband, nods me in with a finger to his lips. Lyla is napping on the couch, and Henry leads me past her scraping snores to the kitchen. He pours a glass of lemonade and jiggles cookies from a box onto a plate, as if I were Lyla's seven- rather than thirty-seven-year-old niece. "Make yourself comfortable," he says, and I lounge against the counter to simulate an easeful pose, but only feel tight and slouchy. Henry stands in the middle of the kitchen, popping his knuckles. "Would you mind," he says, slowly, each word coming with a pop, "staying with Lyla while I run some errands?" He points to her in the adjoining room, and we both look, like visitors at a museum display.

When Henry has driven off in the direction in which I imagine lies the nearest tavern, I ignore the lemonade and cookies, this after-school snack for a child, and I stand in the living room. I watch Aunt Lyla huddled in sleep, her patchy hair smashed flat in places, snarled and spiked in others, her flowered shift caught between her knees, exposing legs to match the kindling that I passed in the yard outside, and I remember what she was like for me then, when I *was* a child of seven. I remember Saturday afternoons on the front porch when she painted her toenails, afterward stretching her long, dancer legs down the steps so we could all admire the effect—all of us except my mother who was absorbed in *True Detective*, *True Romance*, or some other genuine, factual piece of fiction.

Now in her mountain cabin, my worn-out aunt stirs and makes a smacking sound with her gummy lips. I get up to make some tea, and by the time I return with two cups of chamomile, one with a squirt of lemon, the other with a drop of whiskey, my aunt is sitting up, her knees apart for balance, her rough bare feet on the rough wood floor.

She's smiling, not at all surprised to see me. "I've been wondering when you'd be dropping by," she says, as if her California mountain hideout was a leisurely walk from my Seattle neighborhood.

"Come here," she says. "Give your Aunt Lyla a kiss."

I set the tea tray on the table next to the couch and lean down to peck her cheek, careful not to inhale. The smell of her enters my nostrils anyway, and I try not to react to the moldy bread odor that comes from her breath, her hair, her skin. She laughs the way she used to when I would kiss her faintly out of shyness.

I want to cover her bare feet. Too much of her is exposed. Too much of her is lost.

"Bring me my slippers," she says, reading my mind. She points to a pair of fluffy brown moccasins that look like small animals. I retrieve them and bend down to fit them to her wrinkled feet, my hand guiding her veiny ankles. When I stand up, she is already reaching for the tea and soon sipping from the cup meant for me.

I take the other cup, the one with the lemon.

She pats a spot on the sofa next to her, but instead I take the nearby rickety chair. "So I can see you better," I say.

She snorts into her tea, looks around. "Where's Henry?"

I sip my tea, tepid now and strongly citrus. "Errands," I tell her.

"Of course," she says.

Lyla gulps her toddy down, and before she can ask for another, I launch into an admiring monologue about the house, its rustic quality (I don't say charm), the faded rugs that give a lived-in feeling, the sunlight that slants across the floors and makes a nimbus above its splintery boards.

Lyla points to the living room window. "It's pretty out here, isn't it?" She asks the question as if she wants to be convinced.

"Yes," I tell her, because everything *is* pretty except the ugly house, which intrudes upon the pine and dogwood like something deviant and tumorous.

"It's quiet," I say. I wonder how she tolerates it with no one around to gossip with, no one to admire her, no one to jeer at or tease. Except Henry.

"Restful," she agrees, and I remember why she has chosen to live in Descanso, and I remember, too, the skepticism of my mother and my other aunts.

She slumps into the couch, the slippers slide from her heels and dangle from her toes. Her eyes are closed and the line of her once perfectly pouty mouth is limp and uneven. Her hands are open to the sloped ceiling. She stays like that for several minutes.

Finally, I say, "Can I get you anything?"

She doesn't answer, so I rise from my rickety chair, wishing Henry were back in case there is something medical that has to be done—pills to be administered, a syringe full of painkiller to be injected. I lean toward her, see the damage of the years up close. I study her neck for the shiver of a pulse, but the skin is slack and concealing. I have to take her wrist. I reach for it, her palm cooperative, already turned upward and resting on the couch. I touch two fingers to her puckered skin, which elicits a terrible shriek from Lyla's seared lungs, and I scream in reply. I am shaken at the sound of my fright, the way it smacks the air and knocks me off balance, so it is a minute before I realize Lyla is laughing. She has slipped to the floor in her hilarity and is gasping for breath. I sit back down, wrap my hands around the worn, wobbly arms of the chair, and wait for her to recover.

At last, she wheezes, "Gotcha."

We have another cup of tea, this time at the table, this time with whiskey in both our cups. Lyla is garrulous, her speech throaty and aggressive as she recalls old times. Remember how I used to visit on Saturdays? Remember the store at the corner? She is precise in her details, though some are surely made up. I wait for her to mention Fat Allen, but she never does. Perhaps she truly has forgotten. She is done talking now. She rests her hands in her lap.

Henry's truck pulls up, and we are both relieved.

THE NEXT DAY I'm at my mother's again, sitting beside her on her little one-step cement porch. We're sipping iced tea, unsweetened. I think she would like to know about my visit with Lyla, but I don't tell her.

I want to ask her, "Do you remember Fat Allen?" I almost do. But instead I say, out of nowhere, it seems, "You still read those magazines?" I point at the slick pages in her hand.

Now she points at me with the rolled-up magazine. "Are you criticizing me?"

"No," I say, truthfully.

She opens the magazine on her lap, licks her fingertip to turn a page. "I'm still your mother, you know," she says, without looking up.

Later, after I've pulled out of her driveway, my tires squeal a little as I shift gears too suddenly, and when I hit the freeway, I accelerate hard to reach the speed limit and then some. It's a long way back. This time I will stop in Berkeley, and then I will stop in Ashland. But not for long. Ed will be waiting. Ed will be wondering.

3

Leaving Kimball Park

Strong Girls

❖

IT WAS LUNCHTIME, and in our corner of the cafeteria, Ofelia and I were on the second of our roast beef sandwiches with extra mayonnaise. Ofelia stopped chewing, though her mouth was still full. Her black eyes bulged, and I had just decided to administer the Heimlich when she swallowed. It was loud, like a cork popping. Now looking back, maybe that's what really happened after all. Ofelia popped her cork.

I watched as she headed toward Big Freddy Galarza who had collared one of the scrawny kids who played chess or read *Ulysses* at lunch. Freddy was actually dangling the kid so that his Red Wings danced several inches above the food-littered linoleum.

"Put him down, Freddy," my sister said.

And Freddy did, because now Ofelia offered a more interesting object of ridicule. I wished I'd had a chance to wipe the mayonnaise from her chin, pluck the shred of limp lettuce from her lovely black hair.

"Now which twin are you?" he asked. "The fat one or the fat one?" It was an odd question coming from Big Freddy, who was the only boy in the school almost as big as we were. But rather than engender a comradeship or, even more, a courtship or a single no-strings-attached date, our shared physical characteristic only increased the bully in him.

He moved toward Ofelia, and her reaction came from a place out of our childhood. She hefted her leg and aimed a cancan kick into Freddy's gut, knocking him off his feet. That might have been the end of it if she had just walked away. But someone in the crowd yelled, "Go, Ofelia!" It was me.

So Ofelia finished the job by throwing her entire weight on the still-recumbent Freddy and pinning his shoulders to the floor. As it turned out, Mr. Jarvis, the wrestling coach, was on cafeteria duty that day, and he was the one who pulled Ofelia off Freddy and led her away. I followed, expecting him to take her to detention hall, but instead he took her to his office in the gym. He was about to close the door when he saw me and motioned me in, too.

We sat down in two sweaty-smelling chairs, and he leaned against his desk, arms crossed, big-knuckled hands wrapped around his biceps.

"You girls ever wrestle?" he asked.

Given our surroundings, we knew it wasn't a metaphysical question.

"No," we said together.

"Builds character," he said, stroking his biceps. "How much you weigh?"

We told him and he nodded. "Come see me tomorrow after school."

That evening after we finished the bucket of KFC and the bowl of lettuce our mother had left for us on the dining room table, we mulled over Coach Jarvis's invitation. That's what I called it, as if it were a request for our presence at a social event requiring an RSVP.

"I don't think he meant for us to have a choice," Ofelia said.

"Of course we have a choice," I told her.

"Then what's your choice?"

"What's yours?" I asked her back.

"I want to fight," Ofelia said, her broad nose made broader by the flare of her nostrils. "That big oaf Freddy was just the start." Her eyes burned with anger at the Freddys of the world. "I want to win," she said.

I didn't agree with her that Freddy was that big of an oaf, but I realized that I, too, wanted to win, and I pictured myself in a letterman's jacket, medals pinned at the left breast, a place in the yearbook.

WHEN WE WERE eight, our parents, Lyla and Vin, divorced, and the odd symmetry of two hyper-large daughters and two attractive, pleasingly proportioned parents was broken.

Though Lyla was our custodial parent, we spent half our time at Vin's, a more stable household, especially after he settled down with his new wife, Vera, a bubble-haired, hoarse-voiced smoker who called us "Doll." They were managers of an apartment building, and while it was a far cry from the hotel Vin had once hoped to own, they lived rent-free and held pool parties every third Thursday. Lyla, on the other hand, who had never quite let go of her ambitions for stardom, first for her and then for us, channeled her energies into a series of entrepreneurial ventures from raising llamas to cactus farming, losing money but never faith, and finally finding her niche selling cosmetics from a vendor cart at the mall.

Our aunts pitied us, and our cousins envied us for the lives we led. Our grandmother Lupita prayed for us. When we weren't undertaking a new enterprise with Lyla, we were generating tidal waves in Vin's apartment pool as we cannonballed from the high dive. We had grown into large, powerful girls with breasts that floated like rafts, a source of envy for our cousins whose thin, underdeveloped bodies fought for buoyancy when we invited them to swim. On one of these occasions, after they had flailed and we had churned in the water for an hour, we spread our towels on the concrete and lay in a circle. There were six of us, three sets of sisters—Rosalie and Julia, Rica and Bonita, and Ofelia and me, Norma.

We talked about our favorite singers and sang Herb Alpert's "This Guy's in Love With You." We talked about being famous one day, and though Bonita insisted she would somehow gain fame as an airline stewardess, I felt deep in my bones, deep within my adipose layers, that I would be the one to enjoy renown.

We talked about boys and speculated on which one of us would have a boyfriend first. Rica ruled Rosalie and Julia out with, "Boys don't make passes at girls who wear glasses."

Julia shot back, "Boys don't make passes at girls who are stupid."

"We've been to charm school," Bonita said, sincerely believing that a month of Saturday mornings at the Wendy Ward Academy gave her and Rica the advantage.

None of them considered Ofelia or me as candidates for a boyfriend. But it was something we had talked about privately, the two of us, at night in our twin beds when the lights were out. Ofelia would imagine out loud how a boy, someone bigger and stronger than we were, would place his hands in the vicinity of her waist and pull her toward him so he could press his lips against hers. As I listened, I would slip my hand beneath my nightgown and across the bare skin of my thighs and hips, the mound of my stomach, my balloon-like breasts. And even if he wasn't bigger and stronger than we were, Big Freddy Galarza appeared behind my closed lids.

But it wasn't until that wrestling season that we first felt a boy's touch. Then we felt it regularly—and in front of large crowds.

WE WENT TO the gym, thinking we would humor Coach Jarvis just long enough for him to let Ofelia off the hook for decking Freddy in the cafeteria, just long enough for us to take down a couple of guys on the team. But we stayed the whole season, and the gym became our haven and eventually our stage. We met little resistance from the boys on the squad because to them we were a big, fat joke. Nevertheless, we were a joke that kicked butt. During practice, Ofelia and I took turns going against Martin Hardcastle, who was the only one in our weight group and the reason Coach Jarvis had recruited us. Martin was like Play-Doh on the mat, and both Ofelia and I perfected our headlock on him. Coach Jarvis, rather than compliment us, bellowed at the struggling Martin, "Do you want to win or lose, Hardcastle?" Martin would wheeze, "Win." But then Ofelia or I, whichever one of us was wrestling him at the time, would slam his shoulders to the mat, expelling from him a loud gasp that surrendered traces of that day's lunch.

Sometimes Freddy slouched in the bleachers, alternately giving his attention to the pert cheerleaders practicing their scissor kicks at one end of the gym and Ofelia and me pummeling Martin at the other end. He emitted low whistles audible enough to make the cheerleaders toss their ponytails in annoyance, audible enough to make Ofelia maintain her hold on Martin a second longer just to make a point, audible enough to make me spring to my feet as gracefully as my size would allow in a pathetic attempt to appear cute and girlish. Soon, though, Coach Jarvis closed practices to Freddy and all the other looky-loos that came to ogle either the cheerleaders or us. We knew he was frustrated that his plan to use us to build up Martin Hardcastle's repertoire of mental and physical maneuvers was failing. It was true that Martin was getting stronger. But not as strong as we were. He continued to be a pushover. So we practiced on each other, walking through the choreography of a takedown, a reversal, an escape, coaching each other through the moves, eager for our first real opponent.

WHEN WE WERE little—that is, when we were young—Lyla enrolled us in dance lessons. But gravity was our enemy, propelling our round bodies back to the ground almost immediately after we lifted a dimpled knee for a leap or pushed off the ball of a double E foot for a spin. Lyla developed a squint from scrunching up her face as she watched us, her frown encouraging us back to equilibrium. What she could not squint away, though, were the effects of the leotard, the way the stretchy pink fabric clung to us, bundling at the waist and hips and under the arms.

Strangely, though, we liked our leotards, liked how the elastic captured our bodies, showed them as they were. And if we couldn't execute leaps and turns in them, we felt a certain compactness of our large bodies that allowed us to move, if not gracefully, at least more powerfully.

Sometimes after dance class Lyla took us to visit one or another aunt. While Lyla and our aunt drank coffee on the front porch, Ofelia and I strutted in our leotards for our skinny cousins who did not take dance lessons. Aunt Millie said her daughters were graceful enough, while Aunt Connie refused to "parade her girls about like poodles."

It was at my Aunt Connie's house where Ofelia and I were parading about like poodles that my sister and I got our nicknames one afternoon. We were in the backyard prancing in our Pepto-Bismol leotards for our cousins Rosalie and Julia. We twirled in the patch of crabgrass that was their lawn, pushing our ballet slippers into the bristly blades.

"Do a real dance," demanded Julia who was jealous that we got to take lessons.

Ofelia and I stopped and looked at each other. We thought we *had* been doing a real dance.

Rosalie coaxed us. "Just something easy. Like the cancan."

Ofelia and I retreated to the edge of the crabgrass to talk things over.

"Do we know the cancan?" she asked, no anxiety in her voice, just curiosity.

"Of course," I answered, reminding her of the episode when Lucy Ricardo did it on TV. Sometimes while facing Ofelia, I forgot that she was a replica of me and I saw her as someone wholly apart from me. But then her eyebrow would curve upward the way I knew mine did or she would bite her lip, which was my habit, too. That's when I remembered that she was my mirror and I was hers.

"We *can* do the cancan," she said to me. We put our arms around each other's shoulders and strode back toward our cousins. Then in one of those uncannily twin moments, we each lifted opposite legs, kicked each other, and landed on our butts. Our cousins threw themselves down beside us, overcome with laughter.

I'm the one who yelped, "Uffy," but Rosalie was already pointing her finger at Ofelia, rechristening her Oafie as she got up to re-enact landing on her cancan. I also performed an encore, and now I had a nickname, too. "Oafie and Abnorma," Rosalie warbled, and Julia made a chant of it, loud and showy, as they danced around our sprawled and awkward bodies. But Aunt Connie's stinging reproach and Lyla's silent contempt when the back door swung open ensured the ban of the nicknames. Still, they were whispered when we played Red Rover after Sunday dinners, when our cousins would unlink arms to avoid having them broken when Ofelia aimed herself toward their line. And they were whispered again after dark when we went inside to play Twister and I lost my balance and splayed across the mat, burying several cousins beneath me.

Oafie and Abnorma. Maybe it should have bothered us more than it did. Instead, we took comfort in our aberration, in the largeness of each other, the space that we occupied, the molecules we displaced when we sat in a chair, stood in an aisle, rode an elevator. There was something about our size and our twinness that made us feel invulnerable. As long as we had each other, we would be fine.

AS MUCH AS we were reassured by our shared burden, we struggled for selfhood, which is hard to attain when someone is always mistaking you for your sister or her for you. Big Freddy's question to Ofelia as to whether she was "the fat one or the fat one" was the most recent case in point. Being on the wrestling team did nothing to differentiate us from each other. One of us would have to shine. One of us would have to win it all.

One morning we were both in front of the bathroom mirror

brushing our teeth. I gently elbowed Ofelia to gain more of the mirror. She elbowed back, and I rocked sideways, off balance, allowing her to insert herself squarely in front of the mirror.

"I was here first," she claimed.

"No, you weren't." I was standing behind her now but peeked around her to see part of me in the mirror. She immediately moved to block my view of myself.

"You don't own it," I said, referring to the mirror, but thinking also of the face that was reflected there.

"Well, I got first dibs." Ofelia stood her ground, ready to swerve left or right to obstruct me.

So the competition was on—the first one to the mirror each morning was the first to claim the image there for herself. We took to using all manner of ploys to be the first to the bathroom. One morning as I was quietly crowding my feet into my slippers, Ofelia screamed, "Mouse!" and while I jumped onto the bed, she dashed into the bathroom. Minutes later when she came out, face washed, teeth brushed, hair combed, she was composed, almost smug, and I didn't speak to her until lunchtime when I warned her that if she ate a third sandwich her face would explode from an overdose of mayonnaise.

That night after Ofelia was asleep, I grabbed the alarm clock that sat on the nightstand between our beds and buried it under my pillow. If the muffled ringing couldn't wake me, I was sure its vibrations would. But sometime during the night as I wrestled with demons in my dreams, I must have flung the clock onto the floor. When it rang, I vaulted out of bed, startled by the unexpected sound, and collided into Ofelia who had also jumped out of the blocks at the bell. The impact threw us both on the floor with twin thuds against our respective beds where we eyed each other warily, silently measuring the distance to the bathroom door. Our panting was the only sound in the room until Lyla ran in and demanded, "What are you doing?" She had been applying her makeup and only her left eyelashes were glued on.

"Nothing," I answered.

"We fell," Ofelia said.

"Well, be more careful. And quiet." Lyla left to put on the rest of her lashes.

We decided that morning to alternate who had first turn at the bathroom mirror each morning. It didn't matter who woke up first. If I did and it wasn't my turn, I waited for Ofelia to snap out of her deep sleep. She did the same for me. It was not out of consideration that we did this, but a realization that if we didn't, we would hurt each other. The way our parents had.

IT'S NOT THAT Lyla and Vin fought incessantly or loudly or even rancorously. They calmly vexed one another, striking with great accuracy and then retreating to their separate corners, separate worlds even, leaving Ofelia and me to ours. Sometimes our worlds overlapped. Most of the time they didn't.

Lyla and Vin took us to Disneyland when we were seven, though we looked older because of our size. By the time Lyla finished dressing us in babyish sailor suit outfits, we looked like outlandishly oversized dolls, as much a part of the scenery as the Disney characters parading along Main Street or posing in front of the magic castle.

We wore vertical-striped blue-and-white pedal pushers that I suppose Lyla meant to have a slimming effect, but our calves strained at the short hem like bulldogs at the leash. Luckily for Lyla, the fashion dictated three-quarter-length sleeves, so our sailor blouses, each embroidered with a large blue anchor, covered our upper arms, and left only our sturdy forearms exposed. It was the sailor hats that Lyla had screwed onto our heads with bobby pins that made us feel conspicuous. She had tilted mine to the left and Ofelia's to the right for a quick way to tell us apart. Otherwise we looked so much alike, Lyla sometimes had to take my chin in her hand and angle it this way and that to view my profile—my double chin was plumper than Ofelia's.

"For heaven's sake, Lyla," said Vin, "those hats."

"Vin," was all Lyla said, was all she had to say, her voice throaty like Barbara Stanwyck's in *Crime of Passion*.

So we walked down Main Street dressed as short, pudgy sailors between our two movie-star-attractive parents. Lyla wore Audrey Hepburn sunglasses and high-heeled sandals, and Vin wore Troy Donahue sideburns.

Ofelia asked, "Mama, why do people look at us?"

"Because, honey . . ."

"We're all so doggone beautiful," Vin cut in.

Lyla shushed him as if he'd said something cruel and she adjusted our hats just so.

It was only after the Alice in Wonderland ride and our reaction to Tweedledee and Tweedledum that we were allowed to ditch the hats. The sight of that paunchy pair in their silly hats made us scream, and Lyla gave in when Vin took us to the hat shop. Ofelia chose Mickey Mouse ears and I, in keeping with my second banana status, went for the Donald Duck hat that quacked when its bill was squeezed. It was lost on me that Donald Duck wore a sailor hat.

Now our heads at least blended in with the throngs of other kids in the park, and we raced for the Dumbo ride. With Ofelia in front and me behind, we filled the cavity of the elephant.

As we circled above the crowd, Ofelia operated the lever that raised or lowered our elephant, and each time we passed our parents she brought Dumbo to his base altitude as we tried to wave to them where they sat on a bench below. Lyla, mysterious and unreachable behind her dark glasses, faced one direction and Vin slouched nearby, squinting upward, but not at us. When the wind gusted my Donald Duck hat from my head and into the crowd, neither of them saw to rescue it.

WORD THAT KIMBALL Park High School had two girl wrestlers got around fast, and at our first match the bleachers groaned under the weight of the curious. Newspaper photographers blinded us with their bulbs as we stretched on the sidelines, and Morocco Smith, the town's hippest DJ, was doing live feeds to the local radio station. Our team had only a small lead when I stepped to the mat, and a hail of cheers and hoots set my ears pounding. I felt a trickle of sweat between my breasts, knew it was darkening the wrestling outfit that was so reminiscent of the leotards that had once put us on display in dance classes. The suit's elasticity made me feel resilient and robust, and I bounced on the balls of my feet as I waited for my opponent—and waited some more, until I realized he had refused to come. The referee held my hand up for the victory—but I felt as if I'd been spurned at a dance.

So it was Ofelia's turn, and the boos for my opponent's forfeit turned to wild whoops as her opponent bounded onto the mat like Sylvester Stallone. I understood then that the crowd not only wanted to see the fat girls wrestle, they wanted to see us lose.

The ref blew his whistle, and Ofelia and Sylvester circled

each other. In the din of the gym, I shouted to Ofelia to let Sly make the first move. Of course she couldn't hear me, but she did it anyway—waited for Sly to lunge at her for a single-leg takedown. She eluded his grab and took advantage of his momentary imbalance with a duck under, seizing him in a body lock and throwing him to the ground. A singular gasp from the crowd swooshed through the hot gym, ruffled Ofelia's bangs as she sat astride the futile writhings of the boy pinned beneath her.

Ofelia's win made every boy in the league want to put a headlock on us. We were objects of conquest now. So there were no more forfeits, at least not for the next five matches. By that time Ofelia was undefeated and I'd only lost once—to a pervert who blew obscenities in my ear and pinched my nipple on his way to a half nelson. I was disqualified when my heel involuntarily found his testicles.

Parents of the boy wrestlers petitioned the league to banish us from competition, claiming we corrupted the sport. When their petition was denied, the forfeits began again. Though our muscles clenched and our glands swelled with adrenaline, we had no release.

MOROCCO SMITH CALLED one day and asked to meet with us. At a deli near the radio station, he bought us club sandwiches and fries, and while we chewed, he talked in his smooth DJ voice about our stunning ability, how we were natural audience-pleasers, how we were being cheated, deprived of fans and a venue for our talent. Lyla, who had come as chaperone, beamed *I-told-you-so*'s at us, her motherly instincts about our star potential confirmed by this scrawny man who called us "young ladies" as if we were debutantes, though we could have bounced him like a toddler on our knees.

"You deserve better," he told us.

"Absolutely," Lyla said, and we silently agreed.

"I got a plan," he announced, and in the end we went along, not because Morocco promised us a fortune, or Lyla predicted a spread in *People* magazine, but because we had so much unspent power that we were willing to use it against each other.

The Battle of the Big Girls was booked at the community college, and tickets were sold at TicketMaster outlets. Morocco was already pitching a ten-city tour to promoters. Lyla was shopping for a new outfit, and Ofelia and I were preparing to beat the crap out of each other for a trophy, a title, a little bit of fame.

We hit the weight room twice a day. I spied on Ofelia as she did squats and hammer curls. When I caught her counting my reps on the lat pull-down and bench press, she pretended to be humming.

Though we still looked alike, we didn't recognize each other. Or ourselves.

By the time the Battle of the Big Girls was upon us, we had stopped speaking to each other. We ate lunch at separate tables, took separate routes home from school, ignored one another as we settled into our twin beds at night and tried to be the first to turn out the beside lamp and leave the other in the dark.

The day before the match I did a light workout—squats and curls and some agility exercises. Then I went to scout out Ofelia, who was going a few rounds with Martin. He was no match for her, could no way give her the fight I could. It was a mistake for her to train with him. I knew her moves, her strategies. I knew that I could beat her. I wasn't the only one who knew this.

When I left the gym, I saw Freddy leaning against a pillar near the handball court as if he had been waiting for something. Or someone. My heart had been racing all afternoon in anticipation of the next day, but it quickened even more as I walked past Freddy, intent on snubbing him, playing hard-to-get, maybe. I wasn't sure. But when he called my name, I stopped so suddenly my sneakers made skid marks on the cement.

"Hey, Norma," he said. I turned around and he took a step toward me. Though my palms began to sweat and I regretted not spraying on a little fragrance after my workout, I stood my ground. We'd never really spoken before, and I'd never noticed the details of his face—the slight hook in his nose, the way his eyebrows took too long to taper at his temples. One of his front teeth bent outward a bit, which made his mouth almost sexy, except when he spoke and the wonky tooth seemed to leap out with each syllable.

"My money's on you, Norma."

It hadn't occurred to me before, but of course, there would be bets, people taking sides, laying odds.

"Make me a rich man, champ." Freddy punched me lightly on the shoulder. It was gentle, playful. Then he held out a hand for a high five, and I pressed my palm gingerly to his.

"For sure, Freddy," I said and walked away a little giddy, partly from his touch, partly from guilt. I knew I should have been angry at his motives, but what mattered at that moment was that Freddy believed in me.

WE ENTERED THE gym from opposite entrances as a band played a gladiator march. Television cameras panned us as we strutted the sidelines, and the crowd stomped and waved. Some high school boys came dressed as us, in long black wigs, their wrestling unitards stuffed with foam breasts. The perky girls from the cheer squad pranced and wiggled in tiny skirts and arced backward in flips or were hoisted in the hands of muscly boy cheerleaders. Our skinny cousins munched popcorn in the front row, and our grandmother Lupita worked a rosary. Beside them sat Lyla, who held two bouquets of roses in her lap ready to present to us as if we were contestants in a beauty pageant. "Remember, you're both winners," she had said to us in the car. Vin, who had patted us on the head as if we were large pets, sat with Vera, both of them wearing T-shirts silk-screened with our portraits overlaid with Lucha Libre masks.

It was a spectacle, I thought. But then as I met Ofelia on the mat, the referee between us, I realized we, Ofelia and me, were the spectacle. I looked at her, but I could see it was too late. What was inside of us needed release, and so when the whistle blew, we set upon each other with an aggression that went beyond competition. I took Ofelia down first, but she made a nifty escape and then returned the favor with a gut wrench. But when she followed with a near cradle, she grabbed my top leg, leaving me my bottom one to leverage a breakout. We were both on our feet again, facing each other, and the fire I saw in her eyes was the same that I felt burn in my sockets. We were fighting each other because boys could only deal with our strength by making us demolish each other. "Ofelia," I pleaded. But she lunged at me, and I ducked so that in her momentum she soared over me to smack the mat in a slapstick spread-eagle landing. In the laughter that erupted, amid the hoots and catcalls, I heard the screeching of my cousins as they urged us on. "Go Oafie! Go Abnorma!"

We hadn't heard those names since we knocked ourselves on our butts when we were kids. But I took my cue without further prompting. I launched my body over Ofelia's and did a belly flop on the mat. Then I raised my butt in the air and pushed off into a forward roll and made a clownish attempt to land in cheerleader splits—a move that spurred the real cheerleaders to toss their pom-poms in appreciation. The hilarity was in full swing as Ofelia, aware now that the competition had turned to farce, happily revived that joke of our youth—the cancan dance. The audience had just begun to clap in rhythm when Ofelia lost her balance. As she stumbled toward me I put my hand up to break her fall, but her own outstretched hand plowed right past mine, hitting my nose dead center. There was a snapping sensation between my eyes, and as blood poured from my face, down my chest, streaking my leg as it puddled on the mat, I remember feeling, through the penetrating pain, a great sense of relief.

IN THE AFTERMATH, there was no fame or fortune to be had as a result of our big girl bodies (for us or the Freddys of the world). We declined Morocco's proposal to tour as a comedy team, to make Oafie and Abnorma household names. Our bodies would remain ours, and so would our names.

A few days later we gathered at Vin's pool with our cousins. We were still minor celebrities, willing to recount the details of our short-lived glory.

"So what was it like wrestling boys?" our cousins in their slinky bikinis asked.

"Anticlimactic," Ofelia said, getting up to climb the ladder to the diving board.

She was right, that in the end, that physical contact with boys—their sweaty bodies against ours, their grip on our flesh, ours on theirs, our eventual pin of their shoulders to the mat—it was nothing compared to what we had known all along about our strength.

I stretched my body across the deck chair, settled some sunglasses gingerly on my swollen nose, and watched Oafie cannonball from the high dive.

Bonita

❖

THE FIRST TIME it happened, Bonita was sixteen. Her parents took her to Children's Hospital, which, even in her hysteria, Bonita protested. "I'm not a child," she wailed. But to herself, she whispered, *am I?*

During her two weeks of confinement, she pretended she was at boarding school, like the rich girls in novels. Except there were no math or English classes, only the group meetings and craft classes and the game room with puzzles and Ping-Pong, checkers, dominoes, and incomplete decks of cards.

There were other girls her age and a few boys, dangerous-looking, with long, greasy hair and lidded eyes. But everyone was more or less the same—tranquilly bewildered. It was knowing that they were all alike in this way that lent a sense of camaraderie to their small crowd. Not unlike the camaraderie she almost felt the night of her slumber party, the night of too much laughter.

Her mother had insisted that she invite her cousins. The skinny ones, Rosalie and Julia, and the fat ones, Ofelia and Norma. And, of course, her sister, Rica. That meant that with the limit of ten girls her mother had imposed for the slumber party, Bonita could only invite four girls from school. But of those four girls, three were unavailable—a cold, said one, and she sneezed into the phone to prove it; grounded, said another; homework, said the third. In a way, even Rowena who *could* come didn't count since she was a neighbor and a grade younger than Bonita. So now there would be no one in her class with whom she could giggle on Monday at lunchtime about all the fun party stuff and make everyone else feel left out.

THE SLUMBER PARTIERS lay in a circle on their sleeping bags in the family room. They were on their stomachs, leaning on their elbows talking about Sean Connery and what it would be like to be a Bond girl, and that led to the topic of bikinis and breasts and sand. Big-breasted Ofelia and Norma complained about having to dig holes in the sand at the beach to accommodate their D-cups. Rosalie and Julia, unembarrassed by their freakishly flat chests, lifted their torsos and brandished airplane arms, shouting, "Look, Ma, no bra!" Then they slammed their chests onto their sleeping bags.

Rica's breasts were round and firm, and she had adopted a bouncing walk so that even the slim distance from bed to bureau produced a vigorous action. But Bonita believed her breasts to be the perfect size and she had proof: *Seventeen* magazine. According to an article in the recent issue, the French declared the perfect size breast to be one that fit inside a champagne glass. Bonita confided to the others that she had actually done this very thing, sneaking two glasses from her mother's hutch, locking herself in the bathroom, removing her blouse and her bra, slipping a champagne glass over each breast—kind of like fitting the glass slipper on Cinderella.

Bonita was not at all prepared for the laughter that ensued. Of course, they had laughed at her before. But the laughter had accumulated. And now it stayed with her, infected her like a flu, filled her chest, stopped up her ears. Later, it exited her at inappropriate moments through her carefully lipsticked mouth—in church, in class, and then one night at the dinner table when the laughter, triggered by her mother's request to please pass the chicken breasts, became uncontainable. At first, her mother thought she was merely being rude, then unforgivably defiant, then utterly selfish for attention. Almost no one counted on Bonita being crazy.

But after two weeks at Children's, she was back to her old self, or nearly so. The only problem was that she had lost track of what was funny and what was not.

THE SECOND TIME it happened, Bonita was twenty and married to Nestor. They had met at the community college where Bonita had learned data processing and Nestor had been in the medical technology program. Bonita had never faced a shortage of boyfriends. She was pretty and she knew how to flirt. It came naturally, something that was passed through the womb like corpuscles. The trouble was not attracting boys and men. The trouble had always come in keeping them around, when conversation petered out after the third date. Bonita didn't mind covering the same ground, and when that failed, she didn't mind the silences. But for some reason the boys did. Except Nestor. He seemed content to have her just the way she was, just the way her mother had trained her—willing to please.

She liked their apartment, didn't mind all that much that the Kmart sign loomed just two streets over or that their yard was tiny and bone-dry or that the sun burned mercilessly through the living room window, appearing to set the puce carpet afire.

She kept a tidy household, matched her tablecloth to her curtains, had Nestor install a lazy Susan in the cupboard on which she could arrange and spin the condiments, and stacked the coasters evenly at the four corners of the coffee table. She went to the beckoning Kmart and bought a plastic ficus to set next to the TV and brushed its leaves twice a week with a dust cloth soaked in Pledge.

On weekends, Nestor made omelets and Bonita made toast. They ate while the radio played and tapped their feet under the table to the beat. On weekdays they ate cold cereal for breakfast and left for work at the same time, parting at the curb, Nestor in his Trans Am to the phlebotomy lab at the community hospital and she in her Datsun to the county licensing department. She typed up forms as customers gave answers to the questions she asked: name, address, phone number.

One day though, her supervisor called her into his office. "What is the meaning of this?" he asked, holding up a stack of forms in triplicate, each with her own name, address, and phone number.

Bonita could only answer honestly, "I don't know."

They moved her to the back office, away from the customers, where she did not have to type. Instead she sorted things by color, paper-clipped them, and packed them into boxes.

At home she had begun to burn the rice, the fault of the electric rice cooker, she claimed. Soon Nestor took over that job and so she made Jell-O. Nestor took over other things—the shopping, the vacuuming and all things electrical, the dusting of the ficus.

One day she was sent home from work early. It was the day Nestor came home and found her watering the ficus.

"What are you doing?" he asked. There was fear in his face,

which made Bonita tremble with her own fear and a glimmer of some awful force inside her.

"The plant," Nestor said, his hands gesturing accusingly at it, at her, his voice rising with each word, "is not real!"

This time she went to Paradise. A month, at least, the doctor said. A respite, her mother called it, a word she learned from the doctor, but even Bonita knew her mother pronounced it wrong, with a long *i*, so it sounded rude and hateful.

And now she was back again.

She was at the breakfast table at Paradise Hills Sanatorium, not exactly wondering what she was doing there. She knew that. She wasn't stupid. And yet, she did sort of wonder. A pancake and two slices of bacon sat on the plate in front of her, scrambled eggs in a bowl on the side. Across from her sat Wanda, the sullen teenager who had attached herself to Bonita during her first stay—those initial days when, thick with lithium, she was marshaled everywhere by the nursing staff until she could grasp the routine on her own. Wanda followed her like a puppy. Bonita had been afraid of Wanda until she understood that this plain, fleshy girl with the unbecoming bowl-cut hairdo admired her, thought her pretty. And that's what Wanda called her ever since Bonita explained the meaning of her name, a Spanish word common and recognizable to everyone except Wanda.

"Why did you come back, Pretty?"

"It was a mistake," Bonita said. She dumped the eggs onto her plate and used her fork to rake the soft yellow clumps to frame her pancake with curly tresses, vaguely aware of the contrast to her own stiff and ropy black hair, once as lush as the mane of any of Charlie's Angels.

"We all make mistakes," Wanda shouted triumphantly. It was something they'd heard repeatedly in their group work, and

Wanda had glommed onto it, pocketed it like a lucky penny, tossing it out at the slightest cue.

Wanda grinned at Bonita across the pancake, and Bonita aimed a grin back, though hers sat on the threshold of a sneer. Really, it was difficult to contain her impatience with a girl so pathetic. Bonita picked up the syrup dispenser and dripped the raspberry maple over her pancake, two fat drops for the eyes, a small puddle for the nose and a loopy smile that slanted off the edge of the pancake and onto the industrial-strength tablecloth. She arranged the two slices of bacon under the pancake face like legs. Only the torso that housed ribs and heart and stomach was missing.

Bonita assessed her handiwork, then picked up her plastic cutlery and sawed the pancake in half between the eyes and through the loopy smile. She shredded the halves into bite-size pieces and ate slowly and methodically in front of Wanda. Poor Wanda. Tormented, unwanted Wanda would probably stay forever in the Paradise Hills Sanatorium. Even though Bonita was back in Paradise, hadn't her conditional release just a day ago proven the temporary nature of her stay? As her mother used to say during Bonita's adolescence, "It was just a phase."

Suddenly Bonita hiccupped, a piece of pancake having slipped down her throat partially chewed. Bonita was startled by this sharp protest of her digestive system. Even as she took the glass of water that Wanda pushed toward her, Bonita let herself be lurched by the hiccups without embarrassment, so fixed was she on this automatic response out of her control.

When the hiccups subsided, Bonita sat a moment, dazed, having lost her train of thought. As she brought her chin to rest in her hands, her elbow caught the rim of her plate and sent her plastic utensils flying. Bonita retrieved the fork that landed in Wanda's hair, but the knife had sailed over her head and was out of reach.

"Wanda, get the knife," Bonita said.

"You get the knife," Wanda said back playfully.

Bonita was startled by Wanda's words, and as tears gummed her vision, her memory was jarred. "Get a life," she said, not to anyone in particular, though Wanda gave a shrieky laugh and bent to pick up the sticky utensil after all.

It's what she thought she was getting when she married Nestor. A life. Away from the peach-colored stucco house that smelled of her mother's perfume and her father's fish soup, that vibrated with her mother's voice and the hush of her father's stockinged feet. Smug that she was marrying ahead of Rica and happy to leave the fussed-over, fussy Mario, she left the family home for the duplex on Morningside Drive a few miles away, a sense of accomplishment flushing her cheeks.

BONITA ARRIVED EARLY for group but not early enough. Iris was already there, seated in the middle of the semicircle, the seat that Bonita craved, the center. The heart.

It had been her seat during her first stay at Paradise, but hard-faced, raspy-throated Iris did not offer it up.

"I'm back," Bonita said, as if she'd only been gone to the toilet.

"Sorry," said Iris.

Bonita stood a moment, wondering what exactly Iris meant, but too afraid to ask. She took a seat at one end of the semi-circle, disconcerted because there was no way to tell which end was first and which was last.

The room was called the salon, a word that Bonita had always associated with beauty as in beauty salon, and that gave her a certain comfort. Even after the commotion of the night before in her parents' living room, her mother's bulging eyes, the grip of her father's fingers around her own, the ride back to Paradise, she still woke up that morning to apply her makeup. She brushed on mascara, skimmed her eyelids with liquid eyeliner, swirled blue powder under her brows in the same way she imagined that crazy artist Van Gogh painted his *Starry Night*. It was one of her cousins who made this observation back when they were adolescents. Her cousins were skinny and wore glasses and read books. They taunted her with multi-syllable words, filling their conversations with references to the Pythagorean theorem, Darwinism, Nietzsche's Superman, all of which Bonita ignored except to offer her own preference for Lois Lane, which always produced gales of laughter from her cousins. She dismissed them. They weren't pretty. They had no choice but to read books.

Wanda came in, followed by the others in the group. Wanda sat at the opposite end of the semicircle from Bonita and copied Bonita's posture—feet crossed at ankles, hands folded in lap. Then she put on a face that alarmed Bonita. Everything was inflated, like a balloon with too much air that distorted the picture painted on it. Nostrils, eyes, brows, even Wanda's ears seemed distended. Bonita stared open-mouthed, and when she saw Wanda's jaw drop as well, she realized that Wanda was mimicking her face as well as her body. She changed her expression and watched it appear on Wanda's face, changed it again and again and saw it repeated across the semicircle from her. Before she could decide whether she liked this game or not, Dr. Boyle ambled in, taking the chair that faced them. Bonita went rigid with concentration. In her one-on-ones with

Dr. Boyle, Bonita tried hard to give the right answers but was frustrated by the doctor's passive expression, which Bonita, inspired by Wanda's example, now copied.

Despite her dislike of speaking in groups, she much preferred the talk circle to the one-on-ones. Besides, sometimes Dirk, the orderly, came in to hand Dr. Boyle a message. Bonita liked Dirk and she liked the name of his job. Dirk, the orderly. Orderly Dirk. Of course, the other women liked him, too, but she believed it was her he noticed most. She was sure his smile was directed at her.

It had been a long time since Bonita had had a boyfriend, yet she was still prodded by a flirtatious reflex. It was an organic part of her like sweat and saliva, and now the taste of lithium on her tongue. Every muscle conspired to lure and fascinate— the dark magnets of her eyes, the baited hook of her smile, her laugh that once rang at just the right pitch, mirthful and spirited, yet not quite crossing into hilarity. These days she often practiced her laugh under her blankets in bed, trying to recover that perfect resonance, though nearly always hysterical gasps issued from her throat instead.

If Dirk came in today, she would be sure to give him her best smile. She already felt the upward tug at the corners of her mouth. As Dr. Boyle began the session, Bonita looked up and was appalled at the maniacal grin Wanda was wearing, so she dissolved her own smile into slack cheeks.

Bonita usually had trouble listening to most of what any of them in the group had to say. She was too intent on waiting for her turn to talk. No matter how much she'd rehearsed new things beforehand, she always told the same story—how when she was a little girl, she was cherished, how her mother curled her hair and tied it with ribbons, dressed her in crinolines and velveteen. She was aware that as she spoke, she was smiling shyly, her lashes lowered, and she was reminded of how her mother taught her when she turned twelve to lengthen them with mascara and to line her lips with color to enhance their shape. And her mother spared no expense with trips to the dermatologist to keep Bonita's teenage skin free of the pimples that plagued her cousins who read books and had no boyfriends.

She wanted them to like her—the girls in the group, all of them together like a club or sorority—but she felt isolated sitting at the end of the semicircle. Bonita's mother had always explained away her daughter's lack of friends. "Other girls are jealous of you," Millie would tell Bonita with the same conviction with which she believed only Catholics went to heaven.

Bonita had never told her group what her mother said to her when she lost her marbles, went off the deep end, went *loca*. But she told them now. While Bonita was strapped to the gurney, her hands tied to her sides to keep her from striking at anyone within reach, as a paramedic inserted a needle into her arm, Millie leaned into her ear and whispered, "How could you do this? Haven't I given you everything?"

"Well, did she?" Iris asked.

Bonita named the things her mother had given her. A slender figure, thick black hair that could accept a vast range of styles, orthodontia, sculpted bras, a bulging walk-in closet, a private bathroom equipped with a lighted makeup mirror, charm school.

"That's not everything," Wanda declared.

"Monthly professional manicures," Bonita added.

They had trimmed her nails off practically to the nub when she first came to Paradise Hills, and they pruned them regularly. She felt them aching to grow.

SHE WAS TEN, and her mother was allowing her to have her fingernails painted for the first time, doing them herself, squeezing Bonita's fingers flat on the coffee table as she brushed the tips a quiet pink—not orange as Bonita had wanted. Rica, who was twelve, was blowing expertly on her freshly done nails. Mario was slumped on the floor in the last throes of a tantrum at being denied fingernail polish.

"You're a boy," Rica told him derisively.

"Anyway, you're not ten yet," Bonita said.

Rica snorted, "That's not the reason."

Even though Rica didn't say it, Bonita heard the word *stupid* in her sister's voice, so she called her sister stupid out loud.

Immediately, her mother pinched her arm and scolded, "How would you like it if someone called you stupid?"

Bonita blinked and didn't answer, because she thought someone *had* called her stupid. She would show them. She would be an airline stewardess when she grew up. She would wear a uniform and a little pillbox hat, a name tag and a pair of wings above her heart. She would greet passengers as they boarded, fill requests for coffee, tea, or the soft drink of their choice.

"I'm going to be a stewardess for TWA," she said.

"I'm going to be one for Pan Am," Rica said, and before Bonita could call her a copycat, their mother broke in sharply, "Never mind that."

She laughed, not one to let them down gently. "There's a height requirement, you know. You'll never get that tall. Besides, what if the plane crashes? Where will you be then?"

"Dead," said Mario, who had recovered from his fit and was coloring his own nails with crayons.

"Better to be secretaries," their mother said.

That night when Rica and Bonita were in their twin beds, they overheard their mother say to their father, "Can you imagine? Airline stewardesses? How many brown airline stewardesses have you seen?"

"Let them have their dreams," their father sighed.

The girls were quiet in their beds for a while. Then Rica said, "I don't want to be a stupid airline stewardess."

"Yeah," Bonita said. "That's stupid." She didn't add that she no longer wanted to be an airline stewardess because she didn't want to crash and die.

"Let's be secretaries," Rica said, as if it were her own idea and not their mother's.

They sat up in bed, placed their pillows on their laps and began tapping their quiet pink fingers.

"Let's see who can type the fastest," Rica said, and they each banged their fingernails furiously into their pillows.

IN THE AFTERNOON, Bonita sat in the art therapy class opposite Wanda. It was the only time Wanda was not wholly attentive to her, so rapt was she in creating collages or sculptures from pipe cleaners, Popsicle sticks, and endless bits of paper and fabric, while Bonita sat stymied at all the ways one could orient a sliver of ribbon on a square of construction paper. Sometimes there was weaving to do, potholders on a loom, and all the while Bonita would resist the urge to unravel each neatly interlaced strand with one sudden and well-placed yank. Today it was just tempura paints and sheets of butcher paper. Wanda was already deep into churning colors on the page, and Bonita watched a picture emerge—arms positioning heads back on shoulders, hands attaching sandaled feet to ankles, fingers pull-

ing words out of mouths—screaming with life and pain and
possibility. Bonita tried to copy the strokes and swirls of Wanda's hand, tried to duplicate the shapes and hues, was desperate
to see objects emerge that she could recognize, but her page
was muddy with no definable images. She was so much better
at decorating herself than a piece of paper.

Wanda looked up from her painting, her face flushed, her
eyes almost wildly lucid, and though Bonita had seen her this
way before, she drew back alarmed. She hastily folded her
muddy painting in half, patting it down, smearing the two sides
together.

"Open it now," Wanda told her.

Unused to obeying Wanda, Bonita nevertheless peeled open
the paper.

"It's different now," Wanda said, clearly satisfied.

Bonita fluttered her false eyelashes in embarrassment and anger as she stared at the marbled concoction that made no sense.

"Put it on the shelf to dry," Wanda said.

Just then Dirk the Orderly came to escort her to the visitors'
lounge.

"*You* put it on the shelf," she told Wanda as she left the room,
and though the words came out mean just the way she meant
them, Wanda took no offense.

In the hallway, Bonita fell in step beside Dirk. He was not
the man of her dreams. He was lanky and his arms too hairy,
his Adam's apple was a disagreeable knot, his hairline was in
retreat. And still, she imagined putting her arm through his,
her bare skin against the starch of his orderly jacket. If only he
wouldn't walk so fast. She had to take too many steps to stay
up with him, and the echo of their heels in the corridor made
a weird clatter.

Her father was sitting in a chair by the window, a cup of coffee balanced on his knee. She knew he would come alone. The visitors' lounge had a view of the courtyard paved with flagstones and planted with fading hibiscus. A birdbath, empty except for a few dried leaves, looked forlorn in the late afternoon sun.

She sat down next to her father, and he patted her paint-dappled hand.

"Have you had time to think about what you did?" he asked.

"Yes," Bonita answered, because she had had time, though she couldn't exactly say she had used it for that purpose. If anything, she might have thought about *why* she'd done what she did, though she wasn't even sure of that.

"We want you home," her father said.

Bonita nodded, waiting for more.

"You've hurt your mother, you know."

"I didn't mean to squeeze so hard."

"But you're sorry, right? You'll be a good girl now?"

She drummed her short fingernails against the arm of the chair. "Yes," she said.

Her father leaned over and kissed her, and she breathed in garlic and peppermint. They sat together while he drank his coffee in gentle, soothing slurps. When he was done, he tugged her hand. "Let's go to your mother."

It turned out her mother was there, waiting in the lobby, and Bonita needed only to collect the few things that had been hastily packed for her in a small tote the night she was brought back to Paradise. On her way to retrieve her tote, Bonita stopped in the art room. It was empty. There were just the paintings on the shelf, dry now, ready to hang. She rolled the painting up and slipped a rubber band around to hold it in place. She peeked through it like a telescope, pretended she could see far into the distance.

Her father reached to carry her bag for her, but she held on to it, the rolled-up poster, too. "I can do it myself," she told him. She let him hold her hand as they walked to the lobby where her mother was not sitting in one of the vinyl chairs, but standing, her arms crossed over her chest. "Stand on your own two feet. That's what you need to do," her mother had told Bonita the first time she visited her in the hospital, and she had remained standing the whole time as if to demonstrate how it was done.

Her mother accepted Bonita's kiss. But it was the painting that pleased her most. "It has strength," she said.

Bonita nodded solemnly.

Then her mother led Bonita out the door and her father followed. Her mother held Bonita's arm as if afraid she might bolt, and Bonita herself wondered if she would. But there was only the parking lot ahead of them, and it seemed to Bonita obligatory to slide herself into the backseat of her parents' station wagon. As the car rolled away from Paradise, Bonita wondered when Wanda would discover that her painting had gone missing.

At home Bonita stood in the living room as her parents bustled around her, her father steering her suitcase past her mother who was moving ashtrays and other breakables away from the edges of tables and shelves. Bonita looked around for changes, but everything was the same. She wasn't sure what she expected to be different—just something.

She sat down by accident, plopping on the couch to avoid her mother's flurry, her mother who was reflected in all the polished surfaces in the room—the mirror, the TV, the glass of the picture frames holding family photos. Finally, her mother stopped scurrying around and sat down across from her. Her father brought in glasses of ginger ale. He raised his glass. "Welcome home, honey." They each took long sips.

Her mother set her glass down. "When you unpack, put everything in the clothes hamper."

"They washed everything for me at Paradise," Bonita told her.

"It doesn't matter."

Bonita watched her mother light a cigarette, suck in deeply, and then blow.

"You're well now. Everything's okay again."

Her father turned the TV on, and they all watched an afternoon talk show where the people sat on living room furniture just like they were doing in their own living room. For an hour they watched the people in the TV living room talk, and every so often the audience laughed and applauded. Amid the TV talk and laughter, Bonita heard her mother's voice over and over in her head: *You're well now. Everything's okay again.*

It was this matter-of-factness so incontestably residing in her mother that Bonita wanted to wring out of her and take for herself.

That's how she tried to explain it later, after her father had peeled her hands again from her mother's throat and called the ambulance while she sat back on the couch, holding her ginger ale gone flat.

Señor Wonderful

———————— ❖ ————————

TONY CAMACHO SAW her as she paused at the entrance of the Three Palms Lounge, the blink of the sign lavishing pink neon applause upon her—the woman of his demographic profile, the kind of woman his mother would embrace if he were ever to take a woman to meet his family. As she strode to the bar, she eyed the three imitation palm trees that sent oversized hands curving toward the ceiling instead of leafy fronds. The hands were labeled with fortune-telling lines indicating longevity, health, romance, and other routes to happiness. She did not seem particularly amused at the joke. She was a tough one. Tony gripped a bottle of Scotch, his muscles flexing as he measured two fingers for a customer.

She took a seat and ordered a glass of wine. Her unstudied assurance and grace discombobulated him, and his talent for charming with small talk deserted him. Tony poured, noticing that the woman's eyes never went to his biceps or the flexors in his forearm. When he placed the glass in front of her, she barely glanced at his smile, normally so infectious. So he turned to his other customers, deftly stirring, shaking, and garnishing drinks, working the crowd, working his magic, but she was unfazed. So he punted, drop-kicking the bar sponge to land squarely in the plastic tub at the end of the counter. Frankie, one of the regulars, led the others in the wave, and a waitress fluttered a pom-pom of napkins.

The woman offered a polite, "Rah, rah."

"Sports fan?" he asked, his knack for small talk weakly surfacing.

"Mmmm," was her answer as she sipped her wine. Encouraged, Tony launched into a monologue the way a desperate man jumps off a cliff. He related his exploits on the football, soccer, and baseball fields, and then despite or because of her cool passivity, he was moved to demonstrate his agility by vaulting over the bar, just grazing a tray of margaritas. To add purpose to this performance, he went to the assistance of the bouncer who was expelling an unpleasant drunk, and on his return, he sparred with Frankie and showed off his left hook, his right uppercut, his dancing Pumas.

"All in the footwork," Tony explained to the woman.

She brushed her wine glass against her lip. "Huh?"

It was contagious, the blankness of her voice, her face. Tony's mind went empty. He was never this confused with one of the endless blonds on whom he exercised his Latin appeal and undeniable good looks. Now he remembered why he seldom dated homegirls. They scared him. So when she looked up from her glass of Riesling, her dark eyes clear and compelling, he capitulated. "I quit," he muttered.

"Good move," she said, and Tony prepared to retire to the sidelines.

"Boxing is so violent." She shuddered, and Tony's eyes rested gratefully on her blue-cashmered shoulders as he realized that, far from being dismissed, he was being offered the chance to declare his own abhorrence of blood sport.

"Vicious," he agreed.

She nodded and his mouth ran on. He told of how he took

up the guitar, learned to strum a few chords, and at parties sent guests falling off the furniture with his rendition of "Bésame Mucho." This set her laughing and Tony could finally relax.

"Music soothes the savage beast," Tony said, grinning with one of his favorite lines.

"Breast," she said.

"Excuse me?" Tony said.

"The line is actually, 'Music has charms to soothe a savage breast.'"

"Breast it is," Tony grinned.

"Beast makes more sense," Frankie said into his beer, but Tony ignored him.

He turned the wattage up on his smile, which he knew to be dazzling, and leaned across the bar, his chin cupped in his hand. "So tell me about yourself."

She nudged him back across the bar, and then, in one of those unexpected moments that made Tony believe in God, she began to, of all things, tell him about herself. Her name was Anita. She had worked her way through college and now taught bilingual special needs children. Tony was floored, and his manufactured adoring pose was now sincere appreciation, except that his mouth disappointed him when it blurted, "Marry me."

"Like hell," Anita retorted, and they both laughed. "Got any more lines?" she asked.

"Just one more," Tony said sheepishly, as Gabor, the lounge owner, took the microphone at the stage and roared his Hungarian accent into the microphone. "And now to kick off our karaoke, here he is, Tony Ca–MACHO, Señor Wonderful."

Tony answered Anita's amused look with a helpless shrug, then bounded on stage and took the microphone from Gabor, who continued to wave his arm in fanfare even after the music swelled and Tony was deep in the throes of "I've Gotta Be Me."

He never had to sing more than a few lines before he got the audience involved. He was Mitch Miller and Harry Connick, Jr., choral leader and crooner rolled into one. Karaoke nights with Señor Wonderful were the most lucrative nights for Gabor and the Three Palms Lounge, and they only enhanced Tony's already enormous appeal with the ladies. But that night when he ended his number and bowed out of the spotlight, he squinted into the darkness to see if Anita was still perched on her barstool.

She was.

They had a picnic on the beach the next day, saw a movie the day after, and from then on saw each other nearly every day. They played miniature golf, browsed a flea market, threw Frisbees at the park for Tony's collies, Abandonada and Bandita. Three weeks of exhilarating romance, and then came the fourth.

"I'd like you to meet my parents," Anita said.

Tony shifted his feet, obeyed a reflex to comb his hair.

"Come to a party next Saturday."

For a moment Tony lit up. He was at his best at a party.

"It's my parents' anniversary," Anita said.

Tony felt the enthusiasm leave him the way an errant billiard ball drops off the end of the table. His own parents had divorced when he was young, he himself had never had a relationship that lasted more than a football preseason, and the only females firmly established in his life were Bandita and Abandonada. Celebrating any number of years of marriage was a startling proposition.

"Terrific," he told Anita. "Right after work."

The following Saturday, Tony called in sick, not to work, but to the party. "I have an impossible headache," he told Anita over the phone, wondering at his use of the word *impossible*. He normally didn't speak like that. "Horrible," he said. "Sucky."

"Well, that's a shame," said Anita, and Tony cowered at his end of the line.

He clutched his fake, sucky headache and hurried off to work.

"Still in love?" Frankie said, sliding into a space at the bar.

Tony could feel the tension in his forehead pull his grin unnaturally wide.

"Going for a record, eh, man?" Frankie held out his hand and Tony slapped him five, but the sting across his palm felt like a reprimand.

"When you find true love, you go for it," advised Frankie who prided himself on being happily married for the fourth time. "It's all about commitment," he said.

"Yeah, commitment," Tony agreed, setting a beer and tequila in front of Frankie. *Commitment to what?* he thought. He looked to the giant palms and their fortune-telling lines for a clue. It disconcerted him that they were all right hands, as if raised in solemn oath.

When he started the karaoke session, Tony felt that burst of song in him waiting to get out. But as he clutched the microphone he knew he was crooning a weak defense. *I've Gotta Be Me.* It soothed neither breast nor beast. With the last long, drawn-out *me-e-e-e-e-e*, he hopped off the stage, pantomimed to Gabor that he was sick, and staggered out the door.

He drove to Anita's parents' house. She had pointed it out to him on several occasions as if it were some shrine. He would pay his respects, offer his congratulations, make small talk with the family, charm Anita's mother, win over her father. But as he turned the corner and saw the driveway and lawn crammed with cars and a bouquet of Mylar balloons tied to the mailbox, heard "Suavecito" wafting above the banter and laughter, his truck seemed to roll on past of its own accord. A half block away he braked so abruptly he launched his face into the steering wheel. He rubbed his chin. He rubbed his nose. He ran his hand through his hair, a strand tumbling over one eye. He peeked at himself in the rearview mirror. There he was—Señor Wonderful.

Determined to live up to his name, he parked his truck, got out, and smoothed his open-necked, short-sleeved, stretchy-fabric shirt and tugged at his jeans. He sauntered boldly but, at the corner, found himself veering into the alley where the backyards were screened by rampant bamboo and unpruned hibiscus. His saunter became a prowl. He crept from shrub to shrub until he came upon the party. He wished he'd worn his green rather than his white polo. He knelt behind a muscular hibiscus and peered through a rift in its branches.

Immediately, he pulled back, because there was Anita staring straight at him. No, not at him. She sat at a picnic table across from her parents, perfectly framed between them. Shrieking children, contemptuous teenagers, and flirty adults mingled and scattered about the yard. Tony recognized the scene. It was like his own family's. Final proof that he and Anita had much in common. Then why was he hiding in the bushes? Suddenly, one of the contemptuous teens pointed at Tony's hibiscus. "Who's that?"

Reflexively, Tony popped out of his crouch, and the collective gasp his appearance elicited brought him, if not to his senses, at least to his feet. Anita's parents twisted in their seats, heads craned toward each other, blinking in curiosity. Anita stood above them, her torso growing up out of their tilted heads. She gaped at Tony. He gaped back. She made a gesture, some kind of question, and he flinched, stepped backward just as the teenager who had first spied him lunged in his direction. Despite his boxing lineage, in a fight or flight situation, Tony invariably chose the latter, disinclined to sacrifice his face for some small injury to his pride. He heard footsteps pound behind him, the tattletale teen, no doubt, and he felt the eyes of Anita's extended family on his back. When he heard Anita shout to his pursuer, "Let him go," he raced to outrun the words.

HE SAT ON his couch, nursing a beer while considering the sad wreck of his big toe. He had stubbed it severely on an exposed tree root, adrenalin keeping him from feeling the pain until he had pulled up to his apartment. He limped inside and swathed the toe in gauze. He stared at the sloppy white turban, could almost see the throb of the bruised nerve endings.

He accepted the commiserating whimpers of Bandita and Abandonada, who sat on either side of him, buffering him with their furry bulk, their steadfastness. He had rescued Abandonada from the roadside, a skittish, temperamental female of uncertain age, and from the beginning unquestionably in Tony's thrall. Bandita, so named because she had stolen his heart, was dignified in her dependence on him. He loved them both. If he had to name a favorite, it would've been—well, impossible, really.

He took the last swallow of his beer and, regretting not ever having trained his dogs to open the refrigerator, began to consider the effort in covering the distance himself when both Bandita and Abandonada raised themselves to full alert, ears rigid, mouths quivering. Then came the no-nonsense knock.

Tony looked at the door, at his toe, at his dogs who were making pleading noises.

"I know you're in there," Anita said. "What do you have to say for yourself? Señor Wonderful."

There was nothing to say. Not out loud. *I've gotta be me*, he mouthed.

There was a thud. Anita's open palm? The sole of her shoe? The door a proxy for his mouth, which still held the shape of the word *me*?

Another thud. Then the tap of heels, fading away.

It was time to get out of this town. At least for a while. He suddenly recognized a long-lurking itch to head north, Montana or Wyoming, Marlboro country with big sky and open land, where he would hunt and fish, climb the rocky face of a big mountain.

He got an early start, before the sun was up. He wanted to avoid the traffic and see the dawn of a new day, he said to Bandita and Abandonada, who were squeezed beside him in the cab of his truck. Though he didn't expect an answer from them, their silence discouraged him a little. He felt a pang in his chest. "That 7-Eleven breakfast burrito," he explained to his companions, who had yet to offer any corroborating dog noises. He turned on the radio and found an oldies station. As he accelerated along the nearly empty lanes of Interstate 15, the sun began to appear on the horizon, making it difficult to see the backlit highway sign. Tony reached for his sunglasses and read the words—Las Vegas 300 miles. Maybe he'd stop a few days, hit the blackjack tables, take in a show, maybe a karaoke bar. He began to hum to the radio.

Lovely Evelina

---·······❖·······---

AT THE BAY Vista Manor, the Saturday evening social was in its last quarter hour. As Evelina narrowed her eyes down the length of her clarinet, her thoughts were not on the senior citizens shifting their feet on the dance floor in front of her. They were instead on her upcoming high school reunion, rearing its fanged and monstrous head, taunting her. Would she go? Would she dance?

Evelina rested her clarinet, allowing Penny, the merry-faced activities director, to eke out a solo on the piano that was as ancient as the Bay Vista Manor residents. As Evelina wiped her lips, she noticed that the perfumed and unctuous Mr. Vega was finally headed toward her mother. Why he danced with the other ladies first before Alma Munger, the best dancer at the retirement home, Evelina could not fathom. Why her mother always obliged Mr. Vega's belated invitation, she understood quite well. After dancing with barely ambulatory but chivalrous septuagenarians sorely lacking in rhythm, it was bliss to be in the arms of a man who could dance—an experience that Evelina knew far too rarely herself. Evelina would have settled for being in the arms of a man, period. Her transformation from a girlish-looking man to a woman with the hint of something mannish about her was as complete as it was going to be. And yet she had to believe that there was a partner out in the world for her. So she felt it personally, her mother's limited options and, despite herself, sometimes blew a wrong note in protest. She picked up her clarinet and joined Penny's foxtrot.

Since moving her mother into Bay Vista a year ago, she had been the woodwind section of the two-piece ensemble that provided the live music for the socials. These monthly engagements were in addition to her weekly visits to sit with her mother on the terrace offering not a view of the bay, but a strip mall, and beyond that the freeway. The bay did exist, green and spiritless on the other side of the freeway, its shores claimed by industrial and commercial interests, billboards, lofty car lot signs, and dusty palm trees serving as skyline for this little city of low, flat buildings. Evelina, at forty-three, well-traveled and remade, was surprised that she still lived here in Kimball Park, a pit stop between the bars of Tijuana and the beaches of San Diego, a place with no natural attractions of its own.

She watched her mother and Mr. Vega command the linoleum as most of the others retired to the orange plastic chairs lining the dance floor. Alma Munger, neé Rosas, was a tiny woman who, at age seventy-five, was still nimble in high heels. She was a perfect fit inside Mr. Vega's embrace, and his polished black hair was a perfect complement to her own bottled shade. Evelina tossed her own locks as she brought the number to a close.

Mr. Vega led Alma back to her chair. He never gave her the last dance, and neither did any of the other old men who shambled over to find partners more suitable to their puttering steps. So Alma sat, the flush of her cheeks showing through her powdered rouge, hands in her lap resting among the lilacs printed on her dress, her foot tap-tap-tapping as Evelina and Penny drew a tender waltz from their instruments.

When the music ended and the dancers clapped their slow, arthritic hands, Evelina packed up her clarinet and joined her mother. She settled her strong frame into an adjacent flimsy chair, hating its orangeness, since she believed that even the least association with the color gave her skin an unhealthy appearance. Interracial unions could produce tepid results. Her father's sandy looks and her mother's caramel cast had combined to produce Evelina's dun-colored skin, a color that was neither this nor that, a color of great uncertainty. Such thoughts always made her miss her father, his clueless, grinning face full of love for his only child. He had not lived long enough to see the woman she had become. She could only hope that he would have approved.

Some of the dancers were drifting toward the parlor for cake and cocoa and checkers before bedtime. As they passed, the women patted Evelina's knee. "Lovely music, dear." And when they thought they were out of earshot, they clucked to one another, "Still not married." Some of the men also tried to pat Evelina's knee, which at first she thought was a paternal gesture until Mr. Della had actually managed to move his hand under her skirt. So now she made sure to intercept each hand and shake it firmly, sometimes alarming the old men with her grip. She wondered how much more alarmed they would be if they knew she had once been Alma's son. She supposed it was a good thing that the imperfections of her womanhood escaped their diminished eyesight.

"Good night, Sam," Evelina's mother called out as Mr. Vega passed by.

Mr. Vega, ever polite, smiled his large silky smile, though his small brown eyes shied from eye contact. "Good night, Alma. Until next week, Evelina."

"Evelina won't be here next week," Alma said. "She'll be at her high school reunion, dancing herself."

"Yes," Evelina said. Maybe, she thought. Maybe she would go. Maybe she would dance.

"Well, knock 'em dead, eh?" Mr. Vega, still smiling, nodded at them and left to join the others for cocoa.

Evelina took her mother to her room where they sat by the window to look out on the neon-lit asphalt and the invisible bay beyond.

"Why does Mr. Vega sit out the last song? Why doesn't he dance it with you?"

"Silly man," her mother sighed, "thinks I have the hots for him."

Evelina hooted. "Shouldn't you set him straight?"

Now her mother hooted. "Oh, Evelina, I'm hardly capable of that." She lowered her voice, though there was no one else to hear. "The man is gay as Hercules." Alma had seen a show on TV about homosexuality in Ancient Greece and had since attributed the preference to the entire Pantheon.

"Oh," said Evelina, enlightened. "Of course," she said, looking in the direction of the unseen bay.

AS SHE DROVE home in her Camaro, she felt conspicuous amid the Saturday night parade of teenage couples in souped-up cars. At a traffic stop, she ignored the rev of the engine next to her. Sometimes she thought about trading in for a foreign-made subcompact. But she had always driven Chevrolets out of loyalty to her father who had made his living selling them. When the light turned green, the car next to her shot forward with a squeal, and she could see the boy check his rearview mirror as his girlfriend tossed her head in triumph.

Evelina eased forward, and when she shifted into second, she accidentally pulled the hem of her skirt back with the gearshift and thought of Mr. Della and the other old men at Bay Vista and their feebly probing hands against her thigh. She sighed at how squeamishly obscene a gesture could be in one set of circumstances and how thrillingly erotic in another. She had experienced both (though her share of the latter had been less than fair, for which she tried hard not to feel aggrieved), but the most unforgettable experience was one that had not even happened to her, and only peripherally to who she used to be—Chuck.

IN HIGH SCHOOL, Chuck belonged to the band, where the notes from his clarinet combined with the notes of the other instruments to form pretty much the extent of his social interaction. In the mornings before classes began, when the bell rang for lunch, and again at the end of the day, Chuck headed straight for the band room, avoiding the halls where the popular kids promenaded—the unpopular ones huddled in corners or skirted the halls like mice, and the toughs slouched against the lockers, hands jangling unknown metal objects in their pockets. Chuck acknowledged the social need band filled for him, and deep down he admitted another truth—he had a crush on the trumpet section. On Donny Wiley in particular.

One day after school, Chuck lingered in the band room. There was no practice that afternoon, and he was alone, sitting on the floor behind a file cabinet, browsing through sheets of music, when the door opened. Without needing to peek from behind the file cabinet, Chuck knew it was Donny. It wasn't just the telltale scent of marijuana in his hair or motorcycle grease on his pants. There was something electric about his presence that made Chuck's ears buzz.

He put his palms to the wall to steady himself when he heard a girl's voice, giggly, and piercingly pitched. It was Missy Montoya (Missing Montoya behind her back because she was forever missing notes on her flute). Chuck sat quietly and listened to Missy's muffled shrieks and mild murmurs of protestation to Donny's whispered overtures. Chuck's hands went clammy, and he could feel his pulse thrum in his neck as he leaned his head cautiously around the file cabinet. He didn't have to worry about being seen though. He could have stood up naked in plain view and still have gone unnoticed. Donny, his back to Chuck, had his face buried in Missy's neck, and Missy though facing Chuck, had her eyes closed. Chuck watched in astonishment as Donny's hands moved up and down Missy's miniskirted hips, circled round to her buttocks, and then came back to spread across her breasts. And at that moment Chuck wanted to be, despite her middling musical skills, Missy Montoya.

EVELINA HAD HAD dates over the years, but they were just that— dates that never evolved into relationships. A fastidiousness on their part. Or was it hers?

She expunged them from her memory, their tense jaws and their curious, tentative touch, or at least she reduced them to blips on the screen of her consciousness, as noteworthy as the chain of look-a-like shops she drove past now—a tedious suburban-scape. Most of the development that had occurred over the years in Kimball Park had been commercial, with strip malls strung neatly over the once scraggly lots. But a few condominiums had sprung up here and there like exclamation points across an otherwise dull page. Evelina's was in the old business district that no longer saw much business. Besides a bank, there was an ice cream parlor that had persisted since Evelina's grade school days, the church where she had made her First Communion, and a collection of cheerless storefronts.

Her building was at the corner of a once-busy intersection, but now that the strip malls drew the traffic away, she could look down from her second-story unit at the oddly quiet street, shaken from its lethargy one day each spring when local high school bands and drill teams marched the mile and a half from the old Woolworth's to the city park. In all her years in Kimball Park, the route for the Maytime Band Review had not changed, and though the parade had grown smaller in recent years, Evelina remained fond of the tradition. She, or rather Chuck, had marched in it in high school, though now the experience seemed far removed, as if it had happened to someone else—which, technically, it had.

When Evelina got home, she watered the philodendron that occupied a stool in the living room. Evelina kept no pets. She was away too often to be a responsible caregiver to a dog or cat. For a while she had kept a goldfish, a lovely spurt of orange in a clear glass bowl on her coffee table, and when it died, she got another, but that one died, too. So now it was just the philodendron.

Evelina aimed the remote at the television. She searched for an old movie, hoping for something with Deborah Kerr or Barbara Stanwyck, but settling for Jane Powell in a perky musical. There was something about those women back in the forties that made them seem both vulnerable and tough. Or maybe it was just the clothes, those padded shoulders.

She kicked off her lamentably large shoes and stretched out on the couch. She was comfortable here in her living room ornamented with souvenirs from her travels—carvings, wall hangings, pottery, not to mention the photographs of her atop pyramids, aboard cruise ships, astride an elephant. When she entered the travel industry she had been amazed to find how many women owned or managed travel agencies, how many wanted to escape or plan escapes for others. She booked solo trips for many of them, matching their destination to their objective—adventure, study, romance. Though the last she considered reckless. A romantic setting distorted the senses. She knew this from instinct as well as experience.

She had vacationed alone in Cancún one spring, and as the sun lowered itself into the ocean, she saw Reinhard emerge from the surf, backlit by the pink glow spreading across sky and water. He was a tall, straight-shouldered Bavarian, graying at the temples, a transplant to Los Angeles who quoted Rilke and Shakespeare for the five days they were together, sometimes in his cabana, sometimes in hers. He had impulsively invited her to move into his luxury high-rise that had a view of the Hollywood sign in the distance. "Anyone can be at home in L.A.," he told her as she swallowed her daily dose of hormones. A far cry from Kimball Park, she had to admit. But when she closed her eyes to kiss him, it was him she could imagine nowhere else but there on that beach in his swim trunks, his slightly drooping pecs tanned and glossy as if he were part of the scenery or a vacation package option, like a rental car.

Even after she had sunned herself on glittery beaches in Jamaica, hailed taxis on the boulevards of European capitals, trekked the highlands of Peru, fallen for a German, she always came back here to Kimball Park, as if she didn't really belong out in the world.

Her teeth brushed and flossed, her electrolyzed skin cleansed and moisturized, Evelina stood in front of the bathroom mirror and was reassured. The embryological derangement that had given her testicles and a penis and resulted in a confused boyhood, a silent, tormented adolescence, and an approximated manhood achieved by studying the swagger of sailors on leave had been corrected along with that inelegant name—Chuck, a name only a father who bestowed it could love.

"YOU'RE MY LUCKY charm, Chuck." Whenever he came home to report an especially good sale, Russ Munger would say this to his son. As if Chuck's very existence was cause enough for success.

Though he was convinced of his own bad luck, Chuck did not want to begrudge his father's insistence on treating him like a rabbit's foot. So he said, "Thanks, Dad."

"No, son. Thank *you*."

And he really meant it, Chuck knew. Chuck could not return this deep appreciation his father felt for him with complaint or rejection. Or blame.

A teenage boy whose father owned a car lot should have enjoyed some measure of celebrity in high school. But other than his accidental friendship with big Warren Pong, he was a loner. Still, he might have reaped some benefits from his father's car lot had it not been for those commercials.

The unabashed stars of gimmicky TV ads, Russ and Alma Munger were household names not just at his high school, but throughout the entire South Bay community.

"Get the best deal here, or I'll be a monkey's uncle," Russ would promise, pointing at the Munger Chevrolet sign that was adorned with bunting and balloons, and Alma would waltz around him with a live monkey in her arms.

"These prices are out of this world," Russ would exclaim, his hands holding a price placard, and Alma would detonate a toy rocket that blasted from the hood of an Impala.

"What do you think, son?" his father would ask the first time a commercial aired as they watched from the living room couch.

"I like it," said Chuck, who had long known the necessity of a lie.

THAT NIGHT WHEN Evelina went to bed, the silk sheets smooth across her shoulders, her head nestled into the pillow, she dreamed that she was floating, suspended in air, freed from gravity, and determined not to be afraid of the fall.

The next day after an afternoon at the office booking tours on land and sea, in temperate forests and tropical islands, Evelina stopped in at Rita's Used Books, nearly empty as usual except for a few browsers hoping to find something rare and wonderful in the sagging, overstuffed shelves reeking of ancient dust and stale cat pee. Rita herself sat smoking at a scuffed desk piled high with ragged books. She held the cigarette at arm's length behind her as she greeted Evelina with a hug. Still, the smoke crept into Evelina's nostrils and she tried to breathe shallowly, but soon gave up and resigned herself to Rita's toxins, which she endured for her friend's company and advice, unsolicited but always welcome.

Evelina settled herself on a corner of the desk while Rita

lowered her meaty frame back into the large chair that swiveled on rusty wheels.

"How's business today?"

"Booming," Rita said, the bass of her voice evidence that her lungs were powerful despite the years of nicotine. Her laugh resounded in the small store with its crowded bookshelves that did not align neatly but veered and switchbacked like a chain of dominoes. A skittish customer reshelved a book he had been leafing through and left. Rita, unconcerned, watched the screen door bounce close.

"How's business with you?" she asked Evelina.

"Cruising."

"Ha," laughed Rita, politely.

Evelina picked up a book from the stack in front of her and examined the cover, idly paged its contents. It was an illustrated guide to beetle larva, and she pretended interest in a labeled drawing of boll weevil anatomy.

"Well," Rita demanded.

Evelina closed the book with a sudden decisiveness. "I'm going."

"Did I tell you what happened when I went to my reunion?"

"No," Evelina lied. She wanted to hear it again. So Rita told her story of sudden romance, the thrill of a mutual attraction, the frisky, frolicky evening, and the euphoria of the early morning hours, and the best part of all, according to Rita, walking away at the end and coming back here to her own life.

"Love," Rita said, pointing her cigarette for emphasis, "is like a good book. You get caught up in it. But when you turn the last page, it's over. Back on the shelf." She stubbed out her cigarette. "That's love."

She began to light up again when she stopped and eyed Evelina. "Tell me that's not why you're going, honey."

"No," Evelina agreed. "That's not why I'm going."

"The past is the past."

"I know."

"Take it from me."

"I do."

Rita leaned over the cluttered desk and kissed Evelina's cheek. She smelled of tobacco, of lavender-scented shampoo, and, of course, old books.

A FEW DAYS before the reunion, Evelina sat with her mother in Bay Vista's small rose garden. Alma, whose old eyes were sensitive to sunlight, wore large sunglasses on her petite face. An aged Audrey Hepburn, thought Evelina. Or an insect, a needle-thin damselfly, its large oculae mounted on a slender head, seeing the world in mosaic.

Their mother-daughter talks mostly centered on everyday things—Evelina's next excursion, Alma's next medical appointment, the next Saturday night social at Bay Vista Manor. But with the advent of Evelina's high school reunion, their thoughts had turned to the past, each recalling her own singular story.

Alma had been on the dance committee, in the Future Homemakers club, had attended her prom in a strapless organdy number.

"Such exciting times, those high school days!" A smile settled in Alma's soft lacework of wrinkles.

Sometimes Evelina thought that her mother forgot that she had once been Chuck—Chuck who had missed out on committees, clubs, and dances. Not to mention friendships, adolescent high jinks, and teenage loves.

"Will you be seeing Warren at the reunion?"

"Yes," Evelina told her mother, "I'll see Warren."

"I suppose his skin has cleared up by now."

"Mother, that was twenty-five years ago."

The last ones left after all the teams of friends had been chosen, Chuck and Warren became friends by default. Warren was in the chess club and science club and, astoundingly enough, on that most celebrated of clubs at Truman High—the football team. He seldom saw action on the field though, other than stampeding through the goal posts prior to the game as the cheerleaders formed a pom-pom-waving, scissor-kicking gauntlet to honor the rush of cleats and testosterone. Warren always told Chuck how exhilarating that was, and Chuck smiled as if in agreement, thinking only of what it might be like to wear a tiny pleated skirt and matching ribbed pullover while turning cartwheels in the cool autumn air.

It was Alma who had urged Chuck to get involved in school activities. (How about student government, debate team, Key Club?) It was Alma who had told him, "These are the best years of your life."

ON A WARM evening in September, a Saturday when Evelina would otherwise have been playing her weekly gig at the Bay Vista social, she prepared for her first-ever high school reunion dance, brushing delectably named cosmetics onto her full lips, high cheek bones, long lashes—features that had been girlish on Chuck.

She slipped into a turquoise cocktail dress, its scooped bodice tasteful and hardly revealing, its skirt swishing just below the calves. Evelina had great legs, the happy result of the redistribution of muscle and fat as a result of the hormones. She put on her earrings, rhinestone teardrops, but decided against the matching necklace, preferring not to call attention to her less than delicate neck. She slipped her feet into her dyed-to-match turquoise pumps, regretting that her size elevens were too large for the silver, high-heeled sandals she had fallen in love with at the Nordstrom half-yearly.

The organizers of the reunion had eschewed holding it in Kimball Park, home of Truman High, preferring instead a San Diego hotel near the marina, so Evelina steered her Chevy onto the interstate and headed north. She had heard that most of her classmates had settled in the north part of the county after graduation, where the homes were bigger, the streets wide and smooth, the schools better, and the cafés furnished in wood rather than plastic. This exodus of her classmates made Evelina's own escape unnecessary. There was little danger of running into any of them at the bank or grocery store or hair salon. Except when she was out of town on business, she remained rooted to the old stomping grounds and their ghosts. Now, though, as she headed away toward this celebration of her high school years, she felt as if she might finally leave behind her past at Truman High.

Evelina swung the Camaro into a parking space facing the bay with the full moon splashed on its surface. Even with the windows closed, she could smell the salt air, and it made her feel exhilarated and new. From her purse she extracted the name tag that had come with the reunion registration packet. It was a picture of the high school Chuck, and it had come with his name next to it. But Evelina had taken one of her personalized address labels, snipped her first name from it with her nail scissors, and pasted it over the word *Chuck*, so that it now read in mismatched type *Evelina R. Munger*. She had kept her middle initial, which stood for Rosas, her mother's maiden name. She liked to think it also stood for Russ, to whom she owed her metamorphosis.

WHEN CHUCK RECEIVED the news of his father's heart attack, he was in Belize shepherding a tour group from rainforest to coastal resort. He had always meant to bring his parents on one of these jaunts, which were very civilized and replete with amenities, but Russ and Alma declined. They apologized for being homebodies, for preferring the quiet of Kimball Park to the clamor of foreign sounds.

It was against the chatter and shriek of monkeys and macaws that he heard his mother's voice crack.

By the time Chuck arrived home, his father, Russ Munger, life-long resident of Kimball Park, owner of Munger Chevrolet, known for his gimmicky commercials featuring live monkeys and toy rocket ships, had succumbed quietly in his sleep.

"He tried to hang on for you," his mother said.

Chuck felt he had failed his father. No more lucky-charm Chuck.

After the burial, there was the settling of Russ Munger's affairs. "Munger Chevrolet is yours," his mother told him. Perhaps his mother read the fear in his eyes as Chuck tried to imagine himself waltzing with a monkey. "It's yours to keep. Or to sell."

She took his hand. "He always understood, Chuck. It's never been in you. Being a salesman."

And so it was the sale of the car lot that financed the series of operations that had made her Evelina.

EVELINA PUSHED ASIDE her hair and pinned the name tag to the left side of her bodice. Then she let her hair fall over her shoulders where it brushed the tops of her breasts like a curtain. She looked at her watch. She had promised herself she would wait until 8:15 to go into the ballroom, when enough people had arrived so that her entrance would blend into the mingling crowd. She sat in the car, turquoise feet planted on the floorboard, and waited, her hands in her lap. At the Bay Vista Manor the Saturday evening social would be winding down now, her mother flushed from her dance with the fastidious Mr. Vega. Soon Penny would be clearing the social hall of the orange chairs.

Evelina looked toward the hotel, its entrance lit by iron-filigreed lanterns. She hoped that Warren and his wife were already there in the ballroom. She hoped she would be able to find them. Evelina checked her watch and followed the slow, steady sweep of the second hand to mark the full quarter hour. Then she picked up her handbag and caught a last glance of herself in the mirror before she closed the door of her Chevy.

She made her way through the lobby, an all-purpose smile on her face for anyone she happened to make eye contact with. She walked casually but resolutely, intent on finding Warren because she counted on her association with him to trigger the memory of Chuck among her classmates. At the entrance to the ballroom she quickly scanned the tables, many of which were already occupied. Even at places where nobody sat, a coat, a purse, or a half-full glass of wine staked someone's claim to a chair. Evelina headed for the bar, her eyes peeled for a familiar face as she weaved her way around knots of people, avoiding the sudden thrust of an elbow here, the jab of some knuckles there as her old classmates swapped handshakes, hugs, and backslaps. Squeals of recognition mixed with the music pumping over the speakers—seventies hits with their themes of peace, love, and alienation—and Evelina caught herself stepping to the beat.

She hadn't seen Warren in years, but it didn't occur to her until that moment that she might not recognize him. She had assumed that because she had changed so radically in her appearance, changes in others would be mild in comparison. But as she looked around her, she realized how little she had counted on the altering effects of receding or absent hairlines, bellies that floated toward chests or dropped precipitously over belts, cheeks and chins that had acquired storage space. The once-lean track team could now pass as linebackers, while the former football players had expanded so impressively at the middle that they themselves with their elliptical shapes resembled giant footballs. Even though the women had, in general, fared better than the men against time and gravity, at least a few cheerleaders and homecoming princesses had achieved near-spherical contours. Few people, though, had changed beyond recognition, and this gave her hope that she would detect Warren in the rapidly filling room. At least Warren had a picture of Evelina that she had sent him at his request. Surely he would recognize her.

At the bar, Evelina ordered a glass of wine, and the white-jacketed bartender winked at her as he poured the Chablis with a magician's flourish. Evelina pretended not to notice, simply turned sideways and sipped her wine, nursing it the way she had learned, having long ago switched from drinking calorie-packed lager beer. She surveyed the room for Warren once again.

"You look lost." It was a man's voice, not solicitous and full of concern, but salacious and full of motive, and vexingly familiar. Evelina turned to find Dwayne Burton at her shoulder, staring at her chest. In P.E. class in high school, when the boys did their warm-ups on the exercise quad, Dwayne would grunt and make lip-smacking noises as the girls, a few yards away, went through their own routine of torso-twisting windmills and jumping jacks that made their breasts leap. Later, on the handball court, Chuck, despite his hopelessness at sports, always imagined himself slamming a ball into Dwayne's Adam's apple.

"You know what's great about this reunion?" Dwayne said. "I have to look at name tags to find out who I'm talking to. And guess what?" Dwayne raised his hands helplessly. "I'm forced to look at a woman's breasts."

Evelina's hair covered her name tag, and when Dwayne reached to brush it away, Evelina slapped his hand.

"Grow up, Dwayne," she said.

"No fair," he bleated. "You know my name."

Evelina crossed her arms over her chest, which only served to lift her meek cleavage and, simultaneously, Dwayne's point of focus.

Dwayne slapped his thigh and gleamed triumphantly. "I remember you." He launched a finger at her, pointing it like a missile at a target, and Evelina prepared to rip it from his hand should it touch down on any part of her. She looked him in the eye, hardly daring to breathe as she waited for Dwayne to be the first to identify her.

Dwayne was nodding his head and grinning, and Evelina braced herself so tensely that with Dwayne's next sentence she nearly toppled off her heels.

"Drama class. You were the dead girl in 'Our Town.'" Dwayne clasped his hands theatrically. "Am I right?" he asked, clearly convinced that he was.

Evelina laughed outright, which Dwayne took to be corroboration. "So what's your name?" he asked flirtatiously, trying to peek again at her name tag, still obscured by her hair.

"Evelina," she said, determined not to lie, not even to Dwayne. "Munger," she added tentatively.

"Munger," repeated Dwayne. "Sounds familiar." His eyes rolled upward in concentration, which Evelina quickly suspended. "So what are you up to these days, Dwayne?" she asked.

"Retail sales by day," he said.

"And by night?" Evelina asked obligingly.

"Stand-up comedian."

Evelina was politely impressed. "There's no business like show business," she said agreeably.

Dwayne evidently regarded Evelina's response as encouragement. "So what's your business?" he said. "What do you do?"

Then he touched her on the arm casually, and Evelina felt his fingertips press against her breast, and she curbed her instinct to send her elbow into his gut. She was certain that she would soon have another opportunity to double Dwayne over in shock. For now, she shook him off like an insect.

The tables were nearly filled now, and there was a buzz at the bandstand with instruments being tuned and microphones being adjusted, which made Evelina anxious to be seated. Resigned to not finding Warren, she began heading for a table in the corner where she could feel safely inconspicuous, a tactic she recommended to lone women travelers when eating in restaurants. As she kept her eyes on the unoccupied table, she realized she was rushing, but she could not help herself, and the sense that she was fleeing to the empty corner made her clench her teeth. When a hand grasped her shoulder, Evelina whirled around, this time willing to perforate Dwayne's neck with her White Seashell–glazed nails. Instead she threw her arms around the bald, sallow-skinned man before her with delighted relief. Warren was a large man, not so much fat as thick and squishy, and the embrace was hugely comfortable.

"Well," Warren said, looking at her admiringly, "the years have been kind to you."

Evelina stared at him a moment and then laughed. Warren blushed. "Well, have they?"

She nodded. It would be selfish to ask for more, she told herself.

"C'mon," he said. "I've scored a table right where the action is."

As she followed Warren, she saw how his suit jacket strained at the armpits, how his trousers hugged him at the waist and flooded at his ankles. *Lovely man*, thought Evelina, as she guiltily remembered that Chuck had secretly coined the term *blobular* to describe his locker partner of three years.

Their shared sense of being outsiders had cemented the friendship, and Warren and Chuck had stayed in touch with each other over the years. Except for a long interval during which Chuck was gradually becoming Evelina and too focused on the social complications of her second (this time female) puberty, their contact was regular, with annual Christmas greetings and one of those humorous Hallmark cards each June that joked about high school graduation. When Evelina resumed communication with Warren, she was both excited and anxious about what Warren's response would be, certain that there was no Hallmark card that offered congratulations on a sex change. Warren sent a postcard instead that read, *Dear Evelina, Marry me. Ha Ha. Just kidding. But now that you've found your true self, I hope you find your true love. Your friend, Warren.*

That's when Evelina realized how lonely Warren was and regretted all the times she had secretly and not so secretly ridiculed his pudgy body and bad skin. She was overjoyed when, a few years ago, he wrote of his marriage to Mary Etta, the woman in the office cafeteria who always spooned extra mashed potatoes on his plate next to his hot roast beef sandwich.

Warren stopped at a table already packed with people and held out one of the two empty chairs for her. After he settled his bulk in the other, he leaned back to allow a small woman peeking around him to extend a bony hand.

"I'm Mary Etta," she said in a voice as thin as her body. "I'm glad you could come." Evelina took Mary Etta's hand, and the unexpected strength in it pleased her.

While Evelina and Mary Etta elaborated on their greetings, Warren looked on, a grin pushing his cheeks against the lower rim of his glasses. Finally, unable to contain himself any longer, he bubbled, "Isn't this great?"

"It's absolutely great," said Mary Etta, patting her husband's arm in a way that Evelina found touching.

"Look at us. After all these years," Warren said, lifting his hands and then dropping them in his lap to indicate the profundity of his words.

"And there's a memento of the occasion," Mary Etta said. "We saved one for you, Evelina. I'm sharing with Warren."

Evelina set in front of her the program printed with the Truman High mascot, a snarling tiger in the blue and gold school colors. While Warren and Mary Etta leaned their heads together over their copy of the program, Evelina took the opportunity to look around her. She recognized many of the others at the table as facsimiles of former chess club members. They were reminiscing among themselves about some unforgettable match, of which they each had conflicting recollections. None had yet noticed Evelina's presence. So Evelina's eyes roamed the room, and it was only when she saw Donny Wiley that she admitted to herself that she had been looking for him all along.

Despite a paunch so minor as to be forgivable and a decline in the wave and density of his hair, it was unmistakably Donny—suave, confident, and still the center of attention. Evelina watched Donny, following his every gesture, trying to read his lips, looking for a sign, though of what, she wasn't sure. Suddenly, Warren exclaimed, "Missy Montoya!"

Evelina turned around, expecting to see Missy but encountering only the disconcerting sight of Warren's gaping mouth. "Where?" she asked.

"Here," answered Warren, pointing to a page in the souvenir program.

Missy's senior picture, along with those of a dozen or so other classmates, bordered the page that read *In Memorium*. Evelina was stunned. "How?" she said.

"Breast cancer," whispered Mary Etta as she leaned across Warren. "I heard it from the other table." Then she proceeded to relate the cause of death for the others memorialized in the reunion program. Drug overdose, car accident, asthma attack, AIDS, cancers of every category.

Evelina was saddened by all the deaths, but it was the news about Missy that she found the most distressing. She had never forgotten that image of Missy and Donny in the band room.

It had lodged in Chuck's fantasies and haunted Evelina's con-
science. When she recalled that memory, it was sometimes with
envy of Missy, sometimes with scorn for her, but always with a
vivid awareness of Donny Wiley's embrace.

"Death, now that's a big change," someone said. It was one
of the chess players across the table, whom Evelina recognized
from the permanent furrow between his eyes as Bob the Brow.

"Glad I haven't changed that much," said another chess
player.

"That's a matter of opinion," said still another.

"Say, Warren," Bob said. "Whatever happened to that sissy-
face you shared a locker with? Old Woodchuck."

"Yeah," came a chorus from the chess club as they all turned
to Warren in anticipation, as if waiting for the punchline of a
very funny joke. Evelina turned to Warren, too, who looked
genuinely surprised at the question as if the situation was self-
explanatory, the answer sitting right next to him. Evelina knew
that it was unfair to expect Warren to enlighten the others on
the turn Chuck's life had taken. She was about to speak out
when Mary Etta broke in quietly, "Warren, tell what happened
to Chuck."

Warren nodded at Mary Etta and then turned to Evelina
who saw twenty-five years' worth of Hallmark cards in her
friend's uncomplicated face. "This is Evelina Munger," he said
to the chess club. "The real Chuck."

There was a moment of silence before Bob let loose with a
loud guffaw. "Good one, Warren." Relieved, the others joined
in the laughter.

"No, wait," said Warren, and the urgency in his voice si-
lenced the chess club, which turned a collective stare first on
Warren and then on Evelina.

"I was Chuck," she said, returning the chess club's stare with an unswerving look of her own. "I'm Evelina now."

"Wow," said Bob, setting off a string of exclamations from his cohorts.

"Incredible."

"Great job."

Evelina listened with equanimity, patiently waiting as the story of Evelina Munger spread to the four corners of the ballroom. She could almost see the news travel as heads turned this way and that in waves that were not fluid and gently rippling as she had hoped, but rumbling and percussive.

Warren grasped her elbow, quietly urging her to stand. Amid the gaping rubberneckers, he led her to the dance floor, and she concentrated on Warren's lapel as they slow danced. Warren was a surprisingly able dancer. Nothing fancy. A workman's by-the-book box-step. But without fault, which allowed her to demonstrate her own ability to travel to the rise and fall of the music. She smiled.

She was grateful to Warren for breaking the ice. She took her eyes from his lapel to tell him so, only to find Bob at his shoulder. He tapped Warren. "Mind if I cut in?"

Warren, gallant, stepped aside. Bob grinned like an idiot as he swayed back and forth with Evelina. Within minutes, one of the other chess players cut in, and Bob with a gracious sweep of his arm passed Evelina along. Her new partner was named Art. She remembered in biology class he had pocketed the organs of a dissected frog. He smirked at her now as one sweaty palm took her hand and the other gripped turquoise chiffon at the small of her back. Evelina could feel the smile on her face deaden. After a few turns around the floor, Art handed her over to someone whose name tag read *Bobo*, a nickname she recalled, though she didn't bother to glance up at the face, and by the time she was on her fifth partner, she had even stopped looking at name tags. It didn't matter who she was dancing with anymore.

And so it went, until she had danced, fast or slow, in holds that were probingly firm or squeamishly light, with the entire membership of the chess club and then some. When Evelina saw that the line to dance with her was beginning to rival that of a ride at Disneyland, she tried not to panic. She was a grown woman, she reminded herself.

Suddenly the line began to buckle and tilt, and finally gave way to a surge of bodies that carried Donny Wiley at the forefront. Evelina's dance partner was abruptly yanked out of slow-dance position by a tangle of arms, and for a moment she thought she was being rescued by the mob. But then Donny was thrust in front of her. Chants of *Don-ny, Don-ny*, interspersed with *Munger Chevrolet*, filled the room and vied with the beat of the music.

There was nowhere to turn. Evelina covered her face with her hands. She felt Donny's arms around her, felt his body next to hers, and then she was being maneuvered in a way that she knew was not a dance step because he had bent down and now was scooping her up and lugging her (as she was strong-boned and not light) across the room. She felt her high heels raking wineglasses off tables, snagging on coats and shawls, and overturning chairs. She even connected once or twice with someone's stomach and though the anguished *oomph* surely belonged to Dwayne Burton, it gave her little comfort. Her hands still covered her eyes, but she could sense that the crowd had receded as if the spectacle of her as plunder in Donny's arms was merely a segue to the next number by the band.

It was quiet where they were, a small space—she could tell by the acoustics of Donny's exhalations as he deposited her rather harshly on a vinyl bench. "Whew, you're not exactly a feather."

They were the first words Donny Wiley had ever spoken to her in her or Chuck's life. She took her hands from her eyes but could not look at him yet, because though she was shaking with hurt, the only thing she could think to say back to him was, "I'm average," and she had wanted it to be more substantial than that, about who she was and why she mattered.

She looked around. They were in a small foyer with the bench on which she sat, an armless chair in which Donny sprawled with his eyes fixed on the ceiling, exhausted from the effort of carrying her, and a large fig plant that shielded them from passersby. She looked down and contemplated her turquoise shoes while fingering her teardrop earrings. The band was taking a break, and she could hear classmates mingling in the lobby. She was inexpressibly tired and wanted to close her eyes.

"So you used to be Chuck, huh?"

Evelina nodded. Donny was still breathing from his exertion. He smelled of spearmint. Even Chuck, during all those years in the high school band, had never come this close to Donny. And now he had manhandled her, picked her up, trundled under the solid weight of her, and heaved her onto this bench. She understood it now. He had saved her. The realization made her heart flutter with gratitude.

"Used to be," Evelina confirmed, looking at him now from the corner of her eye. Up close and in the foyer lighting, the effect of the years on him was more apparent, and Evelina felt a sadness overcome her.

Donny gave a low whistle and she saw a small spit bubble

on his pursed lips. He straightened himself in his chair and reached in his pocket. He offered her a Life Saver, and they sat in silence for a while sucking the candy. Evelina couldn't help thinking of the smacking sounds she had heard in the music room that day when Donny's hands had roamed Missy's body.

"So what is it you do? I mean, you have some sort of job?"

"I lead travel tours."

"Seen the world, huh?"

"A lot of it. And you?"

"Naw, I'm a bartender. I meet a lot of people, from all over, though. Hear lots of stories. Crazy stories."

Evelina imagined him regaling his customers with the story of how he carried a woman in turquoise chiffon off the dance floor, a woman who in high school had been a sorry-assed nerd of a boy.

"So you married or anything?"

"No," Evelina said. "Single." She saw him fidget, clearly wishing he hadn't opened this door. Still, Evelina asked, "You?"

"Me, no. But I'm seeing someone."

"Is she here?"

"No, couldn't make it."

"Shame," Evelina said, not quite sympathetically.

Donny had run out of things to say. He scratched his head, left a piece of his hair sticking out to the side. "That Chuck, he was a good clarinet player."

Evelina found herself blushing. "Do you think so?"

Donny nodded.

Evelina smiled. "Do you still play the trumpet?"

"Not much." He shrugged. "Well, never, really."

"Shame," Evelina said again, this time more genuinely.

More silence ensued. Finally, he asked, "What about you? Do you play an instrument?"

"Me?" Evelina said, confused for a moment. "Well, the clarinet, actually."

"Oh . . . right," Donny said. It was his turn to blush. "That's good."

The music from the ballroom started up again. It was the class song, "We've Only Just Begun," and the minglers in the lobby could be heard rushing back in to join the nostalgia. Evelina sang the words softly. She had always loved the Carpenters, still mourned Karen, the anorexic drummer/singer. She thought about playing the tune at the next Saturday evening social at the Bay Vista Manor.

Donny rose, coughed in his sleeve. He held out his hand and Evelina, charmed, put her own large one in his. But then all he did was shake it. "Well . . . good to meet you."

He turned to leave. "Donny," Evelina blurted. "Would you like to dance?"

Donny took a few steps backward, scratching his head. "Uh, no thanks. I don't think so." He took more backward steps. "I'm not much of a dancer," he explained. And then he was in full retreat.

Evelina watched him, noticed a spot of thinning hair at the back of his head. "You know," she called after him, "it's not as if I want to marry you or anything."

He turned around. He was sheepish and uncomfortable as he came slowly forward, but Evelina would show no mercy. She looked him in the eye until he submitted and held out his arms. She stepped into them and placed her hands onto his shoulders, which were broad but not as muscular as she had imagined. As they moved to the music, she closed her eyes and smiled. Donny was a lousy dancer. She took over the lead, and though Karen Carpenter kept crooning the word "together," Evelina waited for that line about "life ahead." Yes, so much of it, she thought, as she spun herself away from Donny Wiley.

Cursos de Verano

———————— ❖ ————————

THE SEVENTH WEEK of my summer in Mexico began on a bus with Margie Bier. I'd hardly known her during the summer session, had had no classes with her, and talked with her, or rather listened to her talk, only a few times. Now we were seatmates on an eight-hour ride to Mexico City.

Margie won the coin toss for the window, and as we headed out of Guadalajara, she had the better view of this lively and lovely city that had been our home for the last six weeks. As we drove past churches, plazas, and parks, then through the cracked and muddy streets of the poorer districts and eventually out onto the highway, I tried to gather images of that summer that would, when pieced together, provide a pictorial narrative with the sweeping symbolism of a Diego Rivera mural.

But I was distracted by Margie's birdlike profile against the window. Every so often she would wrinkle her nose and her glasses would lift slightly to meet her eyebrows. She had small ears that peeked through stringy strands of squirrel-brown hair that trailed to her shoulders to harmonize with her orange muumuu covered in coconut trees. Earlier as we waited to board the bus, people in the terminal had stared at this tall, gaunt gringa, incongruous in the Hawaiian dress so conspicuous among the crowd of Mexican travelers. I wondered if Margie was aware of the looks she drew, the double takes, the outright stares, the quickly averted eyes.

She turned from the window and fixed her small eyes on me. "La vida diaria es lo que cuenta," she said with a sigh of contentedness, a quietness that came, I thought, either from some higher plane of wisdom or a docile acceptance of one's lot in life. At any rate, I was at a loss for a reply.

A wrinkle made a *V* in Margie's forehead to match her widow's peaked scalp. "¿Prefieres que hablemos en inglés?"

"Claro que no," I replied emphatically with a phrase I had mastered that summer. The truth was, I did prefer to speak in English and thought it rotten of her to ask. She could have just begun her insipid conversation in English: Everyday life is what counts.

Then I could have replied *What the hell does that mean?* to make it clear it was elucidation I required, not translation.

But the opportunity was lost.

"Bien," said Margie, and commenced anew one of her monologues, this one about the Mexican countryside outside the bus windows. After a while Margie switched gears, initiating the kind of simple tense small talk that happens in Intermediate Spanish drills, but I forgot to be insulted. I was just relieved at the chance for the give-and-take of conversation.

I learned that Margie was married, which I had already presumed from the ring on her hand, though hearing her confirm it in her agile Spanish did nothing to diminish my wonder. It was hard to imagine a mate for her in looks or sensibility. I learned also that she was a Spanish teacher. Of course she was. Still, it was a blow to me, since I had wanted to imagine her as a clerk in the motor vehicle department snapping photos of driving applicants, or an underwriter making doodles in the margins of actuarial tables.

In exchange for this information about herself and in the spirit of one-upsmanship, I told Margie about my grandmother. That she had been born and grew up here in Mexico. *Aquí*, I repeated, gesturing broadly to encompass the bus and the entire landscape through its windows, as if laying claim to the country, the culture, even the language that eluded me. I fumbled mentally through my sparse vocabulary to tell her about my quest for my roots, but Margie beat me to it.

"Entonces, ¿buscas tus raíces?" She was polite and sufficiently impressed, but her facility with the language of my ancestors compared with my own feeble efforts made my quest seem silly. I shrugged. I yawned.

"¿Tienes sueño?" Margie asked me, making a pillow of her hands against her cheek.

I ignored her condescending sign language. I just smiled, made it sheepish, apologetic.

"Pues, duérmete."

It was what I wanted her to say, to tell me to sleep—only she said it as if she were giving me permission, a teacher to her student.

I folded my arms against my chest and closed my eyes. It was going to be a long trip.

THAT SUMMER OF America's Bicentennial, I had enrolled in *cursos de verano* in Guadalajara. I had come to my grandmother's Mexico, determined to do the Alex Haley thing despite the twitterings of my mother and aunts back home.

"You're American," they said. "We're American."

Yet they would speak Spanish among themselves and, of course, to my grandmother Lupita, who after all her years north of the border could produce scarcely a dozen words of English. Somehow, their professed motives for raising monolingual children—completely assimilated citizens—had them in the end feeling rather embarrassed at the linguistic deficit of their offspring. So I packed my bags, my feelings of inadequacy, and my dreams of recovering a lost identity. I left Kimball Park and headed southward to the tiny spare room off the patio of my Tía Olga and Tío Chano's apartment on Avenida Tolsa.

I spent those first six weeks attending classes until noon like the other students, and like most of them (Margie Bier being among the few exceptions), I treated my studies casually, subscribing out of laziness to the theory that the real lessons lay outside of the walls of the classroom. With Leo and Sylvia, he an amateur lepidopterist and she a bookmobile librarian from Pennsylvania Amish country, I visited churches—gothic, baroque, and neoclassical. While my companions delighted in spires and apses and naves, I was distracted by the locals in prayer. I wanted to take the hand of every small, gray-haired old woman with a black mantilla who looked like my grandmother and say, *Look at me! I'm here to find you. To find me.*

With Jackie, a math teacher from Santa Barbara, and Doris, a heavyset grandmother from the Scottsdale suburbs, I roamed the labyrinth of the Mercado Libertad. There were colorful woven blankets, painted pottery, and stone *molcajetes*—things that had always lived in Lupita's house. I wanted to touch them and say, *I know you.*

With Yolanda, the Chicana from Oxnard, I met men, unctuous smilers who pointed to their bare wrist and suavely inquired,

"¿Tiene la hora?" even while a watch showed from under the cuff of their pointing hand.

Most often these requests were directed at Yolanda, who returned the smile with a regretful shrug. "No tengo reloj," she said pointing at her own slender, naked wrist, a response that invariably provoked an invitation to dinner. Sometimes she accepted, and these allegedly watchless men never failed to have a friend for me. More often, though, Yolanda declined these invitations—disappointing given the beauty of some of these men. Yolanda preferred instead to be the one to ask for the time of day or, as the occasion demanded, for directions. If we lost our bearings, Yolanda would wait until an *hombre muy guapo* came along and ask him to *por favor, haga un mapa*, and she extended a fragile sheet of her baby-blue, scented stationary.

This is how she met Rafael Villa, who offered to draw a map to his heart. Rafael jokingly claimed lineage with Pancho and offered his mustache as proof. "Tócalo," he would tell Yolanda, and she obliged, grazing it tentatively with her pinkie, with a laugh that I could tolerate and a coo that I could not. Rafael and Yolanda were giddy in love and began to spend every opportunity together before the end of the summer session put an end to their romance. Sometimes I was invited along and paired with Rafael's stunning cousin Jorge, who barely spoke to me, which Yolanda explained away as shyness or the obstacle of language.

Still, I felt left out and inadequate and spent many hours wandering the city alone. As I stopped in the Hospicio to lie on the benches beneath the dome of the chapel and stare up at the Orozco murals, rode the city bus north to the end of the route at La Barranca de Oblatos to stare down the gorge at the river, or browsed bookstores to leaf through paperbacks and run my thumb over the indecipherable pages, I occasionally thought of a young Lupita newly arrived in the States without English, without friends. It made my solitude seem romantic, like a black-and-white art house film. Except that nobody else perceived me as the heroine.

Wherever I went, I was immediately recognized as an *extranjera* by the locals and mistaken for a local by the English-speaking tourists. The latter would invariably approach me, map in hand, and stammer out their guidebook phrases, and I would answer in my flawless English, impressing them at first until they realized it was no feat at all. And then before they walked away, I would blurt, "Do you have the time?" But no invitations to dinner ever sprang from these inquiries. Something was definitely lost in translation.

Yet for most of that summer in the land of my grandmother's birth, I persisted in the belief that at the end of my stay, the cumulative experience of my days struggling to grasp idioms and conjugate irregular verbs, riding the city buses festooned with the image of la Virgen de Guadalupe, eating my Tía Olga's real Mexican cooking and smelling my Tío Chano's real Mexican farts, taking weekend excursions to cultural points of interest (the mummies in Guanajuato, the butterfly fishing nets on Lake Pátzcuaro, Elizabeth Taylor's villa in Puerto Vallarta)—all of this would connect me via some meandering but inevitable path to that fundamental point of origin that would root me in this world.

I persisted in this belief even as total cultural immersion failed me. There were loopholes in the system after all—the largest being the summer school I was attending, which purported to create an intensive language learning environment but instead served as sanctuary to the terminally English-speaking. Margie Bier not included.

Her linguistic prowess was not the first thing you noticed about Margie. It was her resemblance to an ostrich in an image-stretching fun house mirror. Long-necked, long-limbed, and lacking even an awkward grace, she was nearly six feet tall, and from the giant stride of her sandaled feet to the black-framed glasses clamped to her small, sharp nose, she was a concatenation of bony angles over which she hung sleeveless shifts dotted with coconut trees, koi, or other tropical life. Margie Bier was from Hawaii by way of Kentucky but apparently had expertly adapted her bluegrass origins to the Polynesian costume that now grew on her anatomy like limp feathers on a gangly bird.

By the middle of the first week of classes, we students had instinctively distributed ourselves into social clumps. I was in two. Margie Bier was in none.

Yolanda, the Chicana from Oxnard, and I had bonded. She had made a beeline toward me in our Mexican Folk Dance class, having spotted me as the only other brown person in this school of *gabachos*, a term I picked up from Yolanda, who hooted at my use of *gringos*. I was honored and flattered to be chosen, ignoring the fact that had we been back in either Oxnard or Kimball Park, where I paled in comparison to the genuine Spanish-speaking *raza*, I may have been left to only one social clump, the one consisting of the fiftyish Leo and Sylvia, forty-year-old Jackie, and Doris the burly grandmother.

It was with this group that I was sitting between classes when Margie Bier, loping in our direction, abruptly stopped in front of us. She wore a turquoise muumuu decorated with white scallops the size of human fists. She held her books close to her flat chest, her bony forearm underlining the title of the bottommost book, the diary of Sor Juana, the sixteenth-century nun who had defied the Inquisitors. It was big and impressive and untranslated.

"¿Alguien tiene cambio?" she inquired, holding out a twenty-peso bill.

While the rest of us dug out our wallets to make change, Sylvia made introductions in English. Sylvia even pronounced my name *Julia*, rather than *Who-lia*. I'd never liked the sound of my name in Spanish. It was the call of an owl, a jeer, a question about identity, and wholly appropriate to my sketchy twenty-two-year-old self.

"Mucho gusto," Margie said. "Soy Margarita Bier."

"Beer?" chortled Doris, whose Spanish vocabulary encompassed little more than favorite food and beverage items. "Margarita Cerveza!" she exclaimed, delighted with her wit and rewarded with laughter from the others. Margie herself seemed pleased and lowered her books away from her chest to better exhale her guffaw.

"But wait," I said, noticing the name tag on her book. "It's spelled B-i-e-r. How do you say that in Spanish?"

But nobody knew, except, of course, Margie, who did not offer to tell, and the others didn't care. Later I looked it up. In Spanish, bier is *féretro*. Her name should have been Margarita Féretro, which was not quite as amusing as Margarita Cerveza.

"¡Lo tengo!" Leo shouted the winner's phrase we used in the Bingo game we'd played that morning in Intermediate Spanish. He handed over an assortment of coins and small bills in exchange for Margie's twenty.

"Gracias," said Margie, dropping the money in the leather *bolsita* she wore around her neck like an amulet. She pulled the drawstring tight and hefted her books back to her ribcage. "¿Qué libro es?" asked Leo, though the title was plainly evident. I understood he lacked the vocabulary to ask what the book was about, that he desired a simple response. But Margie proceeded to explain in her nimble Spanish what we supposed was the art and wisdom of Sor Juana. Doris gaped incredulously at the feat. Leo, Sylvia, and Jackie good-naturedly laughed at their language gap while I pretended to understand more than I did, even offering a canned "qué interesante" during pauses.

"Bueno," Margie announced to end her soliloquy. She waved her big-knuckled hand at us. "Nos vemos."

WHEN I WOKE on the bus, Margie Bier was asleep. Her mouth was open and long strings of snores gargled up her throat. For the next half hour I tried to ignore Margie's gaping mouth as I looked past her at the scenery and the Coca-Cola billboards along the highway.

Finally she woke. "¿Dónde estamos?" she asked with a yawn, her long thin arms stretched above her, knuckles cracking against each other.

It was five o'clock, and we were entering the megalopolis that was Mexico City. Low murmurs began to fill the bus as we approached the center of the capital lit by neon and the sherbet sky. Margie offered an occasional observation on a landmark, spoken softly, it seemed, out of awe for this vast city. I remained resolutely mute, as if to prepare myself for its assault on my senses and expectations.

From the bus station Margie and I took a taxi to the Hotel Ritz, having agreed to treat ourselves to one of the deluxe downtown establishments. It was along the Avenida Juarez, walking distance to the Zócalo, the Latin American Tower, and a short bus ride to Chapultepec Park, all the places we would visit—separately, as it turned out.

I had imagined that I would be stuck with Margie Bier for the duration of our stay, but after we had settled into our room and Margie had hung her muumuus in the closet, she sat on one of the beds and took out a steno pad. I sat on the bed opposite her and watched as she studied a meticulously drawn chart with color-coded entries. She looked up and caught me staring.

"¿Tienes un itinerario?" she asked.

I shrugged, hesitant about what a definite response might bring.

"Debes hacerlo," she advised, snapping shut her notebook. Then she stood and dropped her room key inside the *bolsita* around her neck, giving it a tug as she walked past me. "Hasta luego," she called at the door before shutting it behind her.

And so I was left on my own, not that I was unhappy about it. It just wasn't what I had expected. I lay on the bed, deciding what to do next. Whatever it was, it was not going to be part of a rigidly scheduled itinerary. I jumped up from the bed, determined to be impulsive, and headed out of the hotel into the teeming streets of Mexico City.

I was in the beautiful historic part of the city with its sixteenth-century buildings and imposing wide avenues where pedestrians passed each other in an exhilarating, seemingly endless two-way parade. There were handsome men and exquisite-looking women, soap-opera attractive people with fair skin, aquiline noses, and faultlessly proportioned bodies. And every so often a small Indian woman with a coarse shawl at her shoulders or a young child, huaraches worn to scraps, would surface, hand outstretched, a dark flash among the glitter and polish.

I was carried along with the crowd. Ahead of me was an elegant couple with gleaming shoes. Hemmed in as I was on all sides, I followed them until they turned into a set of gilded double doors that swung shut to a posh restaurant. I faced my reflection in the heavy glass.

I looked lost.

At the moment, though, all I felt was hunger. My peek at the restaurant had made me aware of my empty stomach, and I yearned for a street vendor or hole-in-the wall taco stand, which were nowhere to be found in that part of the city. I began to zigzag the side streets, slowing occasionally to peer into one or another café, and then passing it by, too craven to face a menu and waiter on my own. A twinge of resentment at Margie Bier for deserting me mingled with my hunger pangs, which set my head to throbbing as I retraced my steps to the hotel. Just before turning onto the main boulevard, I noticed a small bistro tucked inside the arch of a building. It was a modest little eatery with a narrow counter, a few booths, a half dozen or so tables, and only a smattering of diners. Unassuming and unintimidating, it was a refuge for me, and I had my hand on the door ready to enter when I saw Margie Bier seated at the middle table deep in dialogue with the waiter at her side, a margarita in front of her. I watched Margie point to herself and then to her frothy salt-lined drink, and as the waiter laughed, I realized she was telling him the Margarita Cerveza joke.

Why couldn't she have taken her amusing name, her fluent Spanish, and her obliviousness to stares into any of the other restaurants I had passed up that evening? I considered going in and joining her, laying some claim to the comfort and ease she was enjoying, but instead I stepped back from the door to spy on her from the other side of the arch. The waiter left and Margie sipped her drink, her long, lank fingers wrapped inelegantly around the bowl of the glass. Between sips she scribbled on her steno pad and occasionally looked up as if to take in the atmosphere. Wasn't she aware of the surreptitious glances directed her way by the other diners? Didn't she know she was an oddity with her birdlike profile and weedy limbs? How much did I really need her company when she had so summarily dispensed with mine with her *hasta luego*? I left Margie to her enchiladas and headed back toward the hotel.

Avenida Juarez was bustling even more now, as if the whole population had turned out for the evening paseo. But the crowd was no longer enlivening, only wearisome as I felt the hunger grind a hole in my stomach, for which I blamed Margie. No longer trying to take in the sights, I kept my eyes peeled only for the gold cursive *R* of the Ritz, causing me to collide with the overstuffed handbag of an overstuffed woman who recoiled as if I were one of the city's perils. I backed away from her in fearful apology into the entrance to a magazine stand, which proved to be a welcome but weak deliverance from my hunger. Packaged snacks in cheerful, shiny wrappers sat in rows atop the counter. I seized a bag of potato chips, a packet of cookies, and a couple of candy bars and lay them in front of the clerk.

"¿Es todo?" she asked.

"Sí," I said, then, "no, espere," as I spotted an English-language newspaper behind her. She turned around. "¿Quieres esto?"

I nodded. "Por favor."

My first transaction in Mexico City had produced food, or at least comestibles, and a newspaper I could read without a dictionary. I swung the plastic *bolsa* at my side as I walked the block and a half to the hotel. In the plush lobby, I felt self-conscious carrying my cheap snacks, and once inside my room I spread them on the bed like a criminal counting her loot. To get rid of the evidence, I ate it all, one thing after another until the sweet, greasy paste from the chewed-up chips, cookies, and candy clogged my esophagus, requiring me to help myself to Margie's stash of bottled water lined up in the closet beneath her muumuus. I gulped half a bottle and hid the rest in my backpack, then settled in to read the newspaper, the latest on Jimmy Carter, Nadia Comaneci, and the Viking lander, all of which was a week old. I tossed it in the trash.

I decided to plan an itinerary after all, informally at least, and so mentally noted the sights I most wanted to see: Chapultepec Park, the Zócalo, the Latin American Tower, the pyramids. Satisfied with this promise of a strategy, I went to bed, though with a vague concern that Margie had not yet returned. Just when I began to imagine grim and ghastly consequences for a solitary, muumuu-clad American on the perilous streets of Mexico City, I heard the key turn in the lock. I wanted to know where she'd been, what she'd done, what new things she learned, but instead I rolled over in bed and pretended to sleep. I listened to her movements. Even after I heard the rustle of sheets, I waited and listened until she was asleep, and even then I listened.

I had a fitful night, the junk food I'd eaten slouching through my intestines. Even so, my hunger reasserted itself, and when I slept, my dreams were of want. I was sitting at the kitchen table in Tía Olga and Tío Chano's apartment on Avenida Tolsa. They were passing platters of food back and forth between themselves and heaping large servings on their plates. Whenever I opened my mouth to ask Tía Olga to pass the pozole or

Tío Chano to pass the frijoles, no words came. As I was about to stab my fork into the *chuleta* on my uncle's plate out of frustration and yearning, I found myself sitting in a booth at Denny's just off the Calzada. I was opposite Yolanda and Rafael, watching them share a plate of French fries. I sulked as they slipped the hot, greasy strips into each other's mouths. Then the fluorescents overhead blinked and dimmed and strobes flashed suddenly from the ceiling. Music blared from the artificial plants that had become speakers in the La Girafe nightclub. I tapped my foot as Yolanda and Rafael got up to dance to Donna Summer, leaving their French fries unattended. When I reached for the abandoned plate, I bumped the table, sending the French fries to scatter across the floor and under the heels of the dancers who had now formed a conga line that was snaking out the door. I got up to follow it, but when I reached the street, the conga line, now with Lupita at its tail, had turned the corner and disappeared.

I woke up then to Margie's soft snores. It was early morning and the noises of the city were getting underway. I drifted in and out of sleep, the honk of a taxi or a snort from Margie yanking me awake. Finally, I got up to shower and dress, and though I made no extra effort to be quiet, Margie was still slumbering when I slipped on my shoes and headed out the door. "Hasta luego," I muttered as I left.

I took the bus down the Reforma where the pricey restaurants and boutiques looked self-important and contemptuous with their doors locked and lights down, where the monuments of Columbus and Cuauhtémoc stood at the center of endless traffic, where the stately and imposing colonial architecture was, like all of the city, slowly sinking.

When I reached the park, I breakfasted on mangoes and

churros bought from a cart vendor. I sat among ancient trees in their pained and twisted postures and waited for the anthropology museum to open.

That morning I spent four and a half hours agape at the enormity of the collection of artifacts, moving from *sala* to *sala*, finally resting on a bench in view of Coatlicue, the goddess of birth and death, creator of gods and man. It was a formidable statue of a formidable deity. The serpents, talons, and human hearts that made up her anatomy and dress were impressive, though I regretted her headless state. I was pondering this proclivity for decapitated goddesses, the lovely bodiless head of the moon goddess not far away, when I saw the tropical flash of Margie's muumuu. I followed her into the next *sala*, staying well behind her. I watched her study the exhibits, lingering at some, jotting notes in her steno pad, consulting her guidebook every so often. I watched her make occasional comments to other visitors, her Spanish echoing in the hall. I trailed her from display to display, stopping to look again at the ones she seemed to reflect on to see what she had read there, to know what she knew. At the same time, I strained to hear what she said to whoever happened to stand near her or pass by. Then the unthinkable—that perhaps I was jealous of the person Margie shared her comments with—occurred to me, and I immediately turned and left the museum.

I was hungry again, and outside I assured myself that that was the reason for my exit. I sought out a cart vendor, ate two tacos, and after dripping grease and salsa onto my shirt, headed back to the hotel for a siesta and a change of clothes.

When I walked into the lobby, Rafael was waiting there. I wanted to wrap my arms around him with relief, except that I was embarrassed that I had neglected a promise to Yolanda to call him. When the summer session had ended (and I had skipped my final exams), I comforted a disconsolate Yolanda whose parting from Rafael was the next day when she would return to Oxnard. I, on the other hand, who had not spent my money on gifts for a boyfriend or on slinky clothes to wear on the dance floor with said boyfriend, was heading to this swarming, choking, magnificent valley of lost civilizations, Mexico City.

Yolanda had pressed a tear-dampened slip of paper into my hand. "That's Rafael's cousin's phone number. Rafael will be in Mexico City the day after you get there. Promise you'll call him." She was all high-drama and desperation as if she thought she could somehow prolong their relationship through me.

"I'll call," I had assured her, folding the slip of paper and stuffing it in my pocket.

She must have been skeptical, given my pattern of speaking in Spanish only when spoken to and when there was no one else around to speak for me, and she had apparently given Rafael instructions to look me up. He greeted me with a friendly *abrazo*, and I contained my urge to cling to him. He looked gorgeous and endearing, simply simpático as Yolanda and I used to say in monstrously bad British accents, after we had heard a woman in the *mercado* so exclaim about the "native peoples."

But Rafael looked different now without Yolanda on his arm, in his lap, or in synchronized gyrations on the dance floor. Rafael looked like someone for whom a summer romance was just that. With him was another man, a taller, heftier version of him, his cousin Eduardo—not the stunner that the silent Jorge was, but more sociable. It was he who suggested we all go upstairs to my room.

We sat on the beds. Eduardo had plopped his bulk down next

to me and Rafael perched on the edge of Margie's bed. Without preamble, Eduardo began rolling a joint while Rafael made small talk about the weather and traffic. I could hardly concentrate, either on the neat spindle forming under Eduardo's thick but agile fingers or on Rafael's polite prattle, distracted as I was by the inglorious prospect of being burst upon, handcuffed, and strip-searched by the Mexican police. I kept my eye on the door as Eduardo offered me the first toke, which I took timidly and inexpertly. I went a few more rounds before I felt I could comfortably decline and practically held my breath until they finished, at which point the door suddenly opened and I gasped in relief at the sight of Margie instead of the brown-shirted *policía*.

Margie was no less surprised at the sight of two men in our room, and suddenly I was pleased with the situation. I made the introductions, but when I referred to her as Margie, she corrected me. "Margarita," she said, offering her hand in turn to Eduardo and Rafael. "Margarita Bier," she added. "Como cerveza."

"¡Margarita Cerveza!" exclaimed Eduardo, and Rafael laughed approvingly.

Abruptly seized by a fit of language competence, I formed a rather articulate Spanish sentence with hardly a blunder. "Actualmente," I said, "su nombre se traduce como féretro, porque se llama Bier, como B-I-E-R. Entonces, Margarita Féretro."

The three of them looked at me.

"No importa," Rafael explained after a clumsy silence.

"El sonido es lo que hace el chiste," said Eduardo. "Es a joke," he translated for me.

Margie looked at me with a sympathetic expression. I wanted to insist that I hadn't missed the joke. Of course, I understood it, but strictly speaking . . .

It was no use. I sat silent as Margie took the first turn at answering Rafael's polite question about what we each had done that day. Margie burbled in fluent detail about the museum and its remarkable contents. I saw the look of approval pass between Rafael and Eduardo over Margie's command of Spanish. Big deal. Old news. I listened with envy and reluctant admiration as she described the social inventions, the conquests, the cultural triumphs and political failings of the various indigenous groups. Creeping into this recitation of facts was a passion in her voice, an intensity of inflection, a prolongation of vowels, a musicality that gave great poignancy to her topic. I stared at her. Where had it come from, this wisdom and affection that sprang from somewhere beneath the tacky scenery of her muumuu?

After a short awe-struck hush, Rafael turned to me, "Y tú, Julia, ¿qué hiciste hoy?"

"Lo mismo," I mumbled. "I saw the same things," I said, though I wondered if I really had.

"Qué bueno," Rafael said absentmindedly as he watched Eduardo begin rolling another joint. We all watched. I also watched Margie to see her reaction, a tightening of her small face underneath her glasses, which she now pushed farther up her nose. When Eduardo offered her a smoke, I thought her entire skeletal self would snap from the offense. Instead, she declined with a simple, "No, gracias."

When I accepted the joint and pulled long and hard on it to show Margie that her own decision mattered little to me, she peered down into her *bolsita*, ever present around her neck, as if taking strength from its contents and then announced that she was going for a walk. After the door shut behind her, I left it up to Eduardo and Rafael to finish the joint, and as I watched its diminishing length pass between these two men I hardly knew,

I felt like an interloper in my own hotel room, abandoned by my roommate.

I suppose it was a need to fasten myself to someone and my readiness to be escorted about the city by the local boys that caused me to blurt affably, "Ahora, ¿que hacemos?" But Eduardo and Rafael smiled sheepishly as they dusted the bedspread of stray flecks of weed.

"Tenemos una cita," Rafael explained, pointing at his watch. They took turns in the bathroom to pee and then were out the door, Rafael blathering something about *pasado mañana*. I waved at the closed door.

I FOUND MYSELF wondering what Margie was up to, what discoveries she was making, what knowledge she was hoarding. Over the next few days I didn't have to wonder for long—about her whereabouts, at least. Though we never discussed our separate plans for the day, I invariably saw her at the sights I chose to visit. I saw her and I avoided her. Sometimes I followed her—like some crank stalker or, worse, I thought, a hopeless wannabe.

I saw her in the Zócalo, her elongate figure so obvious even amid the jam of tourists that drifted about the enormous square. I saw her in the courtyard of the Palacio Nacional, her long neck craned upward toward the high reaches of the Diego Rivera murals. I followed her to each of the fifteen altars in the baroque interior of the Catedral Metropolitana, and then, behind the cathedral, I watched as she trod gingerly among the remnants of the Templo Mayor, ran her fingers along the ravaged stones that once were the temple of the Aztec war and rain gods. I stood behind her on the observation deck of the Latin American Tower, trailed her around its perimeter to gain the various perspectives of city, valley, and mountains. In the Palacio de Bellas Artes, I leaned against a column, chilling my skin against the white Carrara marble as Margie passed by. And in the Museo Frida Kahlo, the black eyes in Frida's self-portraits blazed at us in different corners of the room.

On the eve of my last full day in Mexico City, as I planned my excursion to the pyramids at Teotihuacán, I wondered if I would see Margie there, too. It seemed a simple thing to call into the bathroom where her long bones, stripped of their muu-muu covering, were well into a half-hour bath, and ask her. But it was too chummy, exclaiming through doors as if we were in a sorority house. I waited until she came out in her orange bath-robe that took all the color from her already pasty complexion, watched her unwrap the turban from her wet hair, shaking wa-ter onto her steamed-up glasses. She looked in my direction, but I couldn't tell if she could see me, so I waited.

"¿Qué vas a hacer mañana, Julia?" she asked, beating me to my own question.

"No sé," I said surprising myself, because I did know what I was going to do, had even meant to tell her, perhaps suggest we go together.

Margie shrugged. "Tener espontaneidad es bueno," she said, taking off her glasses, wiping them on her orange sleeve, and then settling them back on her pointed nose.

"Sí," I agreed, glumly thinking of my need to choreograph and rehearse my every syllable in Spanish.

"¿Te diviertes aquí en México?" Margie asked, her eyes nar-rowed in concern.

"Claro que sí," I answered, almost shrilly. Of course I was enjoying myself in Mexico. Why wouldn't I be? Certainly as much or more than she was.

Margie took up her guidebook and steno pad to study her itinerary, and I grabbed the American newspaper I'd picked up that morning and read or pretended to read the old news. In fact, I, too, was pondering my strategy for the next day, wondering how I would get to the pyramids that were 48 kilometers away. There were tourist buses, of course. But it seemed like cheating—a sheltered, mollycoddled way to go. So far I had done things on my own, a solitary wayfarer among the other tourists in pairs, families, study groups, or busloads. I was certain Margie would shun the tourist bus in favor of local transportation. I decided to do the same.

The next morning Margie slept in as usual while I took my time getting ready, looking at her as I dropped my brush onto the nightstand, knocked my backpack against the lamp, kicked the dresser. Still she slept. There was no point in lingering. In the lobby I asked for directions to Teotihuacan, eschewing the desk clerk's offer of the tour bus schedule. He gave me a map of the Metro, circled the station I was to get off at, drew a line to the connecting bus, and handed it to me skeptically. I took the map with a casual, sure smile and headed serenely out the door. But outside, my hand closed tightly around the map.

The subway wasn't crowded, so I spread the map on my knee and fixed my eye on the circle the hotel clerk had drawn. But the propagating mass of passengers at each subsequent station required me to scrunch the map in my fist again. In the jostle and crush of the growing crowd, I lost my seat and at one point was nearly swept out the door in the riptide of an exiting throng.

I emerged from the Metro battered but not beaten, ironing out my map between my hands as I made my way to the bus stop. There was an Indian woman and her two small daughters on one end of the bench, and I sat at the opposite end, looking and not looking at them. The woman's face was expressionless while her body, dense from two layers of sweaters over an apron, a skirt, and a blouse, agitated with the clash of plaids, stripes, and paisleys. The little girls, also dressed in mismatched clothes and poorly fitted shoes, stared at me. I smiled at them, and they lowered their eyes for a moment and then continued their staring. Their mother nudged them, and they shuffled toward me with extended palms, their black eyes boring through my unease. I dropped a few pesos in each hand, not out of pity or conceit, but with the matter-of-factness with which one remits a toll. The girls returned to their mother who had withdrawn a coin purse from the folds of her clothes, now held open to accept the pesos. There was a modest jangle as she restored the purse to her thicket of garments. With that business done, we all sat in silence as we waited for the bus.

It arrived nearly empty, but as it wound its way off the main highway onto narrow dusty roads through villages and farms, it collected a few more passengers. We were a small band of travelers, and I was the only tourist among them. I was smug as I imagined the tourist bus whose sightseeing passengers had only themselves for company—not laborers, farmers, and housewives going about their daily lives in the heart of Mexico.

Pleased with this special cultural vantage point, I acknowledged with a smile the young man who sat down next to me after boarding at the roadside near a crumbling Pemex station. I glanced only briefly at the straight, coarse hair that fell in uneven shanks over his ears and the wide grin that showed short, yellow teeth overlapping each other before resuming my meditations on the gratifying aspects of mingling with the local populace. Soon, though, I was aware of the young man sloping into my shoulder, his breath a sour wind against my neck. I leaned away toward the window where I could see a small fly wedged in the groove at the bottom. I focused on its papery wings, its hairlike limbs, a remarkable and disgusting creature, utterly vulnerable to the whack of a human hand. And as the young man invaded my seat further, his arm actually reaching around me, his mouth with its wide grin grunting a fervent "Te amo, te amo," I slammed my hand against the window, smearing the fly on the pane and jarring myself free of the young man's looming embrace. Pushing past his legs, I made my way up the aisle to an empty seat toward the front, my head and chest thumping. After a moment I turned around to look at the young man. He was still grinning his silly grin, though his face was unfocused and blank, and I saw from a distance what I had overlooked up close. He was slow-witted, his perception of the world defective, his declarations of love distorted.

I took out my map again and with my finger followed the lines that led to my destination. I was suddenly gripped with anxiety. How would I know when to get off the bus? Would it pull up like a taxi to a loading zone right in front of the pyramids? Would there be signs saying *Aquí están las pirámides*? I craned my neck to either side of the bus to find some clue along the road. Then I looked ahead of me through the wide front windshield and studied the yellow line in the center of the highway as if trying to match it to the line on my map. Finally, I approached the driver. "I want to go to the pyramids," I told him in Spanish, sounding like a frightened child.

He was a slight man whose small hands, dwarfed by the

large steering wheel, lifted noticeably from it as he shrugged his shoulders. "Las pasamos."

"¿Cuándo?" I cried. I hadn't been aware of stopping anywhere near such a prominent tourist site as the pyramids. "¿Dónde?"

"Paramos allá hace unos minutos." He gave a backward gesture with his head. I looked behind me as if I could see the spot he had indicated, but all I could see was the interior of the bus, the incurious stares of the other passengers, and the grinning countenance of the young man whose ardor I had escaped. It must have been then, during my annihilation of the fly in the window, my scrimmage with the grinner, and my flight toward the front of the bus that it had stopped.

"Pero tengo que ir a las pirámides," I exclaimed with urgency, fearful of where I would end up if not at my destination.

The driver shook his head, and I began to resign myself to riding the bus indefinitely into the Mexican countryside. Then he pulled to the side of the road, yanked the lever that wheezed the door open, and pointed to a dirt lane. "Anda por allá."

Walk over there. So I set off. As I followed the dusty path through a village of small huts, thatch houses, and adobe structures, I could smell simmering beans and the musty odor of livestock and the rankness of their droppings, saw faded wash hanging on lines and here and there TV antennas sloping from roofs. But I saw no one. I imagined they were in the fields, in their kitchens, at the market, living their lives, while I, a lost tourist in search of the pyramids, was becoming unsettled at the quietude after the commotion of the city. There I had merely been an outsider; here I was an intruder.

Though there was no obvious danger, I wished I was not alone. The solitude I'd been pretending to enjoy since my arrival in Mexico City made itself unequivocally known to me for what it was—loneliness. I told myself the fear and loneliness would disappear as soon as I found the pyramids. I focused as far ahead of me as I could to a spot where the path curved around a stand of trees. Just as I reached it, hoping to see the pyramids rise around the bend, a man stepped out from the trees and nearly collided with me. I startled him and myself with a scream—a rather wimpy one since, even in the middle of nowhere (or at least nowhere I knew), I was still self-conscious about making a scene. The man was not much taller than me and wiry in the same way I was. I wondered fleetingly if I could take him down.

He wore jeans, a cotton shirt, and dusty sneakers. His sombrero flattened the hair on his forehead. His face was dark and deeply creased. Was it a deliberate thing that I noticed all this first before I let my eyes take in the machete in his hand?

I opened my mouth to speak, but made only an unintelligible sound.

The man, composed now after the initial surprise of finding me in his path, asked, "¿Quién es?"

I pointed to myself, a question on my face as if stumped by his question.

"¿Está perdida?"

I started to cry at the sound of the word. I remembered the times in Guadalajara when Yolanda and I would act lost and ask for directions and some suave, oily-haired hunk would draw a map. How sometimes we would end up with dinner dates.

"Sí," I cried. "Lost," I said in English as if that would clarify it.

"¿Dónde quiere ir?"

I was tired. I wanted to say *home*, because suddenly I did want to go home. "Las pirámides," I said, feeling silly that I had ended up here in a village amid cornfields, trying to get to the most frequented tourist spot in the country.

"Venga," he said. I stood rooted momentarily. He turned to look over his shoulder to see if I was following him and his machete.

He said something else I couldn't understand. I thought of Margie and her annoying fluency. What would Margie have done? But then I realized she would never have been in this situation. She would have known when to get off the bus.

I had two choices: I could follow him, or I could turn and run. But run where? So I followed him, expecting to be pointed to a road that led to the pyramids. But he led me down a lane, narrower than the path we'd been on. Was it a shortcut? Vegetation thickened on both sides of us, and once the man swung his machete to sweep a branch out of his way. The movement was swift and efficient, arm and machete a single unit, the quick swoop of the blade like the flash of bird wings.

He stopped abruptly at an open doorway and indicated that I should go first. I hesitated.

"Pásele," he said.

It seemed more of a command than an invitation. I could still run, I thought. But the machete, which the man used to point at the doorway, was persuasive. I thought of my mother and my aunts as they chided me around the kitchen table about safety in numbers. I thought of my grandmother who, upon hugging me goodbye, had whispered, "Que te vaya bien." I thought of what I had come to find in Mexico, and it seemed so ridiculous now, like Dorothy's quest in Oz. Whatever lay ahead of me through that door, I thought I deserved. I decided to go bravely. Headlong.

I stepped over the threshold of the adobe structure to find

myself in a classroom of a dozen or so children hunched at makeshift desks, busy with fat pencils and tablets. They all looked up to stare at me as I charged in. Then they began to giggle. A young woman, kneeling beside one of the students whom she'd been helping, rose and greeted me, then motioned for me to take a chair in the front of the room. She conferred with the man with the machete for a moment in a language I didn't recognize.

On display as I was in front of the giggling children, I smiled at them, which made them giggle more. I giggled, too, at my predicament. And at my fears.

The teacher saw the machete man to the door and then turned to quiet the children. With that settled, she approached me and surprised me by speaking English. "I am Jacinta. I will show you the way to the pyramids. But first I will finish the lesson."

I nodded, grateful and embarrassed.

She gave the children instructions, and they continued to work at their desks, sometimes stealing looks at me. One by one they brought their finished papers to their teacher, who surveyed their work, offered what seemed like words of correction or commendation, and then allowed them to leave the classroom. When the last child had handed in her work and left the room, the teacher turned to me, "And now, I will show you the way."

It sounded profound to my ears, though I knew it was no more than an act of courtesy setting a lost tourist back on the beaten path. We backtracked along the way I had come with the machete man and came out on the path where I had originally encountered him. She asked why I hadn't taken a tourist bus. "I thought I could get to the pyramids by myself," I told her, trying not to show my embarrassment again.

"If you live around here, it's easy," she said. "If you're a stranger, not so easy."

Yes, I nodded, and though I didn't think she meant her words to be scolding, I felt chastised.

We hadn't walked far before she pointed me to a path that merged with a road. "There, you see." I wondered silently why the machete man hadn't just brought me to this path. The teacher read my mind.

"Ignacio. He thinks you have some fear of him. He asks me to show you how to go to the pyramids."

I wanted to deny Ignacio's claim.

"I'm sorry," I told her, barely meeting her eyes.

She nodded. "Que te vaya bien," she said.

I hurried away, spraying dust with my hasty steps, my eyes straining ahead to discern the course of the path. Finally, it intersected a larger road, and as I approached it with relief, a shiny tour bus rolled by—a welcome and maddening site. I looked down the road after it and saw a high chain-link fence beyond which rose the pyramids. I ran to join the other tourists.

Inside the gate, it was a vast and beautiful place, rendering the tourists there insignificant. I stood in the Caldaza de los Muertos, the wide avenue named for the dead, and looked around me, saying the names of each structure according to the map provided at the admissions booth. But before I could decide whether to start at the museum or head directly to the Ciudadela, I spotted a flash of papaya-colored fabric trotting at Margie's unmistakable gait a distance away down the Caldaza. Of course she was here. I followed her once again as she

headed toward the Pyramid of the Moon. She was far ahead
of me, but her height and her muumuu made her impossible to
miss. By the time I reached the pyramid she had already begun
to scale it, taking the steep narrow steps with a surprising agility
and pace. I took my time, feeling that the ascent of this ceremo-
nial structure demanded a more deliberate approach. Every so
often I would look down toward the bottom of the pyramid and
then back toward the top, and the motion produced a dizzying
effect that seemed a requisite and proper part of the journey. I
made sure to keep Margie in view, picking her out easily from
among the less tropically outfitted tourists. I was barely halfway
up when she disappeared over the top. I started to climb faster,
and when I clambered over the last step, I was puffing slightly
as I faced a tranquilly seated Margie, her legs crossed yoga-
style, her small backpack in the bowl of her lap anchoring the
hem of her muumuu to the ground. She was scanning the view
with a pair of binoculars pressed against her small face, looking
like a giant insect. I stood waiting for her to catch me in her
line of sight. When she did fix her binoculars on me, she didn't
lower them, but I saw them jar against her glasses. I'd made her
flinch.

"Hola, Julia," Margie said, still holding me in zoom view.

Did she see my frustration and weariness, magnified, the way
it felt in my chest and head and the arches of my feet as I stood
my ground and stared into the wrong end of her binoculars?
Could she guess that I'd been lost out there in a village amid the
cornfields, seen the glittering edge of a machete up close, been
laughed at, however gently and innocently, by a classroom of
children?

"Hola," I said back, making it sound less like a greeting than
a returned volley thwacked across a net. Margie let the binocu-

lars drop to her lap where they hung heavily from a strap around her long, thin neck. Having lost her insect eyes, she seemed also suddenly to be missing functioning mouth parts.

If she had nothing to say, then neither did I.

I turned my attention to the expanse around me—below to the Caldaza where pre-Columbian peoples once walked and now tourists wandered, across to the enormous and precisely aligned Pyramid of the Sun, and beyond to the mountains. I felt small, which was the point of all the grandeur. I felt exhilarated by the elevation. And I felt annoyed at Margie's presence on my pyramid, which I had earned more than she had.

"Siéntate, Julia."

I couldn't tell if it was a command or invitation. I sat down. Because I wanted to. I needed to after my ridiculously roundabout journey.

"Interesting, isn't it?"

I was surprised that she had spoken in English, wondered at her motive—whether she was finally declaring me a lost cause in the language department.

"Sí, interesante," I agreed, assuming she'd been referring to our surroundings.

"You know," I said, "I can speak in Spanish, si prefieres." The delicate air atop the pyramid and the panorama below gave me a feeling of possibility despite my earlier distress at being lost. Plus the air and sky made me punchy.

"Of course, I know." Now she sounded punchy.

I waited for her to lead the conversation, but she was silent, her beaky face serene.

"Umm," I said. "Can I borrow your binoculars?"

They were bulky, and I wondered how she had scrambled so nimbly up the pyramid with the weight of them. I held them up to my eyes and scanned the grounds, and then beyond to the surrounding fields, trying to locate where I had become lost and encountered Ignacio and his machete. *There*, I thought. *No, over there.* Even from my vantage point atop a pyramid I could not trace with certainty where I'd been when the bus driver had told me to *anda por allá* or when Jacinta had said *I will show you the way*.

"Interesting, isn't it?" Margie repeated her earlier conversation opener.

I dropped the binoculars and took in the sweeping view unaided. "I would call it amazing," I said, even though I knew her question was not in reference to the view.

I looked at her and waited for her to get off whatever was on her chest besides papayas.

"Don't you find it interesting," she said, "that we've seen each other at all the places we've gone to?"

I looked through the binoculars again, this time at her, close up, the way she had looked at me earlier. "Coincidence," I said. "We're tourists. Of course, we're going to end up at the same places." I wanted to scream at her that she was ubiquitous. Inescapable. But most of all conspicuous. So, yeah, I really hadn't wanted to be seen with her.

I lay on my back, my face to the sky. I looked through Margie's binoculars at the blue blankness. After seven weeks in Mexico—learning to convert dollars to pesos and miles to kilometers; learning to say *mánde?* or *cómo?* instead of *huh?*; learning how to recognize the sweetest mangoes and eat them with salt and lime; learning that it's *un tamal* and *unos tamales*—my experience was going to be reduced to my irritation that this Spanish-speaking gringa had left me to fend for myself?

"So, no, not very *interesante* at all," I said. "Lo contrario,"

I added, wishing more than ever I had more Spanish at my disposal.

She didn't answer, and I kept looking at the sky, watching for a bird or a plane or a cloud to pass above Margie's binoculars. I heard her sigh.

"You were right about my name," Margie said. "It should really translate as féretro."

A concession. But I was ambivalent about the gesture. I sat back up and started to hand back her binoculars.

"Rafael agreed. He said you were smart to know . . ."

"Wait a minute," I halted her, ignoring her flattery and keeping a grip on the binoculars. "When did Rafael say that to you?"

"The day after the three of you smoked in our hotel room. He said he had told you he was coming by. But when he came you weren't there. We, uh, he waited, and when you didn't show up, we went to a café to talk."

I pictured them together, long, bony Margie and beautiful Rafael, and because I was irritated that I'd failed to understand Rafael's invitation to meet him, I found myself near tears. What else had I missed out on because of my Spanish language deficit? I looked away at the horizon, swallowed hard, and took a deep breath to push the urge to cry back inside me. I turned a composed face to her and said rudely and ridiculously, "He's Yolanda's boyfriend."

Margie nodded, and then she started crying, quietly so as not to attract attention, or at least any more attention than her dress and stork-like figure already had. She bent over the backpack in her lap and tears leapt onto her knees, splotching the papayas on her muumuu.

I stared at her, wanting to back away and somehow blend into one of the clusters of tourists atop the pyramid with us.

Instead, I moved closer to her to try to shield her from the eyes of others.

"Sorry," I said. I was moved yet mystified by her tears. I found myself resisting the pinpricks of guilt annoying my neck and cheeks. I considered putting my arm around Margie's shoulder, perhaps even dabbing at her tears with the back of my hand, the way I'd done for Yolanda when she'd sobbed like a child upon her parting from Rafael. I could at least place my hand on Margie's.

But all I did was loop the binoculars around her neck.

I didn't want her to explain why she was crying. I'd seen it but I'd ignored it. All through the summer session I'd seen her trotting about alone with her armful of Sor Juana and other esoteric untranslated tomes, the only company she kept. I imagined again her and Rafael together in a café, he gentlemanly and attentive, she reveling in nonromantic, run-of-the-mill, necessary human connection. Was it too late for apologies?

Margie unfolded herself and rose, her limbs snapping into place. She shrugged her bony shoulders into the straps of her backpack and tucked the binoculars inside the neck of her muumuu. Apparently, she was done with me. "My tour bus is leaving."

"Your tour bus?" I sputtered.

She turned to me, her stork legs straddling two steps. "Adiós, Who-lia," she said. Then she started the steep trek downward, and I meant to call out *que te vaya bien*, but after a few steps she turned around and called up to me. "Did you find them?"

I looked around me, gave her a questioning look.

"Tus raíces."

I didn't know if she was being curious or mean. *Wouldn't you like to know?* I thought, though I might've also asked, Wouldn't

I like to know? I didn't answer, and Margie turned and continued her descent.

"Adiós, Margarita Cerveza," I said to the back of her muumuu, even though I knew I would follow Margie one last time, through the gate and onto one of the sleek and gleaming tour buses. For now, I stood and did a slow turn to take in the view. Maybe this time I would spot it—the place I had been lost before finding my way here.

Sunday Dinner

———————— ❖ ————————

IT WAS LUPITA's idea—Sunday dinner. Just like the old days. When she had proposed the idea, they all protested. Too much trouble, her daughters said. It'll tire you, her grandchildren said. Ha, she thought, never once believing it was her trouble, her tiring they were worried about.

She was ashamed now to think that she had pouted. Like a child. Like an old woman. So they gave in—with a condition. She was not to cook a thing. They would all bring something. Potluck.

She pouted some more, so they threw her a bone. "You can cook the beans," said Millie, the bossiest daughter.

Of course she would cook the beans. Who else would do it?

So now the pot of beans is letting off steam in the middle of the table, waiting to be noticed, waiting to be loved amid the potato salad, Jell-O salad, green salad, buckets of Kentucky Fried Chicken, a sizeable tuna casserole, and a pot of chili beans, which Connie has brought as a backup in case Lupita forgot or otherwise failed to produce her beans. Some picked-too-late hollyhocks droop over the food from a chipped vase.

A couple of throw cushions boost Lupita at the head of the dining room table, and four of her daughters and several of her grandchildren have wedged themselves around the rest of it. More grandchildren overflow to the tiny table in the tiny kitchen. Others, along with the sons-in-law (the ones who have not yet succumbed to the heart condition that seems to be the lot of those marrying into the family), balance their plates on their laps in the living room where the TV belches forced laughter.

Her grandchildren are all grown up into people she hardly knows, some even having given birth to children of their own who will know her only in a passing reference as the great-grandmother from Mexico who spoke no English and who cooked the beans for Sunday dinner. And, once upon a time long ago, she slapped tortillas from freshly worked masa. Or have they forgotten—these grandchildren eating two kinds of beans with store-bought tortillas? When they were little, she would interrupt her tortilla-making to peel off balls of dough for them to pat between their unwashed hands. She cooked their fat, misshapen lumps on the griddle and handed them back to them to eat while her best friend Rosa sat at the kitchen table, sipped her beer, and made a face at the indulgence.

Rosa, who still hates indulgence, wanders among them, alight-ing on the end of the sofa or leaning, arms crossed, against the door jamb, or even parked atop the china cabinet, her fat legs, now with no heft, dangling above their heads. Of Lupita's dead family and friends, Rosa is the only one who has come back to keep her company, though she does so at her own whim and never at Lupita's bidding. Sometimes she declines to show her-self but makes her presence known by a waft of air against Lupita's cheek or the levitating of hair at her nape—intimate gestures with a hint of bullying.

THIS MORNING LUPITA woke early as usual but lay in bed, trying to decide if she had imagined the blanket at her feet lifting on its own or whether it was the splay of her ankles beneath the covers, the scraping of her toenails against the sheet. There was no urgency to the day. After all, there was little to do beyond rinsing the beans, setting them on the stove to simmer, adding water at intervals. The trick was the seasoning—the timing of it, the perfect amounts. She knew it all by heart, by instinct. By smell.

There was not even housework to do. After Sergio died, Tony came to live with her so she wouldn't be alone. Tony hired a service to come in twice a week to scrub the floors and sanitize the bathroom and kitchen. Between cleanings, bleach fumes lurked in the crevices, masking the smell of Sergio's cigar that had, over the years, filtered through the wallpaper and into the plaster.

Tony's snores thundered at her from the next room. Her bleary, belly-scratching grandson would not emerge before noon. Always, she listened for the discreet rattle of the front doorknob in the early morning hours when he returned from his weekend job. Always, that little sliver of fear flickered beneath her ribcage that maybe this time it wasn't her grandson, but some intruder with no good purpose. Though, of course, those burro-sized dogs of Tony's would take care of strangers.

Tony's snores were musical, as if in his sleep he retained the memory of his performances at the club where he was prized as much for his karaoke singing as for his deft pouring of drinks. He had insisted on taking her one night when he was off shift. Even on the slower weeknights, patrons hailed him like a celebrity. A few times Tony excused himself from the booth where they sat and slid behind the counter to mix a margarita on request. When the karaoke session started, he was wheedled to the stage by the regulars. He pointed out Lupita to the small crowd of customers scattered in the half-dark, their faces lit by sconces etched with the Dos Equis logo. "Mi querida abuelita," he said, and they turned their heads to smile and nod and make the same noises of approval made over babies and small pets. She smiled and nodded back and made her own maddening noise at the back of her throat, which only she could hear and which had been happening with regularity of late.

When Lupita roused herself from bed, she wondered how to fill her day before Sunday dinner. The dogs, hearing her stir, trotted into her room, their feet making dainty sounds beneath their big, hairy bodies. At the sight of their copious fur, Lupita tried to rustle some life into her sleep-crumpled hair. She decided she would walk down the street to Ramona's and see if her friend had time to set and comb the limp, gray threads that still managed to grip her scalp. Ramona would also be simmering a family-size pot of beans for dinner, even though *her* family never came to eat.

The dogs followed her to the bathroom where she lowered herself carefully to the toilet. She had fallen once and still ached at the indignity of having her grandson lift her naked *nalgas* off the floor and help her pull up her baggy panties. The dogs stood sentry as she peed, whipped their tails as she stood and adjusted her pants, and nuzzled her knees as she doubled over the elastic waistband so the fabric wouldn't sag in the butt.

The dogs led the way to the kitchen where they waited by the door for Lupita to release them into the backyard. "Perritos molestosos," she muttered, and yet she didn't really mind having them underfoot. She looked out the kitchen window at the dogs circling the yard, sniffing and pawing, inspecting the grounds for unexamined clues to something, anything. The yard was a shambles, her roses were diseased, the grass high with weeds. Sergio's old wooden shack had collapsed long ago and had been replaced by an even uglier prefabricated shed. The clothesline, unused for decades, still stood, a wobbly roost for pigeons. The old wooden swing had disintegrated, but Tony had rigged a new one at the whim of one of his girlfriends. Tony pushed the girlfriend in it a few times, but her squeals of delight unsettled him, and he coaxed her out of the swing and eventually out of his life, as he did all the women who could not just adore him, but had to ruin things by speaking of love as well.

At the sink, Lupita poured the water from the beans that had soaked overnight, rinsed them, and refilled the pot. She set it to simmer on the stove. The dogs sniveled at the kitchen door, but she ignored them while she sat at the little Formica-top table to slice and eat an apple. She closed her eyes, making a mental note to check the beans at intervals and to add the seasonings when the time was right.

Her eyes popped open on an impulse, her mouth ceased chewing, a speck of apple teetering on her lip. Flowers. She must get flowers for the dinner table tonight. Then she wondered where that idea came from. It had sailed into her head like something aimed. She stared at the empty chair opposite her until Rosa materialized, her hair mussed, the neckline of her blouse skewed to her left breast. Even a ghost could be disheveled, Lupita noted.

"You're looking tired, Rosa." Not to mention untidy, Lupita added to herself.

"And good morning to you, too."

Lupita picked an apple seed from her teeth. "Life is too short for trivialities. And flowers. Why flowers, Rosa?"

Rosa's face puckered. "Don't you remember? I love flowers."

"Have you seen my yard, Rosa? No more flowers."

"A little testy this morning, eh?" Rosa turned sideways in her chair and rested her arm on the table, her chin clamped to her fist.

Rosa had only just begun appearing again in Lupita's home. Even when she was a living, breathing, old woman with slouching, sulking breasts and a mustache made more visible by a clumpy veneer of red lipstick on her grumpy mouth, Rosa had not been so disagreeable so often.

"Not at all." Lupita flicked the apple seed from her fingers, aiming it at the napkin in front of her, but instead watching it skid across the table, through Rosa's elbow and onto the yellowed linoleum floor. This business of having a ghost at the table was a curious but not entirely mysterious thing.

Lupita took her dishes to the sink, paused for another look out the window at the deterioration, then turned to address her old friend. But Rosa had vanished, and Lupita cursed under her breath this advantage Rosa had over her. When she opened the door to let the dogs in, she felt a faint pinch on her arm.

At midmorning she crooked her handbag inside her elbow the way she had always known to do to guard against thieves and was about to open the door when the doorbell rang. Confused, she jumped, her hand recoiling from the doorknob. The dogs came to her rescue, taking turns barking, lashing each other with their tails. Voices scolded through the door.

"Knock it off, Abandonada!"

"It's only us, Bandita."

The dogs ceased their din at the sound of their names, and Lupita opened the door to her twin granddaughters. She seldom saw them together anymore, so intent were they on establishing separate lives, but failing again and again to let go of each other, leading to a tendency to stumble into and over one another. At the moment, they each tried to enter first, and when they bumped shoulders, they bounced away from each other like balls. Though they were no longer as round as they used to be, they were still big as bears. Bears with bad hairstyles. Norma had scissored hers level with her wide jaw. Ofelia had permed her shoulder-length hair, and now it was frantic with ringlets. They had taken to sporting unbecoming colors like oranges and yellows, and colors with unbecoming names like puce and taupe, which they took pleasure in saying for the release of air as they puffed each *p*.

The twins remained on the porch, having failed to determine who would enter first.

"¡Qué sorpresa!" Lupita said. "Qué buena sorpresa," she clarified to let them know their surprise visit was not unwelcome. But then she blurted, "You're early."

"Can we help you with anything?" Norma asked, twirling a strand of her kinked hair with a fat finger.

Can I help *you* with anything? Lupita might have said to the big, big-hearted sisters still confounded by the oneness and twoness of being twins. Though she wouldn't. She was old. All she wanted was Sunday dinner. But first a hair set. She tugged the purse at her elbow.

"Are you going someplace?" Ofelia asked.

"Where?" Norma said.

Lupita stepped back at the pitch of their voices. They were reaching the age of shrillness in this family whose females tended toward eardrum-piercing volumes as they settled firmly into adulthood, a trait not to subside until old age. "To Ramona's to see if she can do my hair," she murmured, reluctant somehow to reveal her plans. "Just down the street."

"Oh," Ofelia said.

"Well," Norma said.

The three of them stood there a moment, Lupita watching the twins as invisible messages seemed to pass in the air between them.

"We could do your hair, Abuelita," Norma said.

"We could," Ofelia said.

Gone were the days when the twins spoke in unison, which was what made Lupita accept their offer. She was nostalgic for those days when they were a synchronized chorus of two, and yet she held out hope for an easy separateness, one in which they didn't feel obliged to distinguish themselves by a bad perm or ill-chosen wardrobe colors. She gave herself up to their big hands, good intentions, and mediocre artistry with hair.

In the bathroom, Ofelia stacked some ancient encyclopedias and a blanket on a chair that she positioned against the sink. Norma scooped Lupita up and settled her atop the makeshift booster.

"¿Estás lista?" Ofelia said.

"Sí, estoy lista," Lupita said, gripping the blanket beneath her, though it offered no salvation in the event of a fall.

"I'll wash, you rinse," Norma told Ofelia, who accepted the plan and offered her own terms. "You pat dry, I'll comb."

"Deal," Norma said, and they slapped hands. Rather harshly, Lupita thought.

Norma tilted Lupita's head backward into the sink and tested the temperature of the running water. She filled a plastic bowl and Lupita received the dousing with delight. Then Norma began to work shampoo into Lupita's scalp with her big hands, the strength of her fingers sending shivers through Lupita's skull.

"Close your eyes," Norma said, and Lupita obeyed willingly. She remembered these girls so many years ago when they were bubbling, oversized eight-year-olds and they would barge in on her when she was taking a bath. They would take turns lathering her head with shampoo, washing between her toes, rubbing a washcloth over her kneecaps and shoulders. She would think to herself, *Who will bathe me when I'm old?*

She felt the shifting of bodies around her and now felt a new pair of large, strong hands on her head, which was soon flooded with a wave of rinse water. Ofelia's fingers were gliding through her thin hair, shuddering her spine. She was no longer gripping the blanket beneath her for security. She was floating, her hands dangling in the air at her sides.

Ofelia squeezed the water from Lupita's hair and gathered it to make a skimpy handful. Norma swooped in with a towel and rubbed her head until it no longer dripped. Then Ofelia inserted herself again, wielding a long-tail comb whose pointy tip grazed Lupita's shoulder before the teeth raked her head. Lupita imagined tiny furrows being dug.

The twins sat her in front of her dresser mirror in the bedroom and drew a part down the middle of her head. They plucked the little curlers from Lupita's hands and rolled and snapped them into place, working quickly, working quietly, working together but also against each other.

"There," Norma said, making a voilà swish of her bobbed hair.

"Done," Ofelia said, tossing her ringlets.

Tony appeared in the doorway, leaning against the frame for support. He scratched his head, rubbed his face, and then tugged at his T-shirt, which had bunched above the waistband of his gym shorts. The toes of one foot plucked at the cuff of his sock on the other foot.

"Up already, Antonio?" Lupita said.

"We didn't wake you, did we?" Norma asked.

"We've been pretty quiet," Ofelia said.

"Yeah, but it's a loud quiet," Tony said. "Ferocious."

Norma and Ofelia startled, as if caught in some dishonest deed.

"Kidding," Tony said. "I got thirsty. I'm just gonna drink a gallon or two of water and then head back for a little more shut-eye." He yawned and stretched and his T-shirt lifted above his belly, making them all turn away. "See you at Sunday dinner," he mumbled as he shuffled off.

"¡Dios mío, los frijoles!" Lupita shook her fist at no one and everyone and scurried out of the room. The aroma had filled the kitchen, and the taste of the beans landed on her tongue—and it was all wrong. She couldn't remember what time she had started the beans to simmer. She wasn't quite sure if she should add the seasonings now or later.

Tony followed her into the kitchen. He lifted the lid on the pot and peeked inside. "Needs water," he said.

"Déjalo," she said, slapping his hand. His breath smelled, his hair was greasy. He needed a bath. She shooed him away from her beans, out of her kitchen.

Norma and Ofelia squeezed in the doorway. "Need any help?" they asked, eager, needful.

Again, that question. What could they do? What could anyone do?

"Everything is A-OK," Lupita told them, adding a thumbs-up for good measure. "I no need you help." She waved them away, a gesture that seemed to split them, with Ofelia removing herself to the living room and Norma swerving past Lupita to the back door.

When they were gone, Lupita turned off the burner and wept over her beans. What had happened? What had happened to her heart, her instinct? Her unerring sense of smell?

Lupita sighed and sank into one of the two kitchen chairs at the little table shoved against the wall where Rosa preferred to stage her appearances. It was where the two of them had spent so many hours shelling peanuts, drinking beers, and talking. So much talking they did.

"Don't worry about it, Lupita. Who will miss a few beans?" Rosa said, her voice emerging from air, her grumpy self materializing a moment later in the vinyl chair, which did not hiss when she sat her fleshless, weightless butt on it.

Lupita covered her face in her apron, wanting and not wanting to see Rosa.

"I was always irrelevant in this house, among your family. Now you are, too." Rosa's voice held little sympathy. Ghosts, it seemed, pulled no punches.

Lupita dropped the apron from her face. "You were never irrelevant," she countered, ignoring the tail end of Rosa's remark, with which Rosa seemed far too pleased.

"I did not matter," Rosa insisted. "Remember that time Lyla read my fortune with the cards? She made everything up."

"She didn't. She was accurate."

Rosa guffawed. She mimicked shuffling a deck of cards, flipping and twirling the imaginary cards with her see-through fin-

gers. "'Ready?' she asks me. 'Ready,' I say, and I cut the cards."
Rosa's voice even now shook at the memory.

"Lyla arranges a row of cards on the table, tells me draw
a card, move a card here, move a card there. She puts down
another row of cards. I draw more cards, move them here and
there and there. Lyla says 'Hmm,' like she sees something in the
cards. 'So, what do you see?' I say.

"Lyla lowers her voice and makes it mysterious. 'I see a gathering of many people—young and old. A celebration, maybe.
Lots of food. Singing. A toast.' Then Lyla sweeps up the cards
and demands a dollar."

Rosa folded her arms across her chest, indignant at the
memory and ready once again to refuse to pay for the reading.
Except that she did pay back then. It was bad luck to take a
fortune-reading for free. Even if Lyla had only foretold Sunday
dinner, at which Rosa had been a permanent fixture for years.

Being the butt of a joke is not being irrelevant, Lupita thought. *We
all serve a purpose.*

And what was Lupita's purpose these days? To ruin the
beans?

She looked out the window at the little house in the back
near the alley, the front door padlocked shut, the cement porch
cracked, the paint flaking. Tony lived there after Rosa died.
Later, when Sergio clutched his chest and tumbled down the
front steps of their house, took one last look at the watch on his
wrist and closed his eyes forever, it became more convenient for
Tony to occupy the other bedroom in Lupita's house. He was
already taking his meals at her table or reheating leftovers from
her fridge. The little house was empty now and looked smaller
than ever. She, too, had grown smaller with age.

She didn't see Norma in the backyard and found both sisters on the front porch, reunited after their separate exits. The dogs were sitting between them, a buffer, a bond. "Come," she told them, pointing to the curlers on her head.

HER DAUGHTERS, IN their fifties and not a gray hair visible among them, chew and talk, chew and talk, interrupting each other's complaints about their migraines, elevated blood pressure, trick knees, bunions, bloating, psoriasis, and the doctors that failed them. They rant all of this in English, and though Lupita understands it all, every once in a while Millie or Frannie or Connie or Petra, out of some remembered sense of courtesy, or maybe obligation, repeat the harangue in Spanish. Rosa yawns. Lupita nods in sympathy, because hasn't she suffered all those maladies and more? She keeps nodding her freshly coiffed head that despite the twins' efforts looks no different than usual. She wonders when someone is going to comment on the beans. She looks around. Everyone's mouth is busy, talking, eating, laughing. Talking, talking but not about the beans. Not a word.

She mops up the beans on her plate with a tortilla. "Pásame los frijoles," she says.

Instead, Millie snatches up Lupita's plate and sends it down the table to Frannie who ladles a serving of beans and adds a small glop of Jell-O salad on the side. As the plate is passed down the table, it acquires a smidgen of this, a dab of that, and a small pool of Connie's chili beans.

Millie sets the plate in front of Lupita. "Eat," she tells her.

There it is again—the maddening noise in Lupita's throat that seems to happen all on its own.

Lupita aims her fork straight for the beans, her beans, but no one pays attention. Lupita sighs into her plate. Rosa rattles the china cabinet. When the meal is halfway over, still no one has commented on the beans. Lupita imagines launching her tiny, *viejita* self from her padded chair and reaching across the potluck-cluttered table to stir the pot of beans. Rosa, who is now leaning on the back of Millie's chair, is closer. Rosa could do it. But she is busy, winching her eyebrows and widening her mouth as she mimics the talk at the dinner table, which has switched from English to Spanish, from Lupita's daughters' ailments to the absent family members.

Lyla, for instance, who is still living in her mountain cabin, no doubt faking illness. Sure, she has wrecked her health with cigarettes and vodka, but she's a tough bird. Besides, her reputation as a card reader is thriving. Her haggard looks only make her more desirable as a fortune-teller, and she's become not just a local attraction, but a destination for mystic-seekers from both seaside and desert. No, she told everyone who had exhorted her to come, her health did not allow her to travel. But the twins would be there. Her daughters would represent her.

It's true, her daughters are here, right in the next room, counterbalancing one another from either end of the couch, aware that their mother is the topic of conversation, her name like an exclamation point, a recognizable splash in the burble of Spanish.

Lyla. How did she ever get everyone to call her that silly name? Lie-la. Her youngest, Lupita thinks wistfully. The one with the talent to dance. To tell fortunes with cards. The one who bore the good-omen twins. And maybe that was the problem. The expectations that come from being look-alikes. And big ones at that. Strong girls who loved and hated themselves and each other, who once wrestled on their high school team when they expertly harnessed their centers of gravity, but who now grapple with the balance of just being. And where is their mother? Hidden away in a mountain cabin like a fairy-tale witch. And what can she, their old *abuelita* who speaks no English, whose beans are taken for granted, whose garden is devoid of flowers, do for them, for anyone?

The pillows Lupita has been sitting on have lost their plumpness, even beneath her flimsy form. Though her dining room chair is well situated for viewing the goings-on, it takes a great craning effort from her now-depressed perch to see the twins sitting on their opposite ends of the couch, their skinnier cousins sunk in the valley between them. Their newly shrill voices are lost beneath the even shriller voices of their cousins. She thinks she hears one of the twins say the word *beans* in English. *Speak up*, she wants to say to the twins. *Shut up*, she wants to say to the others.

Tony works the room while he eats, shoveling food in his mouth while he flirts with his aunts, his cousins, his cousin's children. Moving from living room to dining room, plate in hand, joining in one conversation only to abruptly jump to another, trying to amuse everyone, but most of all himself. Later they will ask him to sing and he will mug his way through "Volver, Volver." But for now Lupita watches and waits for the inevitable to happen. And there it is—a stumble, a clumsy pirouette. A brush with the floor lamp and his plate suddenly airborne, a literal flying saucer that flips a full rotation, its contents flung like piñata innards and landing in an indiscriminate lump on the rug—chicken bones, lettuce, rice. Beans.

The dogs, well-behaved and tucked out of sight until that

moment, hurl themselves upon the spattered potluck samplings. A commotion arises with shouts at Tony to control his animals, laughter and jokes about the dog farts that are bound to ensue, and a general piling on of napkins to sop up the mess.

The eating slows, then ceases. They suck at and pick their teeth through their gossip. The men amble out to the porch to smoke. There are no more poker games. Too few of them left to play. Full stomachs and the fading light make the women sleepy and nostalgic as they linger at the table of dirty potluck platters. *Remember those Halloween parties, bobbing for apples? The kids hated that. Especially the twins.* "Well, no wonder," Millie says. "Lyla would dunk their heads in the bucket."

No, Lupita wants to say. *It was you who dunked your kids' heads.* Lyla pulled the elastic on the back of their masks, letting it loose to snap the back of their skulls. But she says none of it. They will dismiss her memories as faulty, a circumstance of age.

Dinner is over. The grandchildren with children want to pose their offspring in Lupita's lap. They beckon her to the middle of the sofa. That is her usefulness. A prop for the great-grandchildren. The wrinkled, shriveled contrast to new, downy skin. Some of the children squirm, some stiffen, some flop limp as laundry in her arms. It is clear their mothers don't trust her arthritic grasp on their babies. They hover as the picture is taken, swoop in and reclaim their bundle as soon as the camera clicks, satisfied that they will have a picture for posterity.

She doesn't dare say their names. It's hard to remember them all. But there's the newest one, a little brown bean of a baby. "¡El frijolito!" she exclaims, and they all laugh at the nickname. It's one of the few Spanish words they know. She is and isn't being intentional. The baby does look like a bean, and now an odor rises from his diaper. There are jokes and grimaces and accusing looks all around because haven't they all just eaten beans for dinner? Beans for dinner! But the photo session is over and the grandchildren are dispersing to other parts of the house.

She can't help it. It wells up inside her. She shouts it in English. "You like the beans!" It's meant as a question, but it comes out as a command.

At first, no one hears. Gradually, though, the noise subsides. "What? What did she say?" someone asks.

"The beans. She said we like them," someone else says.

"Of course, we like them."

Then the noise and bustle resume. The plates are being cleared from the dining room table where Rosa has planted herself in a vacated chair, her face turned toward the bent heads of the hollyhocks, her nose working to no avail to capture their scent. Only the twins notice the nearly imperceptible sway of the flowers, moved by some unseen force or perhaps the flowers themselves. The twins reach out to touch the quivering petals but their fingers pull back at the small gust that is Rosa's breath. They exchange looks, accept the shared mystery, then lose themselves among the rest of the family in the rush to clean up.

Leftovers are being divided and wrapped, and some of the grandchildren are packing up their belongings. A couple of the great-grandchildren, fists sticky and chins drooly, toddle to Lupita who holds out a hand to each of them. They grab her fingers. They tug as if she is one of their pull-along toys.

Lupita feels the yank on each hand, thinks that if they wanted to, they could, without much more effort, pull her apart. A wishbone. If only she were capable of granting wishes—like the one Ramona granted her today when she handed over her pot of beans at Lupita's back door, when she tendered the tired bunch of blossoms that graced Lupita's table for this Sunday dinner.

Acknowledgments

THESE STORIES WERE WRITTEN over a period of two decades. Many people helped or inspired me along the way, and I extend my deep thanks to them. First, it was hearing Kathleen Alcalá in 1992 read from her first book, a collection of short stories called *Mrs. Vargas and the Dead Naturalist*, that prompted me to recognize my own urge to write and enroll in extension classes to begin to learn about story from wonderful teachers Jack Remick and Rebecca Brown. Kathleen has remained an inspiration and supporter over the years.

Raven Chronicles, helmed by Phoebe Bosche for all of its twenty-eight years, published my first story "Elena's Dance" in 1994. That story was the precursor to "Ana's Dance" which appears in this collection. Thanks to Stephen Parrish of the *Lascaux Review* for his support for "Ana's Dance," which received the Lascaux Prize in Short Fiction in 2014. Thanks also to these journal editors for publishing other stories that appear in this collection: Don Williams of *New Millennium Writings*, Beverly McFarland of *CALYX*, Jordan Hartt and Jeremy Voigt of *Conversations Across Borders*, Tyler McMahon of *Hawaii Pacific Review*, the editors at *Bluestem*, and Laura Pegram of *Kweli*.

The 1998 Community of Writers at Squaw Valley Workshop was the first writing conference I ever attended. James Brown was my workshop leader and his affirming response to my story

"Rosa in America" gave me confidence in those early years of my writing efforts.

When I attended the Napa Valley Writers Conference in 2000, Lynn Freed told me in her lovely, straightforward, no-nonsense manner that my stories (early versions of "When Danny Got Married" and "Natalie Wood's Fake Puerto Rican Accent") were "flyovers." That was when I began to understand the primacy of scene over exposition.

For many years, the Port Townsend Writers Conference has been a regular place of inspiration, support, and community for me with its stellar faculty, committed participants, scenic setting, and top-notch program director Jordan Hartt. At Port Townsend, I benefitted from the teaching and talents of Bret Lott, Chris Abani, Paisley Rekdal, and Pam Houston.

As I continue to learn to write stories, I still refer to my notes taken in Tom Jenks's 2003 workshop to remind myself about the elements of fiction and how each functions to make a story.

At a VONA residency in 2006, David Mura's helpful critique of an early version of "Strong Girls" led me to deepen the characters and the story, revisions that resulted in its publication by CALYX soon after.

Antonya Nelson's workshop at Bread Loaf in 2008 and the following year at Atlantic Center for the Arts, and Robert Boswell's workshop at the Taos Summer Writers' Conference in 2013 are among the best I've taken.

For over a decade, Alma García, Allison Green, and Jennifer D. Munro have provided me with careful and insightful reading of my drafts and given valuable advice. In an earlier writing group, Larissa Vidal and Florence-Marie Shadlen did the same.

Lauro Flores, Catalina Cantú, María de Lourdes Victoria,

and many other members of the Seattle Latino artist community have supported me with their friendship and belief in my work.

Rick Simonson and Karen Maeda Allman of the Elliott Bay Book Company are big-hearted champions of local writers, and I'm grateful for the support they've given me.

Artist Trust, 4Culture, the Bread Loaf/Rona Jaffe Foundation, and the Seattle Office of Arts and Culture provided grant and fellowship awards that helped me focus on and further my work.

Hedgebrook, Atlantic Center for the Arts, and Whiteley Center provided necessary and precious writing time and space for me to work on many of these stories.

Endless thanks to Randall Kenan for selecting my manuscript for the Doris Bakwin Award for Writing by a Woman and to editor Robin Hollamon Miura and everyone associated with Carolina Wren Press for making *Hola and Goodbye* such a beautiful book.

Arline García generously gave her time and expertise in checking for Spanish language errors. Any inadvertent errors are mine.

Rachel Rauch, Julianna Schaus, Haley Shultz, and Hannah Soltis—smart, creative students in Wendy Call's Publishing Procedures class at Pacific Lutheran University—designed a cool promotional strategy for *Hola and Goodbye*.

My sisters Rose, Sandra, and Diana, and my brother Joe, and the memory of my hardworking parents, Jose and Dolores Miscolta, are a steady source of encouragement.

My daughters Natalie and Ana give me insight into character and growth in the strength and determination they continually show as they move forward in the world. And for making it possible for me to fit writing in with a day job and other everyday demands, biggest thanks to James Cameron for his patience, generosity, kind heart, and ability to make me laugh every day.